LIFE'S A WITCH

The Hollowbeck Paranormal Cozy Mysteries
Book 3

AMELIA ASH

KIM M. WATT

STERLING & STONE

ONE

A bunny too far

I SAT ON THE FLOOR BEHIND THE SHOP COUNTER IN THE Cosy Cauldron, my back pressed to it, both hands clasped over my head in case of unexpected projectiles, as I listened to the sound of shelves being violently emptied in the shop itself. Luckily, very little of our stock was either fragile or expensive, so most of the noise was being made by clattering wooden signs that said things like *Witch Rules Apply* or *Magic Made Here* (for kitchens, but an alarming amount of people told me they were buying them for the bedroom door, which was a lot of information for a novelty purchase), plus boxes of rune stones and divining sticks, which were going to be messy but not unsalvageable.

All the crashing and banging was accompanied by some frenzied shouting, the main thread of which was illustrated by the current yell of, "And why would you give me *rabbits?* Sodding bloody *rabbits!*"

Next to me, Starlight leaned a little closer and whispered, "Do you think it's worth pointing out that we didn't give him rabbits?"

"We already tried that."

"Maybe if we're a bit more convincing?"

I looked from Starlight to the rat sitting on her hindquarters on one of the shelves under the counter, front paws clutched together. She had soft grey fur with a smattering of white on her muzzle, and she was regarding me and Starlight in a way that radiated an astonishing amount of disapproval for such a small creature. Her name was Jacqueline or Jackie, and she offered no advice on the current situation.

"I don't think it'll help," I said aloud. "I think we just wait him out."

In any other place, of course, the response to someone smashing your shop up would be to call the cops. In Hollowbeck, the town's entire police force consisted of one rather elegantly attired sergeant who only came out at night, and given it was currently two in the afternoon, there was no help coming from that quarter.

"He's destroying all our displays," Starlight said, peeking over the counter. "It's taken me ages to get them looking right." She sank back down and looked at me. "You're the boss. You need to do something."

I sighed. I never volunteered to be the shop's owner, and I was unsure if being a boss was something I was suited to. *Boss* seemed very serious and rather excessive for a small magical supply shop that sold a mix of surprisingly effective salves and essential oils, as well as a seaside novelty stand's worth of magic-related tat. And taken the other way, in a sort of entrepreneurial sense, *boss* had all those *girl boss* connotations, which was even worse. At thirty-six, I was too old to remotely consider myself a girl and was pretty sure I lacked the grooming and pastel palette to be any sort of girl boss.

But here I was, the shop's owner. The Cosy Cauldron had been gifted to me along with an old spell book and the title of Town Witch by Jackie. Yes, Jackie the rat. Or technically, by Norma, the previous owner, I supposed, but I didn't think that was intentional, any more than Norma had intended to end up dead in her own cauldron. I'm sure she'd have made better provisions for her book and her shop if she'd known that was going to happen. But however things had occurred, here I was, expected to deal with irate, bunny-fixated customers.

I took a deep breath and stood up, hands spread in front of me, partly to placate the raging man and partly in case I needed to ward off any missiles.

"Warren," I started, using the gentle voice I used on my mum when she was about to spend six months' pension on a rare souvenir plate featuring someone like King Christian IX of Denmark, listed on eBay by an account called SirScamALot.

The man, who had been intent on trying to rip an entire shelf off its supports, spun to look at me. His sparse white hair was in disarray, his blue eyes watering with effort and emotion, and he was so red I wondered if Hollowbeck had an ambulance and, if so, if I should be calling it. One dead body in my shop had been an accident. Two would be careless.

"*Mister Buckley!*" he shouted at me. "Three-time champion radish grower and five-time champion carrots. *Five!*"

"Mr. Buckley, can you please stop destroying our shop?"

"You've destroyed my *life*," he yelled and grabbed a book titled *Building Fairy Doors for Beginners: Guaranteed Safe and Non-Traversable!*, attempting to tear it in two with his bare hands. When that didn't work, he threw it at me. I ducked.

"Mr. Buckley, I don't see how rabbits in your garden could be caused by us. They're... I mean, rabbits get everywhere." I waved vaguely to encompass the fact that Hollowbeck was a small town mired in farmland. Rabbits were the rule, not the exception.

He surged toward the counter, stabbing a finger at my nose, which would've been a lot more intimidating if he didn't look like I could lift him up with one hand. "It's my damn deal! I had a deal with Norma and never had a problem with rabbits when she was around! You take over and"—he waved wildly, arms windmilling—"*rabbits!*"

Ah. The deals. That spell book — grimoire, really — I'd acquired didn't just contain recipes for clear skin and charms for banishing pixies. It also bound half the town — or more, I was still working out the details — to deals that had been made with Norma. *Really* bound them. These weren't handshake deals. These were more like sell-your-soul crossroads deals, and as the new owner of the book, I was now responsible for them.

My immediate instinct had been to attempt to release everyone, as anyone who'd made a deal at any point with Norma, no matter how small, was tied in for life. They could be compelled to do anything the keeper of the grimoire demanded — or face the consequences. It wasn't something I wanted to be responsible for, but I was discovering that trying to break the deals was a fraught process. The book wasn't keen on letting go, and the consequences had so far included plagues of ferrets, carbonated geysers, houses enveloped in spiderwebs (ugh), and one woman who couldn't cook anything except Victoria sponges. As in, she'd put a roast in the oven and opened the door an hour later to find a Victoria sponge, complete with cream and jam, collapsing in the heat. I was still working on that one.

"I'm trying to get everyone out of their deals," I said. "It's the best solution all round."

"It's not. It's worse," Mr. Buckley said, picking up a bundle of sage and trying to rip it apart. Starlight's twine resisted, though, and he hurled the whole thing across the shop with a grunt of outrage.

"Can you tell me exactly what's gone wrong?" I asked.

"*Rabbits!*" he shrieked, leaning so violently towards me I could smell bacon on his breath.

"Um …" I looked helplessly at Starlight, who was still sitting on the floor. She shrugged and petted the ferret on her shoulder, which tried to bite her. Her attempts to turn Howard into a familiar were not going well. Since there was no help to be had there, I looked back at Mr. Buckley. "Rabbits in general?"

"Rabbits in my *garden!*"

"But surely that's not unheard of?"

He looked at me as if I'd just asked if the apocalypse was going to be inconvenient. "I am a *champion vegetable grower.*"

"Oh. Right. So your original deal…?"

He hesitated, looking around as if afraid of being overheard. "To be the most champion vegetable grower in the country, obviously."

"So no rabbits."

"Hard to grow a prize-winning turnip with *rabbits* about."

I couldn't imagine any world in which a turnip could be prize-worthy, but everyone had their passions. "So the deal kept out rabbits and made sure your veggies were … really good, or whatever?"

"Yes."

"And you can't just put the veggies in a rabbit-proof enclosure? A greenhouse?"

This time, he looked at me like I'd suggested making tea in the microwave. "They're *rabbits*."

"Yes, got that."

"They're cunning."

"Oh?"

"And they've been planted. Sabotage, you see."

"Right." I reached down and grabbed Starlight's sleeve, tugging until the younger woman stood up, still petting Howard and looking at the devastated shop with a resigned expression. I needed the moral support. "And why d'you think it's sabotage?"

"Well, it never happened before. I was protected by the deal, see. And now I'm not, and *someone*"—he tapped the side of his nose—"has taken advantage of that to destroy my crops."

"It *is* almost winter," Starlight pointed out. "Do you actually have any competitions coming up that mean someone would want to sabotage you?"

"*Yes*. I was going to enter a beetroot this year. And leeks."

"Do rabbits eat leeks?" I asked.

He glared at me. "They eat beetroot! I've been camping out in the garden, but I'm overrun! And I never had this problem before you did your thing." He waved his fingers at me in what was presumably a magical manner.

"That's unfortunate," Starlight said. "But, on the upside, you don't have to supply Norma with fresh vegetables every week for eternity." She gave him an encouraging smile.

I thought eternity was pushing it. Mr. Buckley looked to be well into his eighties. His vegetable-providing days were unlikely to last into eternity. Although the town already had an eternal ghost mayor, I supposed a ghost gardener wasn't out of the question.

"I'd rather that than rabbits," Mr. Buckley said. "Just you wait. Someone else is going to win the late growers' competition. I bet it'll be that Sally Trimble. She's always sniffing after my secrets!"

"But your secret was a deal with a witch," Starlight pointed out. "This just means you'll have to win on your own merits." She folded her arms, giving him a rather severe look.

Mr. Buckley opened his mouth, closed it, then turned and swept everything off one of the last remaining shelves before storming out, yelling as he went, "I hate rabbits! And *witches!*"

Starlight and I surveyed the wreckage of the shop. Crystals were scattered over the floor, mingled with broomstick magnets, tangled dreamcatchers, dented candles, and packs of tarot cards flung from one side of the shop to the other. Mr. Buckley hadn't managed to topple any of the big freestanding display shelves, but he had tipped our stand of faded postcards over, bending the edges of most of them even more than they had been already.

Starlight sighed. "We're never going to keep this place tidy."

"It's not so bad," I said, emerging from behind the counter to start picking things up.

"It is. We have to figure out how to release everyone from their deals properly. Otherwise, this is going to keep happening. And not everyone's happy about giving them up, either."

We were generous, I thought. Starlight had supposedly

been Norma's apprentice, but the old witch had never let her do much beyond making poultices and salves, meaning Starlight was almost as clueless about the deals as I was. But as the book's new keeper and, therefore, the new owner of the deals, I was the only one who could release anyone from them. So this was really on me, but it wasn't progressing well.

"I'll talk to Grace again," I said. "She said she'd help."

Starlight made a face. "I still don't trust her."

"No," I agreed. "But she's a proper witch."

"We're proper witches," Starlight protested, and I looked at her, raising my eyebrows. She sighed. "We *will* be proper witches. We just need more practice."

I personally thought we needed more witchy ability in general, but I kept that to myself. Starlight had been working on being a witch for years and was convinced we just needed to try a bit harder. I, on the other hand, hadn't even believed in magic a few months ago. Not even the David Blaine sort.

Which certainly made for an easier life.

TWO HOURS LATER, I stood outside Mr. Buckley's gate, Grace beside me. Both of us were staring at his garden.

"That's…" I started, then couldn't seem to find the words.

"Rabbits," Grace said, nodding slowly. It made her long hair ripple attractively, catching the late afternoon sunlight.

"I told you," Mr. Buckley said.

"You did," I agreed, but his declaration that he had a rabbit problem had rather failed to encompass the *scale* of the problem.

The bunnies were packed on the front lawn of Mr. Buckley's little bungalow, so thick he'd had to wade through them when he came to the gate to meet us. They crowded the flowerbeds, munching contentedly, and pushed and shoved for room around the little fishpond. I'd already seen one fall in.

The back of the house wasn't visible from here, of course, but the sides were as packed as the front, so I couldn't imagine it was any different. I'd never thought that rabbits made noises, but there was a wash of sound coming from them, muted clucking and purring, and the sheer number of them meant that it was loud enough we were having to raise our voices to be heard. I couldn't even begin to guess how many were crammed between the low stone walls that enclosed the bungalow, yet the gardens to either side were entirely empty. Not even a scrap of fluff to show where one had been, although a few cats were strolling around, evidently trying to decide if they could pick any stragglers off.

"What're you going to do about it?" Mr. Buckley demanded, then irritably pushed a couple of rabbits away with one slippered foot. He had carrots appliquéd to the slippers, and evidently, the bunnies felt it was worth seeing how edible they were.

"Um." I looked at Grace, who just smiled back, raising her eyebrows slightly. "Right." I took the grimoire from my bag, its cover slick with now-familiar yet still disturbing heat. Every time I touched it, I half-expected it to move, but so far it hadn't. Obviously, I hoped it wouldn't, but the anticipation was also wearing a bit thin. I held the book out to Mr. Buckley and said, "Put your hand on the cover." He did, and I summoned up my witchiest voice. "I release you from your deal!"

He snatched his hand away. "Sod that! I want my deal *back!*"

"What?"

"How else am I going to get rid of them?"

"Oh. But surely you don't want to be tied to the book—"

"I don't bloody well care about that! I care about the next competition! I've moved the beetroots into the bath, and the leeks are in pots in my spare bedroom, and it's all just a *nightmare!*" He was close to tears and took a shaky breath. "*Please.* You have to fix this!"

"I don't know if I can," I said.

He put his hand back on the book. "Please try."

I sighed, closed my eyes, and said, "I reaffirm your deal."

There was no snap of lightning, no surge of heat from the book, no sparks or sparkles. I opened one eye and peeked at the garden, but the rabbits were still munching like furry locusts. Someone next door leaned out the window and shouted, "You best not let them near my roses, Warren!" before slamming it closed again.

"You've got no idea what you're doing," Mr. Buckley accused me, which was fair. I gave Grace a pleading look.

"Try again," she said. "I'm sure you'll get it."

So I did. In fact, I tried it three more times, with different intonations, saying "please" or straight up ordering the book to re-establish the deal, all to no effect.

"You're a terrible witch," Mr. Buckley informed me, his lower lip trembling. "Norma was horrible, but she never stuck me with *rabbits*." He turned and stomped back up the path, nudging bunnies out of the way as he went.

I dropped the grimoire back into my bag with a sigh. "He's right," I said to Grace. "I am a terrible witch."

"You're still learning." She shifted her weight with the

languid elegance of a model, the light doing unfairly beautiful things to her skin. "Do you want me to try?"

Jackie hissed from my shoulder, baring her teeth, and I gave Grace an apologetic look. "Best not."

"Suit yourself." She held out one hand, and a moment later, a wren alighted on it, tipping its little head to the side. She whispered something to it and it shuffled, fluttering its wings. She frowned and whispered something else, and the bird took flight with a shudder. "There. All sorted."

"All sorted?" I asked.

"There's more than one way to skin a rabbit," she said, tipping me a wink, and turned back to where we'd left our bikes leaning against a tree. Or rather her bike and Starlight's, which I'd borrowed. I followed, my stomach uneasy. She hadn't meant *skin* literally, had she?

"What did you do? Did you put the deal back somehow?"

"I can't do that without using the book," she said. "And since *you* won't let me do that..." She shrugged expressively.

"That's Jackie that won't let you," I said hurriedly, and the rat chittered her displeasure in my ear. Okay, I wasn't super happy about Grace's interest in the book, either. Anyone who had control of it had control of the whole town through the deals, as well as the inherent power of the grimoire itself. On the other hand, it wasn't like I was doing much good with it. Maybe it'd be better with Grace, but Jackie had clear views on the matter.

Grace shrugged. "Whatever. But you're going to have to hurry up and learn to use it, you know. Rabbits aren't going to be the worst of your problems if you don't." She swung onto her bike and pedaled off, leaving me staring at the fluffy, moving blanket surrounding the bungalow. She was right, of course, but how was I meant to learn? I'd yet to see witchcraft as a distance learning course.

Sighing, I got back on Starlight's doddery old bike and headed for town. Bewitching Brews would still be open, and one thing I *was* good at was drinking coffee. I'd put in a lot of practice on that, at least.

TWO

The ferrets are fine

BEWITCHING BREWS BASKED IN THE LATE AFTERNOON sunlight, low and gold where it coasted down the main street and reflected off the shop windows, painting the slowly fading blooms still lingering in the hanging baskets in mellow tones. A couple of cars pottered down the road, but most people were on foot or riding bikes (all of which were a lot further from terminal collapse than Starlight's). Everyone nodded and smiled as they crossed paths or stopped for a chat, except for two men struggling to pry a small white poodle out of the pelican's beak, who was proving deeply uncooperative.

A woman chased a pack of kids on bikes straight down the middle of the street, pelting them with potatoes and screaming that she knew every one of their mums and would be "having words" unless they came back and paid for their ice creams.

I leaned Starlight's bike against the wall of the Cosy Cauldron and watched the kids pass, cackling wildly as they went. I'd never really considered that they had parents. They seemed like a force of nature, circling town ceaselessly on their bikes, sometimes with towels tied around their necks like capes, other times with music blaring from a portable speaker as if they weren't sure what decade they belonged to. And honestly, this being Hollowbeck, I wouldn't have been that surprised if they had been some sort of mystical beasts, Tuck Everlasting's long-lost cousins, or something. Anyone being plain old human around here was more weird than the alternative, I'd decided.

I headed across the road to where Bewitching Brew's green awning leaned over the pavement, offering shelter to half a dozen little Parisian-style tables and chairs. There was nothing unusual about things looking so European around here. Hollowbeck's approach to architecture was as all-encompassing as its approach to pets — or familiars, as the case may be. Although, if everyone in town with a weird critter in tow was a magic worker, they'd have no need for a town witch. I'd almost been run over by a Komodo dragon in a fetching tartan jacket the other day. It had been fleeing the little grocery shop with a whole rotisserie chicken in its mouth, hotly pursued by a distraught middle-aged woman in a well-tailored grey suit who'd been screaming, "Steve! Put it back! You *promised!*"

Anyhow, Hollowbeck embraced Mediterranean white-wash and blue shutters, Provençal burnt yellow walls and terracotta tiles, red-painted Nordic wooden cabins, sprawling American-style ranch houses, and the more expected (as technically, we were somewhere in the Lake District, although not on any map I'd seen) grey stone English cottages. So, a Parisian-style cafe was hardly stretching the limits of the acceptable.

I skirted a table full of the Upstanding Ladies, nodding at them in a friendly way while they scowled at me disapprovingly, and one shook an acorn at me. I wasn't sure if she suspected me of being a squirrel or felt the acorn might protect her from my mighty witchiness, but either way, she was going to be disappointed. I pushed through the door into the cafe itself, with its warmly layered scents of freshly roasted beans and brewing coffee, and breathed in deeply. Now, *that* was magic. I was sure coffee had far more powers than I did.

There were only a couple of tables inside and a few stools pulled up to the counter. Half the shop was given over to the roaster, stainless gleaming warmly under the yellow bulbs. In most places in the UK, any cafe with the majority of its seating outside was well on its way to bankruptcy, but Hollowbeck had less of a microclimate and more of a magic climate controlled by my landlady Petunia. It meant the village wasn't subject to the days of endless drizzle and chilly winds that plagued the rest of the country. Instead, it lived in a little bubble in which Parisian-style seating was entirely realistic.

The inside tables were empty, and the only person taking up a stool was my brother, who was mid-argument with the barista, James. They stopped abruptly when the door opened, then relaxed when they saw it was me.

"Tell your brother I'm not serving him," James said, crossing his arms. It made his biceps do very nice things under his T-shirt sleeves.

I reminded myself James was both Starlight's ex and Grace's current … something. They'd been on at least one date anyway, and there was no use my looking at his biceps. Instead, I looked at my brother, who glared back at me. "He won't serve you," I said.

Ruiner (more properly Rainier, but Ruiner suited him much better, and had since I coined the nickname when we were kids) bared his teeth and said, "Why not?"

"You're a cat," I pointed out, taking the stool beside him.

He glared up at me, fluffy tail swishing irritably. "Only temporarily."

I wanted to say *you hope*, but in truth, I hoped as well. My brother being turned into a cat by persons unknown (at least to me) was how I'd fallen out of my life as a perfectly normal mid-thirties divorcee who might've also been having a teeny, tiny, early mid-life crisis (or late quarter-life one) and landed in Hollowbeck as the world's most inept town witch. Among all the other adjustments that had entailed, I hadn't spent this much time with Ruiner since we were in our early teens. He hadn't got any more tolerable.

"Please explain to him that cats can't just walk into a cafe and order coffee," James said, setting my mug up on the machine. "Or drink it, for that matter."

"Did you forget you were a cat?" I asked Ruiner. He narrowed his eyes at me. They were still the same blue they'd always been, making him a very pretty cat with all the long grey fur.

"Did you forget you're meant to be helping me?" he demanded.

"Thanks to you, I'm stuck helping the whole town. Get in line."

"Other cats don't talk," James pointed out, setting my mug in front of me as he addressed Ruiner. "You can't just be wandering in here talking."

"To be fair, after the carnival, I think people might've picked up on him not being an average cat," I said. The carnival was when Ruiner had been found on top of a dead body and then been arrested by the carnival boss. Bit hard to miss when it happened in front of the whole town. Oh, and who had to sort that out? Yes. Me.

"Exactly. Not that I've ever been average," Ruiner added.

"More than average pain in the bum," I said, and James snorted.

Ruiner tried to stick a paw in my coffee, and I pushed him away. He looked at James. "Now we all agree I'm above average—"

"I didn't say that," I said. "I just said not average. That could go either way."

He ignored me. "—can I have that latte?"

"No," James and I said together.

"Why *not?*" Ruiner wailed. "I miss coffee!"

"You can have some lactose-free milk," James offered, and Ruiner huffed.

"I don't want your crappy milk."

I picked up my mug and took a slow sip. "*Mmm.* So good." Then I jerked my arm away before Ruiner could bite it, and we both growled at each other.

"No fighting in the coffee shop," James said, putting a fat piece of millionaire's shortbread next to my mug. "Only eating."

"And drinking *all* the coffee," I said, taking another mouthful with exaggerated pleasure. Not very exaggerated, though. James was good at coffee.

Ruiner tried biting me again, and James sighed, then gave Ruiner some cat biscuits from a jar behind the counter. My brother huffed and knocked them to the floor.

James frowned at him. "You're really far too into this whole cat thing."

"Instinct," Ruiner said without a trace of guilt.

James shook his head and took a tray outside to clear the Upstanding Ladies' table.

"Where'd you go with Grace?" Ruiner asked. We could see James being lectured by the Upstanding Ladies through the big front window, probably about having a cat at the counter or serving witches. He'd be a while.

I broke off a piece of millionaire's shortbread and gave it to Jackie, who was nestled on my shoulder. "To sort out a plague of bunnies."

"Did it work?"

"Not so far."

He watched James for a moment longer, then said, "Did she ask about the grimoire again?"

"Yes," I admitted, taking a bite of the shortbread. It tasted like there was a touch of rosemary infused in the caramel, which was both surprising and ridiculously good.

"You need to stop trusting her, Morgan. You need to figure the book out yourself."

"But there's no one else to teach me." Which was true. After Norma died, the other most powerful witch in Hollowbeck had turned out to be the murderer (and also James' Aunt Edith). She'd been exiled from town, leaving no one to offer much guidance. There was Petunia, of course, but she limited her interest to weather and frogs, so unless I fancied learning to be some sort of amphibian enthusiast, there wasn't a lot of help to be had there.

"How much has she actually taught you?" Ruiner asked.

I took another bite of the shortbread to avoid answering, and my brother arched his whiskers at me. I sighed. "Not a lot. She's very encouraging, though."

"I'm sure that's super helpful. She's not going to teach you anything at all, you know. She's just going to keep *encouraging* you to get things wrong until you give up and hand the book over to her."

"No, I think she just wants me to figure it out myself. She doesn't want to influence me too much." Even as I said it, I was aware of how thin that sounded. But Grace hadn't been *unhelpful*. She'd helped me get into the carnival when Ruiner was arrested so that I could break him out, and while she hadn't exactly helped me get out again, that hadn't been her fault. I didn't think. The carnival had been tricky, and in the end, I'd had to destroy it to save myself and Ruiner. I hadn't wanted to, but it had been that or Ruiner be a sideshow attraction for the rest of his life and me be dead. And I'd used the grimoire to do it, although I couldn't have said *how*. It had just sort of happened.

"Figure it out, then," Ruiner said. "Read a book or something. You like that sort of stuff."

I made a face. Truthfully, I had an entire stash of books on witchcraft that Ben, the librarian, had found for me, but they were so *dull*. Every time I opened one, I'd wake up an hour later with my face mashed to the pages and drool on my chin. I'd thought learning to be a witch would be all casting spells and dancing around cauldrons deep in the woods. It seemed to be more about memorizing the phases of the moon and knowing the difference between which herbs would fix indigestion, which would kill you slowly and painfully, and which would have you running down the main road naked with a chicken on your head.

"How about you, then?" I asked. "I thought you were looking into the whole cat situation."

"I am, but I'm a cat, Morgan. Which no one's supposed to know. How much can I really do?"

I would normally have hit back with something about projectile vomiting hairballs or shedding on people until they surrendered, but he sounded *despondent*. My brother is many things, but despondent has never been one of them. He's so chronically confident in his ability to handle any situation, it's sickening, and it's resulted in a lot of sleepless nights and bail bills for me, the person who gets him out of all the things it turns out he *can't* handle. Ruiner being despondent was more unsettling than the Komodo dragon had been.

I got up, taking my mug with me. "Come on," I said. "Let's go to the shop. I've got some books to read."

"Do we have any cheese?" he asked me, jumping to the ground. "I could just go for some cheese."

"Absolutely not," I said. "I'll get you some cat treats, though."

He made a gagging sound, but I didn't miss that he ate a couple of the spilled biscuits on the way past.

WE HEADED BACK across the road to the Cosy Cauldron, waving goodbye to James as we went and ignoring his desperately pleading look. The Upstanding Ladies didn't look like they'd be releasing him anytime soon, one of them in full cry about having a cat in a food preparation area, but I could only look after one male at a time, and Ruiner still had a droop to his tail. Besides, even James' very nice biceps weren't worth getting tangled up with the Upstanding Ladies. I'd find myself exorcised or signed up for needlepoint classes or something.

I was halfway across the road when there were hurrying footsteps behind me, and a woman's rather deep voice said, "Excuse me, young lady."

Ruiner made a choking sound that I was pretty sure was him trying not to laugh, and I turned around to find a big woman with heavy, solid arms frowning down at me. "Me?"

"I don't see any other young lady I might be talking to."

"No?" I recognized this particular Upstanding Lady.

She'd interrupted when Edith had me trapped in Bewitching Brews when I'd been trying to find out who had killed Norma. She'd probably saved me, but she'd also told me to go home and learn to make floral centerpieces.

The woman held a book out. "For you."

"Me?"

"Can you not talk properly?"

"No. Sorry. I mean, yes." I took the book, my ears burning. It was bound in old burgundy leather, the gold leaf of the embossed title almost entirely worn away. *Miss Edna's Guide to Proper Comportment for Young Witches*, it read.

"If you're going to be a witch, you may as well be a proper one," the woman said and sniffed as she looked me up and down. "And get some decent clothing, can't you? Not whatever *this* is." She waved at me dismissively, taking in my old jeans and well-worn trainers.

"Um..."

"The correct response is *thank you*."

"Thank you?" I said, and before I could say anything else, she'd marched off again, footsteps as firm as if she were determined to stomp the earth into respectability below her. I looked at Ruiner and inclined the book toward him.

He craned to read the title. "So was that Miss Edna, then?"

"No idea," I said, stashing the book in my satchel along with the grimoire. I looked up as Starlight burst out of the shop door, waving wildly. "That doesn't look good."

"She's probably run out of incense," Ruiner said and followed me as we ambled across the empty road.

"*There* you are!" Starlight said as soon we were close enough to talk. "I was about to come looking for you."

"Why?" I asked. "It's not more rabbits, is it?"

"No—"

"Or ferrets? I thought the ferrets had calmed down."

"The ferrets are fine," she said, petting Howard, who was still on her shoulder. I eyed him warily. He looked smug, and I suspected him of peeing on my bag at least once.

"What, then?" I asked, taking a sip of coffee.

Starlight handed me a sheet of paper without answering. For one stomach-churning moment, I thought it was another note of the sort that had been plaguing me since I arrived in Hollowbeck. I had no idea who sent them or why, but they all carried the same warning: I needed to leave, to get out of the magical world. I'd resolutely ignored them so far, but they were yet another thing I had to figure out, and I had no way of doing so. I took the paper with stiff fingers and sighed in relief. Rather than heavy, textured stock, this was a piece of flimsy notepaper torn from a pad.

Starlight took my mug from me and said, "I think it's important."

I gave her a puzzled look, and she nodded at the paper. I unfolded it slowly, barely noticing Ruiner leaping to my shoulder so he could see it, too, provoking a hiss from Jackie. The paper had a line drawing of an old-fashioned phone at the top and spirals, presumably meant to be the phone cord, creating a border on the sides. *Someone called for you!*was printed at the bottom, and in the middle was a note written in blue pen in uneven letters.

Morgan, I need help. Please come. Jason.

I stared at it, my fingers so numb that some part of my mind was amazed the paper didn't just slip through my fingers and vanish.

"Who's Jason?" Starlight almost whispered.

I couldn't find the words, my head too full of questions, and Ruiner answered for me.

"Her crappy ex-husband," he said. "Who we're going to ignore, aren't we? Morgan? Morgs?"

I still didn't reply. Jason wasn't a great person, and he'd been an even worse husband. But if he'd been able to send me a message in Hollowbeck and find me in a hidden, magical town, that meant only one thing.

Whatever trouble he was in, it was all my fault.

THREE

RING-RING!

"Morgan?" Ruiner said again.

I ignored him and looked at Starlight. "Where did this come from?"

She shook her head, pale hair shivering and face pinched into unfamiliar, anxious lines. "It was just on the counter. I was working in the kitchen and heard the bell on the counter ring. When I came through, the note was there. I didn't even hear the chimes on the door for anyone coming in or out."

"Morgan," Ruiner said, as though he thought I'd start listening to him if he said my name enough times. "We're not running off after Jason. He's a git. Whatever trouble he's in, it's nothing to do with you."

"He is a git," I agreed. "But he got a note to me *here*. In Hollowbeck. In his writing. It's not like he looked up my address on Google bloody maps and nipped over, right?" Hollowbeck has ways of protecting itself from outsiders. It's not on any map I've ever found, even though Ben and I had gone through a load of them at the library, just out of interest. And apparently, if someone's not invited or otherwise meant to be here, and it's outside the very limited tourist season, the roads into the valley simply turn away and deliver the car back to the outside world again. There's no mobile phone signal, and the landlines are patchy, rife with echoes and crossed wires. Hollowbeck is entirely happy to have nothing whatsoever to do with the outside world. There was no way Jason could've just stumbled into it.

Ruiner huffed. "You probably mentioned Hollowbeck to him at some point. You did your usual nice person, *oh, come and visit* thing and accidentally invited him. It's not hard for someone to find you once they're in the village."

"I haven't spoken to him since he offered me half my books back, and I told him what he could do with them. Speaking to Jason is not conducive to good mental health."

"Half the books seems reasonable," Starlight volunteered.

"He wanted me to *buy* them back. First option before he sold them elsewhere, apparently. And they were my books to start with."

"Oh." Starlight wrinkled her nose. "I see."

"There's no way I'd even accidentally invite him," I told Ruiner.

"Not even, like, *come here so I can demonstrate exactly what to do with those books?*" he suggested.

I considered it, then shook my head. "No. And that was before I got here, anyway. I haven't spoken to anyone since then." I had a twinge of discomfort at that. I'd emailed Mum a few times, but with the phone lines being what they were, I hadn't bothered calling. I needed to. She'd probably mortgaged the house for a limited edition signed print of Prince Achileas-Andreas of Greece by now. "Ruiner, this is serious. Whatever trouble he's in, it's because of me."

"We don't even know the note's definitely from him," my brother said, his tail twitching.

I held up the note. "I don't know anyone else who writes like a duck on steroids."

Starlight took the note from me and examined it. "This would be really easy to forge, though. I mean, it looks like about four different people wrote it."

She was right. There were capitals thrown into the middle of words, *E*s that looked like *I*s, and the *D*s appeared to have been written backward. "That's just how he writes," I said. "And who'd bother forging it?"

"Anyone who wanted you out of Hollowbeck," Ruiner said.

"Jason is not a good way to get me to do anything."

"Sure he is. Look at you. You're all ready to drop everything and go rushing off to the rescue, and you don't even know what the problem *is*. Maybe he's forgotten to pay the car insurance, or he's had a fight with his girl-friend, or he's got a sodding splinter. Any of those are an emergency in Jason's world."

"But he sent me a message *here*."

"*Someone* did. Let's find out how and make sure we *know* who."

"But what if he's really in trouble?"

"He's a grown man. He can sort it out for himself."

I raised my eyebrows at my brother, waiting.

He glared back at me with those disconcerting blue eyes, then huffed and looked away. "You're my sister. Of course, I come to you for help. He's your ex, and he's got no right to still be doing that. He always was bloody useless."

"You never did like him."

"Was I wrong?"

It was very hard to argue with that. Ruiner was always

the same, constantly sailing blithely into bad situations and expecting me to sort it out. Still, he had also always been right about Jason. He'd disliked my hubby-to-be right from the start, and I'd thought it was because it was taking attention away from him. Well, I'd said I thought that. If I was honest, I'd always known there was at least a little truth in Ruiner's assessment of Jason. But I could hardly admit that. Ruiner was insufferable enough without me telling him he was right about things.

None of that changed the fact that if Jason was sending me notes in Hollowbeck, he was likely in the sort of trouble only I could get him out of. I doubted my feckless ex had suddenly taken up with magic-workers.

"I need to at least check on him," I said.

"Then call him," Ruiner said. "Don't rush to the rescue like some misguided mountain dog."

"Did you just call me a dog?"

"You know what I mean. And I'm telling you, this is some sort of ploy to get you out of Hollowbeck."

"Why would anyone do that?"

"Hollowbeck's a safe space," Starlight said when Ruiner hesitated. "You know, Theodore and Isabella make sure anyone here uses magic to good ends, and no one's doing any creepy stuff. No raising the dead or calling down plagues or that sort of thing."

"Right," I said. "But how does that help?"

"It's also protected," she said. "It's not just that no one can come in without being invited. Things really are just safer here."

I supposed she was right. Crime in Hollowbeck seemed to be limited to the kids stealing ice creams and a little vegetable espionage. Other than the fact that we kept stumbling onto dead bodies, of course.

"She's right," Ruiner said. "If anyone's after you for

nefarious purposes, it's a lot easier to nab you out there than in here."

I frowned. "Why would anyone be after me for nefarious purposes?"

"Oh, I don't know — for the book, maybe?"

I tugged my bag a little closer to me. "Because of the deals?"

"Sure," Starlight said. "But it's an old book, too. It's got a lot of its own power. That's why Aubrey tried to take it from you at the carnival."

Aubrey, the ring woman. Nausea see-sawed in my belly. When I'd all but destroyed the carnival, it had almost killed her, too. I had no idea if she or it had survived. They'd both vanished in the aftermath, and I felt like as much of a murderer as she was for it.

As if reading my thoughts, Ruiner added, "It could be about the book, or it could be a grudge. For destroying the carnival or getting Edith exiled. Loads of reasons for someone to want to have a go at you."

I crossed my arms over my chest and stared at the two of them. "So, what — I can never leave Hollowbeck now?"

"I don't know why you'd want to," Starlight said, mainly to Howard, who had somehow got tangled in her hair. She winced as she tried to unwind the long strands from his teeth. "I mean, it's awful out there. No one's even doing anything about the weather."

I wondered if it was worth pointing out that no one was *meant* to do anything about the weather because everywhere other than Hollowbeck the weather just happened. We had no idea what the consequences of Petunia *doing something* about it would be. Still, it was hardly the most important thing. Instead, I said, "What do I do, then? I can't just ignore the note."

"Sure you can," Ruiner said. I looked at Starlight since she had a distinctly better moral compass than my brother.

She considered it, then said, "Call him."

"How? We don't have a phone, and the library'll be closed." I did have my mobile, half-forgotten, in a pocket of the satchel, but it was useless for anything but photos around here. The only place I knew that had a phone and internet was the library, although the connection was still in the dial-up era and even more intermittent than the phone.

Starlight looked at the clock on the wall doubtfully, then said, "*Ooh!*" and dived through the curtain behind the counter, setting the beads clacking in her wake.

Ruiner and I looked at one another. He arched his whiskers, and I shrugged. A moment later, Starlight emerged, carting an old phone in one hand. Its white plastic body was yellowed with age, it had a black rotary dial on the front, and I was sure it was older than I was. Starlight clutched one end of a phone cable in the other hand, and she looked around behind the counter dubiously.

"There won't be a connection," I said. "We don't get a phone bill."

"We don't use it," she said reasonably.

"No, but we'd need to pay line rental," I started, then gave up when she started digging into the shelves. Starlight didn't come from Hollowbeck to my knowledge, but she certainly acted like she had no idea how the outside world worked.

"Here it is!" She burrowed into the corner where the counter met the wall, plugged the cable into some unseen connector, then clunked the phone onto the counter with a satisfying ding.

Ruiner and I both looked at it dubiously. Starlight sighed, tossed her long pale hair over one shoulder, and picked up the handset, holding it to one ear while she jiggled the cradle with her free hand.

"Nothing yet," she announced.

"Well, of course, there's not," I said. "I told you, we don't have a line."

"Give it a moment to connect," she said, jiggling it a few more times.

"It's not a great advertisement for magic-workers, is it?" Ruiner asked me, and I shushed him.

"I'll go to the library," I said aloud. "Ben might still be there, and I might be able to check my emails." The last time I'd tried, my inbox had been so inundated with junk I'd simply shut the window again without even reading anything, but if the internet was working, I could search for anything from Jason.

"Here it comes," Starlight said and held the handset out to me.

"What?"

"It's connecting." She waggled the phone at me. "Just don't say anything too private. Don at the bank's always listening in."

"You can't listen in to someone's phone call," Ruiner said.

"You could on old lines," I told him, taking the phone. "There was a sort of shared line for the whole neighborhood or street, and you were meant to get off if it wasn't for you. Like listening in on a call in the house."

"That's creepy," he said.

Not as creepy as what I heard when I put the phone to my ear, though. It was a rushing susurrus of disembodied voices, flooding out of a depthless silence, building up and up as if I'd dropped into a conversation of ghosts. I couldn't divide one from another, and I pulled the phone away from my ear as if afraid they'd somehow infect me. I didn't want those voices rattling around in my head.

"Dial," Starlight said, nodding at the phone.

I stared at it. There were only a handful of numbers I knew off by heart. Our old home phone, Ruiner's mobile, and Jason's. Hesitantly, I dialed my ex's number, hooking a finger into the little wheel and spinning it around. With every digit I entered, the voices grew louder, chattering excitedly and setting goosebumps on my arms. As I continued, I realized they were falling into a jumbled chorus. By the time I spun the dial for the final time, they were all chanting the number, not quite in unison. As the wheel spun back into place, they began bellowing, *"Ring-ring! Ring-ring! RING- RING!"*

A shudder went snaking down my spine, but I didn't put the phone down. I clutched the handset so hard it creaked under the pressure.

"RING-RING!" the voices yelled. *"RING-RING!"*

The phone clicked, and Jason said, "Hello," the sound of his voice setting off equal measures of relief and distaste.

"Jason," I started.

"—leave a message and all that," his bored tones continued, and I groaned as the tone bleeped.

"Of course, it's bloody messages. Jason, it's Morgan. Call me back on this number." I had no idea what this number actually was, but hopefully, weird chanting phones still showed up on caller ID. I hung up hurriedly, then looked at Ruiner and Starlight. "I suppose I just wait now. See if he calls back."

"Do you have another number?" Starlight asked. "A home phone or something?"

I shuddered. "No. And those voices are so creepy I'm not about to try calling around anyway."

"What voices?"

"The ones yelling out the number."

She gave me a bewildered look, then picked up the handset and listened. She dialed a few numbers randomly and then held it out to me. "There's nothing there."

I frowned, taking the phone from her and listening. All I could hear was the rush of an open connection, then, very distantly, a tiny voice whispered, "*doot-doot-doot*," and giggled. I put the handset down hurriedly. "Whatever. We didn't have a home phone. I'll just have to wait."

Starlight shrugged. "I can wait. I'm still working on some tinctures, so I was going to stay open late anyway."

"Are you sure?" I asked. The Cosy Cauldron had deeply erratic opening times, partly to cater to Hollowbeck's less diurnal inhabitants but mostly because Starlight seemed to regard business hours as nothing more than suggestions.

"Of course," she said. "You go and see if you can check your emails."

"Or," Ruiner said, "you forget about your pointless ex for the night. Tomorrow he can call you whining about having mismatched socks or something, and you can tell him to sod off."

"I'd rather check my emails."

"Ugh, *fine*. Let's go and talk to Book Boy. He's not quite as useless as Jason, I suppose." Ruiner led the way to the door, fringed tail curving gracefully, and I gave Starlight a little wave, then followed, running a hand back through my hair. It needed a tidy-up after the carnival incident had resulted in some burned bits and a hasty crop, but Starlight insisted she be the one to do it, and I wasn't sure our friendship was ready for that yet.

We walked through the deepening dusk, the sky a rich indigo, stained at the edges with the red lines of the sunset.

The last of the leaves were still clinging to the trees, but the night felt as if it'd be bringing frost, and I tucked my scarf in around the neck of my jacket, zipping it up more tightly. Jackie burrowed into the soft folds of cloth, and I touched the satchel, heavy with both books still in it.

Could someone really be setting this up to lure me out of Hollowbeck? No one could just *take* the grimoire. I had a claim to it, fragile as it was, and that needed to be released. From what I'd read in the books Ben and I had dug through, the longer I had the grimoire, the deeper the connection to it. Even killing me wouldn't be enough because then Jackie would retain the claim and choose who to pass it to. Stealing the book would require me willingly relinquishing my connection or a spell such as Aubrey had tried to use to shatter the bonds between myself, Jackie, and the book (and kill me while she was at it). Or killing me and persuading Jackie to give the book to the killer. And Jackie was very difficult to persuade, in my experience.

We didn't talk as we walked, listening to the quiet sounds of the day's life fading and the night emerging, lights flooding the street with a gently surreal orange glow as the stars bloomed above. It wasn't far to the library, ensconced in its gardens next to the town hall, everything looking a little muted but still rich as the bright colours of summer and autumn faded into the cooler shades of winter.

I tried the door. It was locked, so I knocked firmly, listening to the sound echoing inside. The lights were off, though, and I knew Ben was rather less lax about his hours than we were. He and Dee, the tartan-clad and slightly unsettling assistant librarian, had daytime hours three days a week, alternating with three nights (although I did wonder why they didn't split the shifts between them, as Dee wasn't a fan of daylight. Maybe what Dee did when unsupervised was one of those things I didn't really want answers to, though).

Today had been a daytime shift, and they'd be packed up by now, Ben off making dodgy herbal teas somewhere, and Dee ... I don't know. The question of what Dee did in her spare time could be filed with what she did when unsupervised.

I leaned against the door, looking over the shadowy gardens. I had no one else I could call other than Mum, and if Jason had run to her with any problems, I really would try my hand out at a curse, preferably something deeply embarrassing and impossible to hide. There was nowhere else in town where I could think of to try to get online, and I had to reluctantly admit that Ruiner did have a point about not rushing off unprepared. I looked at my brother, sitting on the library's welcome mat (it had a frog in a smoking jacket reading a pile of books on it, and I wondered if Petunia had been involved in its purchase) with his tail curled over his toes and his snout raised to the night air.

"Drink?" I said.

"Finally, a good idea," he replied and got up, strutting ahead of me back down the gravel path. I followed, and the hair on my arms still stood to attention despite my jacket. Something was up. I was sure of it.

The question was, what?

FOUR

Can everyone stop being logical?

THE WITCHING HOUR'S ROOFTOP BEER GARDEN WAS STILL open, even as the encroaching winter robbed its trellises of their foliage. Huge candles flickered in hurricane lanterns set on the low walls, and more candles in glass vases decorated the tables. Big fluffy blankets were stacked at the end of each pallet sofa, and I wrapped myself in one as we settled down at our usual table. Ruiner complained until I let him sit on my lap, bundled in a second blanket. His warmth was so welcome I could ignore that he was my brother, and judging by the rusty purring emerging from his cocoon of soft fleece, he was pretty satisfied with the situation, too.

Tanya emerged from the stairs to the bar with a tray bearing a large thermos mug for me, a soup bowl for Ruiner, and a little plate of chopped fruit for Jackie, which she clambered out of the folds of my blanket to investigate before snatching a large piece of apple and retreating again.

"Warm enough?" Tanya asked, setting the drinks down and taking a lighter from her pocket.

"Mostly," I said. My nose was sniffly and felt like it was probably an unattractive shade of red, but otherwise, I was pretty cozy among the swaddling of blankets.

"This should help." Tanya flicked the lighter and touched it to a little trough in the center of the table, which immediately leaped into luminous flame

"*Ooh*," I said. "Magic heating!"

She gave me an amused look, lips quirking up. "No. Bioethanol."

"Oh. Right. Well, it's very pretty anyway." How was I meant to know? Magic was a fair bet around here. I picked up my mug in both hands and sniffed it.

"Citrus, ginger, and a touch of thyme in a whisky base," Tanya said.

"Sounds good." No one ordered in the Witching Hour. You got what you were given, and other than one dubious liquorice and candy floss concoction after the carnival and something weirdly mossy on a rainy autumn day that I wasn't even sure had been intended for me (it had been busy and Tanya had had someone else taking the orders out), they'd all been excellent. And I'd still drunk the less-than-excellent ones. It didn't do to upset the bar alchemist. I handed her a large jar of safe-for-canines hair conditioner. Hollowbeck ran, for the most part, on a barter system, and Tanya had very specific skincare needs. Or maybe werewolves, in general, did. I wasn't sure. She was the first werewolf I'd met.

"Thanks," she said, taking the lid off to sniff it. "*Hmm*, nice."

"Starlight's been playing with some new recipes," I said. "She said that one should be particularly good for … for, um…" Suddenly, I wished I hadn't started the sentence.

Tanya quirked an eyebrow at me. She was a tall,

curving woman with strong hands and canines that showed a little more than usual. I could see them now as she said, "For fleas?"

"Not suggesting you have them," I said, and Ruiner snorted into his bowl of chicken broth, which he was trying to eat without leaving the shelter of the blankets.

Tanya laughed. "I should bloody hope not. But good to know. Now, what's up with you? You smell a bit anxious. Not going to start any more wars with carnivals, are you?"

"Not planning to," I said. "Just an issue with my ex."

"Ah." She pointed at my mug. "Want an extra shot in that?"

"Best not." The first sip was already washing heat through my chest and making the lights go funny at the edges.

"Alright. Theodore'll be here soon, anyway. That'll cheer you up." She tipped me a wink as she left, and Ruiner craned his head out of the blankets.

"Tell me you're not going soft for the vampire sheriff."

"He's not a sheriff."

"Not my point."

"Fine, I'm not going soft for a blood-sucking cop hundreds of years older than me with an unreasonable affection for spray tan." Although Theodore also had the sort of cheekbones you could ski off and a weirdly delightful old-fashioned courtesy, so I wasn't objecting to his company.

"Better not," Ruiner said, hooking a strip of chicken out of his bowl with one paw. "Remember, I was right about Jason."

"Don't spill your chicken juice on me," I said, pushing him off my lap.

"Hey! Give me back my blanket!"

We were still scuffling about, Ruiner trying to drag his

chicken into the den he'd dug in the blanket while I tried to convince him we didn't want to mess up a werewolf's belongings (I was sure this was why there were never any fights at the Witching Hour. Having a bartender who could rip your face off goes a long way to keeping things civil), when someone said, "Am I interrupting?"

I looked up to see Ben, a dark green tartan scarf wrapped around his neck and a waxed jacket zipped to his chin. He had a grey woolen hat pulled down over his ears and a thermos mug that matched mine in one long-fingered hand.

"Oh look, it's Book Boy," Ruiner said.

"Ignore him," I said to Ben.

"I usually do." He sat down, pulling a spare blanket over his knees, and wrapped both hands around his mug. "Alright?"

"I came by the library earlier," I said.

"Oh? What for? Not my tea, I suppose." He gave me a sudden, dimpled grin, and I couldn't help grinning back. I still hadn't entirely forgiven him for dosing me with calming tea when I'd just arrived in Hollowbeck. Although to be fair, the first time, I'd found a dead body, and the second time, I'd just thrown myself out of a cursed car. I'd been in need of some calming. And he was hard to stay angry at, especially as he was the only other person here who seemed to have any concept of just how bloody weird Hollowbeck was.

"I wanted to use your internet."

"Good luck with that," he said, sipping his drink and shuddering. "Bloody hell — is Tanya a bit heavy-handed tonight?"

"Maybe," I said, taking a sip of my own and wincing. "Is the internet down, then?"

"It's something. Every time I try to connect, I just get

this awful EEEEE-EEE-EE." He did a passable imitation of the dial-up connection sound, startling a man drinking beer with a miniature horse at the next table. Ben raised his hand apologetically.

"Isn't that usual?"

"No, it's more like someone making the noise than the noise itself, if that makes sense. And I can't get the bloody thing to connect at all."

I thought of the weird phone call earlier and said, "That's not happened before?"

"No. I mean, the phone lines are always a bit dodgy, but they usually work."

"Do you ever get a load of voices on them?"

He gave me a puzzled look. "Voices? No. Only Don at the bank."

I looked at Ruiner, but he was smuggling more chicken under the blanket and was ignoring me. "When did it start?"

"Just today. Why? What's happening?" His voice was warm and concerned, and I reminded myself again that I couldn't trust anyone who served me calming teas, even if it had basically been supercharged camomile, and they happened to have dimples and very nice forearms for a librarian.

"I think I need to leave Hollowbeck," I said.

"What? Why?" He took a hurried sip as if to brace himself, then spluttered. "Oh, hell, that's strong."

"Not permanently," I said, although even as I said it, I realized there was no reason not to consider that too. I wasn't getting anywhere with the book here. Maybe I would out in the wider world. There had to be more witches out there, more chances to find someone who could help me.

"That's a relief," he said, then looked at his mug with great interest. "I mean, we'd all miss you."

I decided to ignore that and said, "You go out all the time, don't you?"

"About once a month," he said. "I like getting biscuits stuffed full of additives and mass-produced baked beans with half a dozen E-numbers in them, not ones made in the home kitchen of Mrs. Betty Baker in Little Oak Farm or whatever."

I snorted. The local grocery store was a hipster's paradise, everything produced in Hollowbeck's long, variegated valley, or at the very least imported from mysterious small businesses elsewhere in the magical community. Every label bore painstakingly detailed stories about the product's origins, often handwritten, and even the eggs had the name of the chicken stamped on them individually. Which was lovely, obviously, but it was also really rubbish when all one wanted was some two-minute noodles and a can of orange Tango.

"Do you have to do anything to leave?" I asked Ben now, and he frowned.

"Do anything?"

"Yeah, like get permission or … or a key or something."

He was still frowning at me, then suddenly, his face cleared. "Oh. You haven't tried leaving since your car was cursed by Edith."

"No," I admitted. The curse had sent my car rogue, jamming the accelerator down on the winding road as it climbed out of the valley. It ended up in my taking an off-road route back, first in the runaway car, then on foot, once I'd thrown myself clear. I didn't fancy a repeat.

"She hasn't even driven since then," Ruiner said, licking chicken broth from his whiskers.

"I have," I protested.

"Moving the car from one side of the street to the other so it didn't get classified as abandoned doesn't count."

I made a face at him, but Ben just nodded seriously, "It makes sense. That must've been a horrible experience."

I poked my drink and made a vague noise of agreement. I wished he wouldn't be nice at me. It made my chest unaccountably tight.

"Do you want me to drive you?" Ben asked,

I blinked at him. "You don't even know where I'm going."

"No, but I'm almost out of custard cremes," he said. "I can stock up at the same time."

"I'm sure I'll be fine," I said, even though the thought of getting in the car was making my palms sweat. That could also have been the cocktail, though.

Ben nodded, took another mouthful of his drink, and made a startled little *wow* sound under his breath. "When are you going?" he asked.

"We're not," Ruiner said

"We are," I insisted. "Or I am. You can stay here and lick your toes if you want."

"Sure, I'm going to let you go chasing off after your idiot ex alone. That sounds like a *great* idea."

"Your ex?" Ben said, with just a little too much interest.

I sighed. "He sent me a message. He needs my help."

"*Someone* sent you a message," Ruiner said. "How many times—"

I cut him off by pulling the blanket over his head. "I'm still figuring things out," I said to Ben. "That's why I was wanting to check my emails. I couldn't get him on the phone to confirm anything."

"Right," he said. "Well, if the message isn't definitely from him—"

"What message is this?" a new voice asked, and I looked up as Isabella, our ghostly mayor, swept across the terrace to join us, all smile and bosom and soft black curls. Theodore strolled after her, looking dashing in an open-necked shirt that set off his luminous orange tan. I don't know where Hollowbeck got its fake tan supplies, but either they weren't well tested, or Theodore was spectacularly heavy-handed.

"Morgan," he said to me. "Delightful as always. And Ben."

"Theodore," Ben said just as gravely, and I hid a grin.

"Do move over, Benji," Isabella said, waving at him, and he sighed, sliding a little closer to me.

"Ben," he said. "Or Benjamin. Either works. Just not Benji."

"Sorry," she said, with no hint of contriteness. "What's this about messages and exes, then, Morgan?"

"Her useless muppet of an ex-husband has sent her a message saying he needs help, and she wants to rush off to the rescue, only we don't even know if the message is really from him or if he's just got a hangnail or *hmmph—!*"

I bundled Ruiner firmly into the blanket this time, ignoring his struggles to extricate himself. "Just some personal stuff."

"Are you thinking of going to find him, Morgan?" Theodore asked. He was drinking from a large insulated cup, and I was just grateful for the lid and metal straw. I'd seen its contents before, and it wasn't Bloody Mary mix, even if it looked like it.

"He sent me a message here, in Hollowbeck. I can't just ignore it if he's in trouble."

Theodore and Isabella exchanged glances, and I had a

sudden surge of irritation. Fine, yes, they were both older than me, probably by hundreds of years, but I wasn't a *child*. I didn't need them being all mature and logical at me.

"Morgan, dear," Isabella said. "Your brother may have a point about waiting to find out if the message is really from this ex of yours."

"Sure. But I've tried calling him back, and there's no answer. Ben says the internet is down. So what else am I meant to do?"

"Perhaps we can help," Theodore suggested, dabbing at his lips with a napkin.

"That's not necessary. Ruiner's probably right and Jason's just making a fuss over nothing. I just need to be sure."

"Do let us help," Isabella said. "Dealing with exes is always so..." She waved expressively, then finished with, "Ugh."

I couldn't help laughing at that. "Yeah, it is. But it's fine, really."

"Fine, as in you intend to go anyway?" Theodore asked, opening the lid of his drink to peer inside.

"Fine, as in it's my business," I replied more sharply than I intended to. But it *was*. Jason was my mess, one I'd hoped not to have to clean up again, but if I had to, I had to. It was nothing to do with anyone else.

"I would suggest that it may not be entirely safe," Theodore said, looking up at me. His eyes were deeply dark, and the light slid off his cheekbones in ways that should be illegal. "I take it you never told him about Hollowbeck."

"No," I admitted.

"That's what I've been trying to tell her," Ruiner said. His voice was muffled, and he seemed to have given up trying to find his way out of the blanket. "I think it's a trap."

Theodore raised one eyebrow. "You have reason to think this?"

"He doesn't," I said. "It's just a bit weird, is all, how he was able to get a message to me."

"Who brought the message?" Isabella asked.

"I don't know that, either."

No one spoke for a long time, and I could feel them all wanting to tell me the same thing — to stay in Hollowbeck, ignore Jason's message, and stay *safe*. Which was all very sensible, of course. If the positions were reversed, I'd probably say the same thing, but this was Jason. He could barely get himself out of a public car park without someone holding his hand. I got up abruptly, shedding the blankets and slinging my satchel over my shoulder. Jackie scrambled up my coat with a squeak of irritation.

"Sorry. I need to go."

"Morgan," Theodore started.

"I'll talk to you later." I headed for the stairs, the grimoire hot and heavy against my hip.

"Morgan, wait," Ben called, but no one followed me as I clattered down the stairs into the warmth of the bar below.

It had filled up since we'd come in, the long, narrow room awash with low music, a rumble of contented conversation, and the competing scents of wintery cocktails. Tanya wasn't at the bar, so I slipped out unnoticed. I hesitated for a moment, then turned left rather than right, heading away from the main street.

Part of me wanted to check in with Starlight, but they'd expect me to go there, and I didn't want them following me. I didn't want to talk about it anymore. I didn't want anyone else being *logical* at me, especially my wildly illogical brother. I couldn't keep justifying the fact that, yes, Jason had been a terrible husband. Yes, he'd somehow managed to come out of the marriage with the house *I'd* bought. Yes, he'd been shagging his much younger girlfriend on the lounge set I'd *also* bought, but if he were in trouble because of me, I couldn't leave it. I simply couldn't.

And if no one had to give me some sort of magical permission slip to leave the valley, I didn't need to talk to anyone about it. I could just go, check he was okay, and be done with it. Or fix things if he wasn't.

I picked up the pace, heading toward Petunia's guesthouse, where we rented a room for the grand total of some digging in the garden (mostly discontinued since it turned out I was really bad at distinguishing between weeds and vegetables), and carting bottles of whisky back from the grocery shop. There was no point procrastinating on this any longer, wondering what was going on. I'd get my stuff together, leave first thing in the morning, and find out for sure. A faint shiver of excitement crept into my belly. Outside. I was going *outside* of Hollowbeck, back where I belonged. Back where I knew how things worked. I'd sort out whatever Jason's little drama was, and it'd all be absolutely fine. It would.

I continued thinking that until I was about halfway home, in the darkness between the streetlights, and the night filled with a rush of whispering voices, spiraling around me, chasing the excitement out and replacing it with dread.

Hollowbeck wasn't letting me go that easily.

FIVE

A haunting call

I FROZE IN THE MIDDLE OF THE STREET, HUGGING THE satchel to my chest with both arms, Jacqueline chittering in my ear. The voices seemed to be coming from everywhere and nowhere, out of the air or out of the dim side streets and unlit gardens, their shadows hiding a myriad of ghosts.

I spun on my heel, not sure which way to run or even if I *could* run. Straight up or down the street would hardly save me, but would banging on someone's door help? What if the voices were *in* the houses, hissing from the curtained windows? Or waiting behind the walls to pounce on me as soon as I opened a gate? Worse, what if someone came to help, but no one could hear the ghosts but me? I looked down the street, but the Witching Hour was already lost a couple of blocks back, and no one appeared to save me.

The whispers rose to a roar, a windstorm of noise bearing down on me out of the chilly night, drowning my own panicked breaths and pounding heart. I could've sworn they were chanting my own mobile number back at me, unused though it was. I tried a step in the direction of

Petunia's guesthouse, feeling like I was fighting against a physical onslaught of sound the way I might a gale.

Then my phone rang. The vibration startled me so much that I dropped the satchel like a snake had unwound from it. Of course, I still had the strap across my body, so it just banged somewhat painfully into my hip, the unexpectedly familiar ringtone jingling out into the night, shrilling through the chorus of gleeful voices.

For a moment, I couldn't move, gasping for air, and then I clawed the phone out of the bag's pocket, almost dropping it. The display didn't say anything, not even *Unknown Number.* It was just a blank green screen, the phone icon looming in the middle of it. I poked answer, and the voices fell silent as abruptly as if I'd shut a soundproof door on them. I looked around, my hands shaking as I raised the mobile gingerly to my ear.

"Hello?" I whispered.

There was nothing but a strange whisper, like an intake of breath, then a click of connection, and Jason's voice said, "Morgan?"

"Jason?" My voice didn't wobble, which was astonishing. "Jason, what the hell—"

"Dammit, is this an answerphone? Hello? Hello? Morgs?" His voice was coming and going, as if he were driving through tunnels, the connection fractured and unreliable.

"Don't call me Morgs," I muttered, taking the phone away from my ear and inspecting it. There was still no name or number on the display, and the little bars at the top had a large and adamant X on them. There was no signal of any sort, yet here I was. Talking to my crappy ex. "Jason? Can you hear me?"

"Morgs, where are you? I need help. I've got myself into a bit of a … situation." He paused. "Why aren't you answering? I emailed, but you didn't answer that either. How'm I supposed to get hold of you?" There was a whiny, plaintive note to his disembodied voice that I recognized too well, even with the distortion. "Can you just come? I don't want to talk on the phone." He paused, then sighed and added, "Please."

I heard the click of disconnection, and a single, oddly androgynous voice said, "Boop-boop-boop-*click*." Then it giggled, and I jerked the phone away from my ear, jabbing for the disconnect button, but the display was already back to my home screen, cluttered with unused icons over a photo of a piece of cake, which I'd chosen for the simple reason that it was the first one on my camera roll when I took the photo of Jason and me down. I thumbed across to the call log, and the last one was to Mum from before we'd arrived in Hollowbeck. I stared at it with no great surprise, then slowly slipped the phone back into my bag and looked around.

The street was still empty. No one had come out into the garden to gawp at the town witch talking to no one on her non-functional phone. The voices vanished as quickly as they'd risen to swamp the night. A dog barked a couple of houses over, and someone was either calling their cat in or had a weird pet name for their partner, and from an open window drifted the sound of someone playing "Highway to Hell" on a flute. Even as I listened, someone bellowed, "S*hut up!*"accompanied by the crash of something being thrown from a neighboring garden to smash into the wall. The flute player paused, then resumed with added rigour.

I took a deep, shaky breath, pressing the heels of my hands over my eyes, and Jacqueline squirmed in the folds of my scarf, nuzzling my ear with her whiskery nose. I lifted her down and examined her. "What the hell was that?" I asked.

She regarded me with beady dark eyes and squeaked in what seemed to be a generally supportive tone, which was largely unhelpful. How come the only animal that talked around here had to be my annoying brother? I returned her to my shoulder, letting her wriggle back into the shelter, and checked the street again. No ghosts, no disembodied heads to go with the voices, no rogue ventriloquists chasing me about. Not that I thought there would be, but after the carnival, I wasn't ruling anything out. I adjusted the satchel strap, feeling both too hot and too cold all at once. I remembered that uncomfortable feeling I'd had on the phone earlier. The one where I'd suspected the voices of trying to somehow infect me.

"Oh, bloody hell, no," I whispered to the night. "Don't tell me I've caught ghosts or something." Was there a salve for that? Anti-ghost tincture? I wanted to laugh at the thought, but I couldn't. The idea that Jason could sort of jump into my life anytime he wanted by way of the spooky voices was intolerable. And what if it spread? What if my *mum* could do the same any time she tried to call me? I had sudden visions of being on a date (if I ever managed to get one again) and ghost voices materializing out of the night to demand I talk to her right now, and what *on earth* was I wearing? No, this was no good. No good at *all*.

I turned back to town, hurrying straight down the centre of the street, as if I thought that would keep me safe. It was pretty clear by now that it wasn't, but one can hope, right?

~

THE COSY CAULDRON was still open, light spilling warm across the pavement, and a squirrel snoozing in the basket of second-hand books outside the display window. It opened one eye as I went past, snuggled its tail a little closer around its neck, and slept on. It was pillowed on a woolly hat that still had a price tag from one of the dress shops on it. I supposed I should try to reclaim the stolen property for them, but it looked far too snug. I just hurried past instead and crashed through the door unceremoniously, setting the bells over it tinkling wildly.

"There in a mo!" Starlight shouted from down the hall.

"It's just me," I called back, skirting the counter with a distrustful glance at the phone, which suddenly struck me as suspiciously bone-coloured.

I hurried down the short hall, passing the downstairs loo, the office, and the stairs up to the next floor. "Did Jason call back?" I asked as I emerged into the big room at the back of the building, which made up the kitchen, living room, and dining room of the Cosy Cauldron. It was also the centre of production for all our — or rather Starlight's — concoctions. A massive hearth took up a big chunk of the wall between the kitchen and the living areas, with a long wooden table set in front of it and a person-sized cauldron squatting over the fire. The table was cluttered with herbs, roots, leaves, jars of spices and dubious powders, bottles of vinegar and oil, and more mysterious things. A big wooden chopping board with an equally large knife resting on it were smeared with crushed plants. The windows were open, but the air was still hot and close, and the fire under the cauldron was burning with flashes of green flame.

Starlight looked up at me, wiping sweat off her forehead with the back of one forearm as the cauldron glooped and burped lavender-scented bubbles.

"No. I thought it dinged just before, but it didn't ring." She hesitated, then added, "The bunnies are gone."

"Oh? Did Grace sort them out?"

Starlight grimaced. "Apparently, there was some sort of mass hawk attack? Most of them got away, but now everyone in the neighborhood is complaining that rabbits are hiding in their garden sheds."

Well, that was unhelpful, although it might appease Mr. Buckley a little. I unzipped my jacket and loosened my scarf, much to Jackie's disgust.

"It's hot in here."

"I'm making some muscle-heating salve. It always sells well in the winter."

If it heated muscles half as well as it was currently heating the shop, I could see why. I stripped the jacket off and pulled my jumper over my head before I could pass out. Jackie huffed and settled herself on the satchel where I'd dropped it on the table. "What d'you know about the voices on the phone?"

Starlight frowned. "Do you mean Don?"

"No, not bloody—" I swallowed. Starlight wasn't being deliberately obtuse. I'd forgotten she hadn't heard anything when she'd listened. "No, not Don. Voices chanting the number, then making ringing sounds."

"When you called earlier?"

"Um. Yes. Also, since."

She frowned. "On another phone?"

"Not entirely." I hesitated. "They were just kind of *around*." I waved vaguely. "And then my phone rang, even though I had no signal."

Starlight stared at me, her frown deepening. "Did you recognize the voice?"

"Voic*es*. Plural."

"And they were just in the air?"

"Pretty much."

"Like a haunting?"

"That's a haunting?"

Starlight hesitated. "Maybe? But then they were on the phone, too?"

"Well, it was mostly Jason on the phone. But he couldn't hear me."

"Maybe you had signal for a moment, and it connected, but then it wasn't enough for you to talk to him."

"But there were still voices shouting my number at me on the street. It was really loud."

"I don't..." Starlight trailed off, looking at the debris-covered table. "I don't know much about voices. You know, other than the usual thing."

I took a deep breath, then wheezed. There were evidently chilies in that pot as well. "The usual thing? Is the usual thing ghosts, Starlight? It is, isn't it?"

"Well..."

"Wait." I was suddenly cold despite the heat. "You don't mean Jason—"

"No! No, I'm sure not," she said, shaking her head wildly. "Just because it sounds like a haunting doesn't mean it is one. Why would it be? I'm sure he's fine. I mean —" She broke off, coughing, then tried again. "I mean—" She wheezed, and I pulled my T-shirt up to cover my nose, my eyes watering.

"Starlight! The cauldron!"

The town's calmest, most peaceful herbalist said something very non-calm and un-peaceful, snatching the big spoon sticking over the rim of the pot and stirring wildly. It was too late, though. The mix was already bubbling over the sides in a great gloopy flood, splattering onto the fire and sending up great scalding clouds of steam that had my already watering eyes streaming.

There were *definitely* chilies in there.

I snatched up the bag and Jackie, who was huffing little

rodent wheezes, and bolted to the back door. Ben had recently repaired it by use of a grinder after I'd managed to seal it shut when practicing an unlocking spell. I threw it open, letting in a gust of cold, fresh air. We stumbled out, doubled over as we coughed and gasped for breath while smoke and steam billowed out of the kitchen in fetching pink and purple shades, and Jackie chirruped in distress.

"*Ooh*," Starlight managed when we'd both stopped choking. "Too much horseradish, maybe."

"Probably not meant to inhale it," I pointed out, sounding like a pack-a-day smoker.

"That too."

We grinned at each other. Honestly, the fact we hadn't blown ourselves up yet was nothing short of magical in itself.

I wiped my nose on my sleeve, snuffled, and said, "Did you mean that? About the haunting? You really think Jason might be..." I couldn't say it. Of course, I'd said I wanted to kill him on a regular basis since we split up (and also when we were together, to be fair,) but I hadn't meant it. I'd never have meant it.

"I'm sure he's fine," she said, wiping her watering eyes. "It was just when you said about disembodied voices following you around, you know?"

I straightened up, shivering a little as the cold reasserted itself. "I need to be sure. I can't just hope he's okay."

Starlight nodded. "Do you want to try calling him again?"

I shuddered, thinking of those giggling, chanting voices on the phone and chasing me down the street. "No. I'm going to go and find him. At least my mobile will work properly once I'm out of Hollowbeck."

Starlight nodded. "Okay."

"Okay?" I said, looking at her with my eyebrows raised. "I thought Theodore was going to lock me up for my own good when I said I needed to help Jason."

Starlight shrugged. "If James called me for help and I didn't know if he was okay, I'd go looking for him too." She thought about it. "I mean, he's a lot nicer than Jason sounds, but still. I get it."

"I'm glad someone does." We both looked back at the still-steamy kitchen as we dimly heard the bells at the front door chiming.

A moment later, Isabella's warm tones rose. "Morgan, dear, are you in here? Benji's a little concerned."

"Ben," Ben said, the voices getting closer in the hall. He started coughing. "What the hell's that?"

"Lavender and horseradish, smoked perhaps?" Theodore's deeper voice said. "It's rather pleasant."

"That's because you're not breathing it," Ben wheezed

"You better go," Starlight said to me.

"What?"

"You said it — Theodore'll lock you up before he lets you run off and get in trouble. Go on! Get moving!" She shooed me away, and I pressed my hands to my heart in a gesture of thanks, then shooed, my breath trailing after me in the sharply cold air. But she was right. The Sensible Squad on their way in wouldn't be here to help me find Jason. They'd be here to tell me it was a trap, and I should be more sensible, and so on and so forth. And while I didn't think they'd *really* stop me from leaving or lock me up, I didn't have time to hang around and argue about it or wait for them to come to some consensus about the most logical way forward.

I ducked down the alley that ran alongside the shop, scurrying to the junction with the main street and checking each way before I emerged. No one was around, and the street was still and artfully lit like a film set. I half-expected a couple to come twirling through the pools of light thrown by the streetlamps or for some private eye with a trilby hat and a cigarette to go skulking past.

Instead, there was just me, breaking into a run as much to stop myself freezing as to avoid being cornered by my self-appointed keepers. I kept Jackie cradled in one hand, chittering disapproval, and clutched the satchel tightly with the other as I sprinted into the chill autumn night.

I'D LIKE to say I sprinted all the way back to Petunia's, but the fact I managed a whole block was already a pretty massive achievement in my mind. It's not like I was in training for the Olympics, and Theodore wasn't actually chasing me down the street. Neither were any ghosts, for that matter. After one block, I was jogging, and by two, I was doing intervals of jogging and spirited power-walking, and by the time I got to Petunia's gate, I'd put Jackie back on my shoulder and was staggering along with one hand pressed to my side to calm the stitch that had appeared around the halfway mark.

I bent over outside the gate with my hands on my knees, gulping air, and my brother said, "So where's the tiger?"

I squawked, jumping violently enough that Jackie tumbled off her perch, snagging her claws in my T-shirt to stop her fall. She hissed furiously, and I grabbed her, cradling her in both hands as I spun around. Ruiner was hunkered on the roof of my old Volvo among the fallen leaves, his eyes reflecting the low light.

"What're you doing?" I managed. "You scared me half to death."

"I thought you must be running from a tiger the way you took off from the shop."

"You saw me?"

"Sure. But cats are a lot faster than middle-aged humans."

"Ruiner, if I'm middle-aged, so are you."

"No, I'm a man. It works differently. I'm in my prime, while you're all shrivelled up and on the shelf. Probably permanently," he added comfortably.

"You're a cat. You should be *dead* at your age."

He arched his whiskers at me, and I looked down the street towards town.

"Where're the rest of them, then?"

"Probably on the way. We should get going."

"What?"

He patted something sitting on the roof in front of him with one paw. "I got the car key. Come on."

"Why? I thought you'd be dragging Theodore in here to *stop* me going."

"I'd like to. But somehow, you'll go anyway, and I'm not letting you do that on your own. So can we just go before Book Boy and the cavalry show up?"

"You are occasionally useful," I said, jogging across the road to join him.

"I am *exceptionally* useful," he said, jumping to the ground as I grabbed the key. "And also handsome."

"For a cat," I told him, but my heart wasn't in it. I could still hear those whispering voices in the back of my mind, and I didn't know what they meant. Didn't know what we were going to find out there in the world.

Or if we were going to be too late when we found it.

SIX

Out in the world

I DIDN'T WASTE TIME GOING INTO THE GUESTHOUSE TO GET another jacket. I just clambered into the car and looked at Ruiner as he jumped across me to the passenger side. I deposited the bag on the floor beneath him, put the key in the ignition, and stared blankly out of the windscreen. I'd evidently parked under a tree very popular with birds.

"Will it even start?" Ruiner asked.

"Soon find out." I still didn't move, though. I really hadn't driven since the accident. Hollowbeck was small, and it just hadn't seemed necessary to drive anywhere. And yes, okay, I was scared. Even now, sitting behind the wheel, I could feel the memory of that helpless seesawing in my stomach as the old car accelerated uphill, far faster than she should've been able to, the pedals locked under my feet, the steering wheel heavy with our lumbering momentum as I wrenched it from side to side, fighting to keep us on the road. I swallowed hard and reminded myself that the witch who'd cursed my car was long-exiled from Hollowbeck. Nothing was going to happen this time. I turned the key.

61

The old car gave a startled groan, coughed a couple of times, and gave up. I patted the steering wheel, muttered a couple of imprecations to the gods of ancient Volvo estates under my breath, and tried again.

This time, she caught, grumbled briefly, and died again.

"Well, it was an idea," Ruiner said. "Shall we go back to the Witching Hour? I didn't even finish my chicken, and I think Tanya's a bit miffed you took off without drinking your cocktail."

I firmly put all thoughts of miffed werewolves out of my head, pumped the accelerator a few times, and tried the key again.

The engine caught properly this time, rumbling into life with only one painfully loud backfire.

"There we go," I said to Ruiner. "She just needed a bit of time to warm up."

"Great," he said, putting his paws up on the dashboard so he could peer down the street. "I suggest we get a shifty on before Petunia comes to see who's taking potshots at her house."

I suddenly wished the car hadn't started. Now I *had* to go, had to drive those winding roads out of the valley, had to go and face whatever had happened to Jason. Happened to Jason because of *me*. I'd been so focused on getting out that I hadn't really thought about what came after. My eagerness to be *outside* dissolved in the face of everything else I would have to deal with.

"The accelerator's on your right," Ruiner said. "Clutch on the left. Clutch in—"

"Shut up," I said and wrestled the car into gear. "I'm going, okay?"

"Could've fooled me."

I ignored him, pulling away from the curb and aiming

the car at the first intersection, heading for the road that would take us out of Hollowbeck.

I don't think either of us thought it'd be that easy to leave. There were really only two ways out of town — the way we'd come in months ago or following the same road out the other side. And given that the mayor was a ghost and the police sergeant was a vampire, it wasn't like they'd find it hard to intercept us. To hear Ruiner tell it, after I'd left the Witching Hour, Ben had basically said I was rushing out to meet my death at the hands of my ex and needed to be rescued from myself, so I fully expected Isabella to do her materializing thing in front of the car and send me spinning into a ditch, or for Theodore to sprint down the street (not one of my sprints either, a proper one) and stop the car with one hand.

But neither of those things happened, which I wasn't sure if I was relieved by or not. Obviously, I *wanted* to leave, but I had to admit it was a little crushing to find their concern evidently only stretched as far as following me to the Cosy Cauldron. Still, it did make life easier.

The streets were quiet and almost empty. Before long we'd left the spreading skirts of the town behind us and were picking up speed, slipping down the field-hemmed main road. It felt like years ago that we'd rolled in here, expecting to find Norma and get Ruiner magicked back to his normal annoying human self, then leave again immediately. We'd never meant to stay, yet the outside world felt oddly distant when I thought about it, like something seen in a movie. Clearly pictured, but not as real as the world we inhabited now. Which was a concerning thought. I was fairly sure thinking plagues of rabbits were more normal than road rage incidents was a slippery slope.

"Do we have money?" Ruiner asked me.

"No more than we arrived with."

He gave me a narrow-eyed look. "Not much, then."

"Basically nothing," I admitted. I did have a bit of cash stashed in my satchel, but with Hollowbeck's entire economy being run on the barter system, I hadn't added to it since I'd got there. And I had a feeling the meager remnants of my bank account in the outside world would've been thoroughly drained by now, between half a dozen forgotten subscriptions and my phone bill. *My phone bill.* "Oh, bollocks."

"What?"

"I don't think my phone will work even when we get out of the valley. They'll have cut it off."

"That's very poor financial management, Morgan."

I scowled at my brother as we passed a farmhouse marooned in a sea of crops and painted sepia by the lights from its barn. A young girl was dancing in their wash to an audience of enraptured goats.

"I'm *sorry*," I said. "Whose car, apartment, and belongings were being repossessed just before we left for Hollowbeck?"

"I'm a cat. You're a bookkeeper. No one expects me to be good with money."

"You realize you can't use being a cat now as an excuse for all the stuff you did *before* you were one?"

"Details," he huffed, then added, "Do we even have enough fuel to get out of here?"

I eyed the fuel gauge, which, unusually, was holding steady. A few years ago, it had developed a tendency to jump about as if the pressure of the job was too much for it. I'd learned to make educated guesses as to what it was trying to say. I wasn't always as educated about those guesses as I'd like.

"I think so?" I said to Ruiner. Petunia had done some work on the Volvo when she'd cleaned the last traces of the curse off it. Maybe those repairs had extended to fixing recalcitrant fuel gauges.

"*I think so* doesn't fill me with confidence," Ruiner said.

"We'll be fine," I replied, watching the darker shadow of the woods lying on the hills ahead like a low cloud, waiting to welcome us in. "This is really the only way out?"

"No," he said. "But the other way would add a few hours on, so probably not what we need when all we've got is an *I think so* on the fuel."

"Fair point," I said, and we both fell silent. My chest was too tight and my face too hot, as if I were getting sick or was back in the middle of Starlight's salve-making experiments. The woods looked impossibly dark. There were no streetlights out here, only the moon offering any illumination beyond the wonky beams of the headlights, and I had the sudden certainty that we weren't driving into tree-clad hills but towards a void that would swallow us up, drowning us in some gaping rent in reality.

"How come Jason's divorcing you again?" Ruiner asked, startling me.

He was sitting bolt upright, front paws pressed neatly together as he watched me with his ears pricked and his eyes reflecting the glow of the dashboard.

I scowled at him. "*I'm* divorcing *him*."

"Really? I thought he must've got sick of the whole cardigan and slacks aesthetic you were rocking. Thirty-nine going on seventy sort of thing."

"I'm thirty-six, and those were my work clothes," I protested, shifting down through the gears as we started to climb into the tree-crowded hills, the engine already labouring.

"Oh, so being a bookkeeper drained all personality from you?"

"You can't criticize my work ethic when you've never kept a job longer than a week."

"I'm a natural-born entrepreneur."

"You're a natural-born scrounger."

"*Scrounger?* When did I scrounge anything?"

"Shall we start with my seventh birthday, which I didn't get to have because you just had to go and drive in a rally race for toddlers?" I demanded, heaving the car through another turn. The trees leaned low and mossy over the road, the sky reduced to a thin trail, and the tarmac was damp and dark as a river in the headlights.

"Hey, that was Mum's call, not mine. And I was *five*, not a toddler."

"How about bail?" I said. "A place to stay every time your current girlfriend threw you out? Paying off some *very* unsavoury types so you didn't lose any fingers?"

"That's just sibling loyalty."

"Funny how it only goes one way," I said. Ruiner gave a theatrical gasp, then proceeded to list all the ways he'd always been my staunchest supporter, which seemed to mostly consist of buying me a round in the pub when he was feeling flush and covering for me the one and only time I came home drunk as a teenager.

We were still arguing as I swung through a turn that was slightly less hairpin-ish than the previous ones had been. The road abruptly leveled out, running along the flank of the hill before curling around it to the other side, taking advantage of a lower point in the range of peaks that surrounded Hollowbeck. I was still unclear on where Hollowbeck actually was in relation to the Lakes themselves, but it was definitely in Cumbria. The heavy, twisted trunks of trees and the lush growth of moss on the stone walls shouted Lake District, as did the myriad little streams and waterfalls that pocked the landscape. As I followed the curve of the road to the other side of the hill, a light rain started, and I switched the windscreen wipers on, peering past them at a billboard looming out of the tunnel of trees.

Thank you for visiting Hollowbeck! Come Back Soon! it declared, and a rabbit peered out of a top hat, waving a paw at us. I'm sure it was meant to be cute, but it had a startling array of teeth, and the paint had peeled on one side of its face, turning its fixed grin into a rictus. I half expected it to lunge for us as we passed, but the only thing that happened was the rain got heavier, the windscreen wipers squawking in protest.

"We're out, then," Ruiner said after a moment.

"I suppose so." It hadn't taken half as long as I thought or been half as frightening a drive as I'd expected. "Thanks," I said to Ruiner grudgingly.

"For covering for you with the smoking?" he said. "Yeah, you owe me."

"I never smoked," I protested. "That was *me* covering for *you*."

"Huh."

We drove on in silence, and I could feel an odd tension collecting in my shoulders. It should've gone after we'd made it up the hill, surely? That had been the bad bit. Now, it was just a plain old, unmagical world, with nothing except how to pay for fuel to worry about. But along with my tight shoulders, an odd, unsettled feeling crept into my belly like a half-digested meal, a growing sense of being exposed and out of place, and I didn't want to think about it too much. I didn't like what it suggested.

The feeling didn't dissipate, either, not all the way to the M6, where we joined the nocturnal flow of lorries and delivery vans rumbling north and south through the country, luminous under the orange motorway lights, little mobile cocoons ferrying everyone about in glorious solitude. The night-time road allowed us a fast run south all the way to Manchester, the suburbs rising around us in a choking tide of red brick and pebble dash, the angular squareness and sameness of it all an assault of uniformity after Hollowbeck. I'd expected everything to feel so much more comfortable, the oases of the rest stops on the motorway, the reassuring loom of city lights and the ubiquitous colour of supermarkets and fast-food restaurants and chain stores, all painting the night with familiarity.

Instead, I longed for the frog-infested bathroom at the guesthouse and the wash of green that surrounded the town, the mishmash of buildings and strangely inhabited garden ponds, the eclectic shops, and even more eclectic residents with their wild assortment of pets. Even the ever present crows that patrolled the place like watchmen, answering to an authority I hadn't worked out yet. Everything here felt sharp-edged and jarring, scraping at my senses.

As I pulled into the little cul-de-sac where I'd once lived and parked outside the semi-detached house that had eaten up my savings, my salary, and far too much of my sanity, I had to peel my hands off the wheel, rolling my shoulders to try to release some of the tension from them.

"Alright?" Ruiner asked, his voice uncharacteristically quiet.

"Not so much."

"No. Let's go ask your useless muppet of an ex what his problem is, then get the hell out of here."

I swung out of the car, stopping to shoulder my satchel, slinging it crosswise over my body, and checking it was securely zipped up. The last thing I needed was to lose the bloody grimoire at an inopportune moment. I let Jackie snuggle into the bag with it. That was a warmer option than my shoulder right now as I shivered in the night, wishing I'd gone back for a jacket after all. I snuffled. The air felt wrong, harsh with city scents, and almost physically scratchy with noise.

Ruiner led the way to the front door, his snout raised and his whiskers twitching,

"Smell anything?" I asked him quietly.

"Someone had fish'n'chips."

"Helpful." I rang the doorbell, hearing it buzz inside, and frowned at the portion of garden I could see from here. The grass was too long, everything in the flowerpots was dead, and the borders were filled with weeds.

No one came to the door. I rang again without much hope.

"I suppose it's too much to suggest we go home?" Ruiner asked. "Since he's not here, and we tried?"

I looked at him. "We don't have a home. We live in a guesthouse."

"Of course, we have a home. The guesthouse detail is irrelevant."

It was really annoying when he was right. "We're not leaving without finding him." I headed back down the steps and around the detached side of the house, following what had been a flagged path. The stones were almost lost among the weeds and encroaching grass, soaking my jeans.

"Can I get a lift?" Ruiner asked from behind me. "I'm going to get my belly wet."

I stopped and looked at him. "Really?"

"What if I catch cold?" He lifted one paw distastefully, staring at the path. I sighed, turned around, and picked him up, carting him with me as we headed around the house again.

"Can't I go on your shoulder?" he asked. "This is undignified."

"I'm not having your claws dig in me. Besides, we're here." I set him down on the back patio, which seemed to have survived the worst of the neglect. The curtains on the kitchen windows were drawn, light shining warmly through them. I knocked sharply and stood back. Still nothing.

"*Now* can we go?" Ruiner said.

I ignored him and went rooting around the flowerpots with their cargo of dead plants. If he'd done so little else to look after the place... Metal scraped as I moved the corpse of what had once been a pretty little bay tree (although to be fair, it had been pretty when I bought it from the garden centre, but my gardening skills were more aspirational than practical, and it had been looking a little tatty even before I left). The back door key gleamed up at me from the pot's footprint, heavily encrusted with dirt but otherwise looking perfectly serviceable. I picked it up, knocked on the door once more for good measure, and then put the key in the lock, holding my breath. Surely he hadn't changed the locks, surely... The key turned, and the lock rolled with a reassuring *clunk*.

I opened the door a crack, not looking inside, and called, "Jason? It's Morgan. Are you there?"

"Morgs," Ruiner said. He was peering in the gap at the door, ears back.

"Jason, I'm coming in," I called.

"Morgan."

"You better be decent," I warned my ex-husband.

"Morgan!"

"What?" I demanded, finally looking at Ruiner.

"I don't think he's going to answer," he said, with a nod at the kitchen.

I stared at my brother, and some instinctive part of me strongly recommended that I just turn around and go, shut the door and pretend I'd never even got the message. Just go back to Hollowbeck and worry about the grimoire and over-cooked salves, and never mind what was going on in the outside world.

But I could still hear the rising, gleeful voices chasing out of the night to find me, and Jason's begging *please*, so I took a deep breath and pushed the door open, revealing dishes still in the sink, a clutter of post on the tiny kitchen table in the corner, and a dirty pot lying on the floor. Which was all fairly normal, other than the pot and, right next to it, the outstretched hand of what was most definitely a body.

"Oh, sodding hell," I whispered. "Not again."

"Yep," my brother said, which was helpful.

SEVEN

Now you see it, now you don't

FOR A MOMENT, I WONDERED WHEN JASON HAD SHAVED his head and why. His thick mess of glossy brown hair had been one of his most redeeming features. But this body was chunkier around the torso and wore the sort of well-tailored suit Jason would've said marked someone as a tool of the establishment, although he'd been keen enough for me to buy him some flash on-trend outfit off the high street for his latest business venture.

I stepped over Ruiner and into the kitchen, skirting the body gingerly.

"Morgan! What the hell are you *doing?*" my brother demanded.

"Looking for Jason. He might be hurt," I said, trying not to look at the body while also trying to avoid stepping in anything gross.

The pot had evidently been full of canned spaghetti, and the squishy orange contents were splattered everywhere. I couldn't see much blood, and I wondered if it had been cleared up or if the man had maybe died of natural causes. I sneaked a little peek at him, trying to pretend I was on a crime show and not in my old kitchen. There was a large dent in the side of his head that didn't look too natural.

"We need to leave," Ruiner said, not venturing over the threshold.

"We can't just leave. There's a dead body."

"That's why we need to leave." He glanced back into the garden, tail lashing. "What if the police are on their way? Or the killer comes back?" He looked back at me, eyes wide. "Or is still here?"

I froze where I was, halfway around the body to the interior door, then crouched down and poked the pot hesitantly with one finger, keeping my eyes firmly on it rather than the body. "The pot's cold."

"And now has your fingerprints on it."

I swore, then grabbed a tea towel off the worktop and wiped the pot frantically. The cloth smelled damp and felt faintly greasy, and I dropped it with a shudder once I was done. I stayed crouched down, giving the body little side-long looks. I couldn't see him breathing, but I had to check, didn't I? I took a deep breath and reached out slowly.

"*Morgan!*" Ruiner hissed. "Don't bloody play with it!"

I ignored him and touched the man's neck gingerly. His skin was smooth, cool, and weirdly firm to the touch, and I could faintly smell something musty and damp over the stink of canned spaghetti and unwashed tea towel. I moved my fingers to the man's wrists, noting that his shirt had grimy cuffs and there was dirt under his fingernails. I wondered if he was a gardener or something, but the suit seemed off. Blinking against a sudden wateriness in my eyes, I rocked back on my heels and looked at Ruiner.

"Are you quite finished leaving evidence all over the bloody crime scene?" he asked.

"It's a dead body," I said to him.

"Really? I thought it was a blow-up doll." His tail was whipping furiously.

"*Another* dead body, Ruiner. That's basically three in three months. That's not normal."

"Your brother's a cat, you've been nominated as town witch, and the *bodies* are what's worrying you?"

"It's all worrying me, but yes. The bodies are an issue. Why are there always bodies?"

He picked his way inside cautiously, then put his fluffy shoulder to the door and nudged it closed. "It's not like we've been responsible for any of them."

"Hardly the point."

"I suppose not." He padded forward, his snout wrinkled in distaste. "Do you recognize him?"

"No." I watched my brother peer at the man's face, whiskers twitching, then examine the rest of him, his gaze lingering on the hands. It was hard to read a cat, but his ears were back. "Do *you* recognize him?"

"No," he said, a little too quickly.

"Ruiner," I started.

"Let's just check the place for The Muppet, then get out," he said. "The police could've been called already."

I opened my mouth to argue, but he was right. It had been bad enough being caught with dead bodies in Hollowbeck and at the carnival when we'd had some sort of support, at least. This time, we'd have no sympathetic orange police officer to help us out, so instead of arguing, I reclaimed the pot and shook the last of the spaghetti out. I held it at the ready as I turned and hurried through the door into the living room, just in case.

The living room was chaos. For one moment I thought hopefully it was just Jason's less than stellar housekeeping skills, but I didn't think even he would've left the coffee table on its side against the bookshelves, spilling half-empty takeout containers and empty glasses in its wake. And he certainly wouldn't have left the TV face down on the carpet. He'd had a more meaningful relationship with it than he'd had with me.

I crossed to the bookshelves and swapped the pot for a copy of *Going Postal*, stroking it mournfully. It had been used as a coaster at some point, red wine by the look of things.

"Morgan," Ruiner said. "Can you pet the books later?"

"He wouldn't give them back," I said. "He said they made the shelves look nice, and he'd only give them up if I paid him enough to buy more."

"You realize he took your whole house."

"Well, yes. But my books." I hugged the old paper-back, and Jackie hissed, craning her neck out of the bag as if she thought I might replace the grimoire with it.

"I did tell you at the time that you shouldn't be the one moving out," my brother said.

"Oddly enough, your life advice is rarely that useful," I said. "And I didn't want the house. He was shagging her here the whole time." *Her* being his unnamed younger woman, who I supposed I should be angry with. Mostly, I was grateful she'd given me the nudge I needed to get out, and I hoped she'd already shaken Jason off like last season's hairstyle. Judging from the takeout containers and canned spaghetti, she didn't seem to have moved in. I put the book back and gave an experimental sniffle, but apparently, my overwhelming emotion was still more relief than grief. Sure, once I left, I'd been living in a dump and working in a dumpier dump while Jason kept our nice, tasteful, sensible house, but it had definitely been worth it.

"Does this mean you've remembered how worthless he

is, and we don't have to look for him?" Ruiner asked. "We could clear the shelves and take off."

That was more tempting than I wanted to admit, but I had no desire to spend the rest of my life haunted by spooky phone calls from my ex-husband.

"No," I said aloud, picked up the pot again, and led the way upstairs with Ruiner sighing dramatically behind me. The pretty hedgehog paintings I'd hung over the stairs had been replaced with photos of cars that looked like they'd been torn from magazines, and everything needed a dust.

Upstairs was as compact as down, just a bathroom (empty and so grimy I didn't fancy using it, even though I really needed the loo after the drive), a small second bedroom (there was a rowing machine and some dumb-bells in it, all dustier than the pictures), and finally the master bedroom, the door pulled mostly closed. I looked at Ruiner.

"I vote we grab the books and get on with our lives," he said.

"Of course you do," I said and pushed the door open.

The bed was unmade, clothes scattered on its end and on a chair in the corner. The bedside tables held pint glasses half full of water, beer, and what looked horrifyingly like pee but which I hoped was Lucozade. Shoes were abandoned on the floor, the wardrobe hung open, and a pervading funk of stale air hung about the place, suggesting he hadn't opened the windows for a while.

"Gross," Ruiner announced. "And you married him."

"You clean your bits with your tongue."

"I still never lived like this."

I ignored him. I knew I should be angry at Jason — I *was* still angry at him in many ways — and that the natural reaction would be to take some pleasure in the fact he really couldn't function as an adult on his own, but somehow, the bedroom and its uni student disorder made me inexplicably sad. Maybe I'd been so used to being the grown-up I'd never given him a chance to be one. Although he'd had time enough now, I reminded myself. And helping with that wasn't my responsibility. Finding him was, though.

Careful not to knock over the Jenga-like collection of glasses, I checked the drawers in the bedside tables. Chargers and condoms and a clutter of change and business cards. No phone, no wallet. I pawed through the wardrobe, but it was so disorganized it was impossible to tell if he'd packed a bag or not. I did find a hoody and a jacket, though, and pulled them both on. Jackie gave a squeak of relief when I lifted her out of the bag and set her on my shoulder, where she snuggled into the soft cloth of the hood.

I slung the satchel back on and trotted downstairs again, Ruiner trailing me. He stood watching me expectantly as I dug through the debris in the living room, righting the coffee table and piling everything back onto it. I checked under the sofa cushions, too, braced for some nasty discoveries, but there were only crumbs, some chocolate wrappers, and a lone sock. Finally, I straightened up and looked at him.

"No phone," I said.

"Does yours work?"

I made a doubtful noise but took it out of my satchel pocket and poked it. It had a signal but with SOS next to it. I sighed. "No service. I think my account's probably overdrawn, and they've cut me off."

"Helpful," he said and looked around. "Does Muppet keep any cash around?"

I thought about it. Muppet didn't, but I'd always had a stash. A stash from him, as well, because stashes never lasted if he knew about them, whether they were stashes of chocolate, crisps, or cash. I reached up to the top shelf of the bookcase, taking down a *His Dark Materials* box set. I took the books out and plucked thirty quid from one, twenty from another, and fifty from the third. I waved it at Ruiner, grinning.

"Oh, we're loaded," he said, arching his whiskers.

"It'll get us some fuel, at least."

"What about food?"

"You can't be hungry. You had chicken at Tanya's."

"I *will* be hungry."

"You'll survive." Although, honestly, *I* was hungry. My cocktail had been both unfinished and distinctly less nourishing than Ruiner's. I led the way back into the kitchen and opened the fridge. There was a packet of sliced ham that still smelled fine and a chunk of cheddar going a bit hard on the edges. I grabbed them both.

"Morgan," Ruiner said, his voice stilted.

"What?" I asked, opening the cupboards. They were pretty bare, but there were some chocolate Hobnobs and a pack of prawn cocktail crisps. Hardly a balanced meal, but they'd keep us going.

"*Look.*"

"*Hmm?*" I turned to look at him. He was standing in the doorway to the living room, staring at the floor. I dropped the biscuits with a yelp. "Oh *sh—*"

The body was gone. Cold spaghetti and luminously red sauce still decorated the cabinets and the laminated boards and created a vague outline of where the head *had* been. There was a little dirt and a couple of coins on the floor, but...

"Ruiner! Where the hell's it gone?"

"Why're you asking me?" His ears were back, and he

backed up, bumping into the door and spinning around with a hiss.

"*How's* it gone?"

"*I don't know!*"

I scuttled to the door and opened it. It wasn't locked, and I peered fearfully into the garden. Nobody on the patio or body snatchers sneaking over the back fence. I slammed the door again and locked it firmly, jiggling the handle.

"What if they're already inside?" Ruiner asked, and we both froze, staring at the ceiling. There was no sound of movement.

"They can't be," I whispered. "We've been through the whole house."

"Someone *stole the body*, Morgan."

"I can see that!"

We stared at each other, his eyes so wide that the pupils had eaten up the blue. I snatched a knife from the magnetic strip on the wall, since I'd put the pot down upstairs and forgotten it, then opened every cupboard in the kitchen, even the little one above the stove, although it wasn't like anyone could stash a body in any of them. Then I stalked across the kitchen to the living room door, knife at the ready.

Well, *stalked* is a strong word. It was probably more of a totter, but I tried to infuse it with stalking energy as I circled the living room, checking the cupboard under the stairs and the folds of the curtains before climbing back to the top floor.

Ruiner followed me, ears back. My heart was beating far too loud and far too fast, and I licked my lips as I paused at the bathroom door and then threw it open. It rebounded, almost hitting me in the face, and I checked behind it, then behind the shower curtain. Nothing. I pulled the door firmly closed, then went through the spare bedroom. Nothing in the wardrobe, which was the only hiding place in the room.

So that just left the master bedroom. I paused on the threshold, then threw myself full-length on the floor, bumping my knees and earning a screech and a nip on the ear from Jackie. There was nothing under the bed and nothing in the wardrobe when I scuffed over to it, still on my knees. I sank back on my heels and looked at Ruiner, swallowing hard. My mouth was sticky with fright.

"A body doesn't just vanish," I said.

"Not usually," he agreed. "But no body, no crime, right?"

"I don't like how comfortable you are with that."

"I don't like how you'd apparently prefer a dead body to no dead body."

I put the knife down and flexed my hand. It was cramping with how tightly I'd been gripping it, and I didn't know why I'd bothered. It's not like I'd actually have stabbed anyone with the damn thing. I was more likely to fall over and stab myself.

"What do we do?" I asked.

"We go back to Hollowbeck," he said. "This isn't some little debt Jason's got himself into. Vanishing bodies are *not* in our skill set, Morgs. Something's way off here."

"I know. That's why I have to help."

"You *don't*. He's a grown bloody human, despite all evidence to the contrary."

I wiped my mouth with the back of my hand, that sticky taste still lingering. "He got a message to Hollowbeck. I'm getting weird calls on my phone. My disconnected, *signal-less* phone. This is about me, somehow."

"Then it's a bloody trap and all the more reason to leave it."

I nodded and clambered slowly to my feet, picking the knife up gingerly. "I can't."

"You *can*. You don't owe him anything. You haven't got him into this, whatever it is."

I waved at the cluttered, musty bedroom. "You really think he can get himself out of it?"

"Maybe he just has to."

"He won't be able to. I have to find him, Ruiner."

"And how are you going to do that? Call the police and tell them your ex, who you've had a nasty breakup with, is missing and the house turned over? How well do you think that's going to go down? Who do you think they'll look at if something *has* happened to him? And how long till the body turns up again at some inopportune moment?" Ruiner's teeth were bared, his ears back. "*Think*, Morgan! This is a *setup*."

"And Jason's in the middle of it. And that's my fault." I walked back down the stairs, my back stiff and my eyes stinging. He'd called me for help. Called me *and* sent a message. I should've left the moment I got the note.

Whatever had happened, my hesitation could only have made things worse.

EIGHT

Mind the hamster wheel

I WAS SITTING ON THE PATIO STEP, HUDDLED INTO THE oversized jacket and munching disconsolately on a chocolate Hobnob when Ruiner joined me. He looked at the dark windows of the house attached to ours, then peered at the fence at the bottom of the garden which divided our garden — Jason's garden — from the next property over. "Should we be lingering at a crime scene?" he asked.

"Probably not," I said around a mouthful of biscuit. "But can things get that much worse?"

"Well, being arrested definitely means you can't help Jason, and you seem weirdly set on that."

I sighed, wiping crumbs off my borrowed hoody. "Wouldn't make any difference. I can't help him anyway. This is evidently some sort of … magic-adjacent thing." I waved vaguely, then took another biscuit. "So I can't go to the police about him being missing, but I've also got zero leads on where he's gone. What do I do? Sit here and hope the dead guy comes back?"

"Creepy."

"Yeah, I realized that as I said it." I looked around the

garden. I'd checked the shed when I came out with my biscuits, but it just held the under-used lawnmower and a clutter of rusting garden implements I'd bought before realizing that gardening would never be my thing. "I thought it would be him owing someone money, but even if that was the problem, we've got about a hundred and twenty pounds all up and a car worth about half that. Couldn't pay off a parking fine."

Ruiner made a thoughtful noise. "So what d'you want to do?"

"I don't know," I said with another sigh. "Wait for another call, perhaps? Jason already figured out how to contact me twice, so maybe he will again."

"If it's Jason. Don't you think it's more likely to be whoever has him?"

I gave Ruiner a dubious look. "Whoever *has* him?"

"Sure. Whoever's setting this up. I doubt he's suddenly worked out how to make magical phone calls."

"Doesn't make any difference," I said. "The only option is to wait for them to call and see what they want."

Ruiner made a doubtful noise. "Or we leave, and you don't answer any more calls. Maybe they'll stop when they realize you won't trade yourself for Jason."

"How likely d'you think that is? They'll just up the stakes somehow." I shivered. "Send me bits of him or something."

Ruiner arched his whiskers. "Wow. *Bits?*"

"They left a dead body here. *Bits* seem mild."

"You know this isn't your fault."

"Of course it is," I said, my tone sharp. "Your average debt collector doesn't have a hotline to ghost voices in Hollowbeck."

Ruiner didn't say anything, and after a moment, I opened

the pack of ham and gave him a slice. We sat there in the cold for a while longer, listening to sirens going past on the main road and munching companionably, then he said, his tone strangely diffident, "What if we try to track him down?"

"How would we even start?"

Ruiner licked his chops and looked at the sky. "I might have recognized something about the dead guy."

I narrowed my eyes at him. "Why would you recognize the dead guy?"

"I didn't say I recognized *him*. Something about him. A mark on his wrist."

"What, like a gang mark or something? Is that a thing?"

"Not exactly," he said with a sigh. "A brand. It bans him from a certain club I happen to know of."

I offered him another piece of ham. "And would your human body have one of these brands, by any chance?"

"No. But I've seen people get them." He hooked the ham with one paw and gnawed on it.

"How did that happen?"

"Because I have not always made good life choices."

"You have never made good life choices. Be more specific."

He sighed deeply. "If you go against the rules at this particular establishment, there are no second chances. Small transgressions get branded, so the door staff know not to let you back in."

"And bigger transgressions?"

"I never asked."

I shivered slightly. If Ruiner never asked, then evidently, the brands were unpleasant enough that I didn't want to know anymore, either.

"What sort of club is it?"

"Somewhere you go for things you can't get elsewhere."

"Drugs?" I suggested.

He grimaced. "No. The owner runs a clean ship, which is why the branding. Often, people get them for thinking they can bring other business in. But it's a gambling club."

"Oh, no."

"Yeah. High stakes, higher odds, different games — nowhere else like it."

"Exclusive, then?" I said.

"Exclusive. And dangerous. And not entirely..." He hesitated.

"Human?"

"Yeah." He sighed. "That's a good way to describe it."

"So there's places like that outside Hollowbeck, then."

He gave me an amused look. "There's nowhere like the Oubliette in Hollowbeck."

"The *what?*"

"The Oubliette."

"How the hell has Jason got tangled up with a magical gambling den called the sodding *Oubliette?*"

"I don't know," he said. "But it's not a great place, Morgan."

"Is it in Manchester?"

"Eh. In a way?"

"Then we go and take a look at it," I said, twisting the biscuit packet closed decisively. "We can ask around, see if anyone's seen him."

"That is a *spectacularly* bad idea. Did you not hear the bit about it being dangerous?"

"Did you not hear the bit about us having no other leads? And you suggested it!"

"I suggested we look for him, not that we go to the bloody *Oubliette!*" We glared at each other for a moment, and Ruiner looked away first, his ears back. "It's not Hollowbeck, Morgan. It's not all love spells and bunny invasions."

I considered it, then waved to indicate his whole fluffy situation. "Did the Oubliette have anything to do with the cat-ification?"

"No. But I might've had some dealings there. Run up a few debts and had to pay them off."

"Which led to cat-ification?"

"Not exactly. Sort of. Maybe."

"Why won't you just tell me?" I demanded. "You keep saying you can't wait to be human-shaped again, but you won't tell me who did this to you, which makes things a bit bloody difficult, to say the least."

"The exact details don't matter. You'll get the hang of the book, and then you can fix it. I'm sure of it."

"I'm not," I muttered, but he didn't seem inclined to say anything else, so I added, "The Oubliette, then."

"This is a bad idea."

"Maybe. But he could be there."

"Not likely, if Dead Guy had a brand marking him as someone who *can't* go there."

"Then we're not going to lose anything by going," I said. "They can't be the ones trying to get hold of me, and someone there might know something."

"Nothing comes for free in the Oubliette."

I sighed. Of course, it didn't. Nothing came for free anywhere. "The other option is we sit here and wait for a phone call or to get jumped by whoever took Jason. So either you show me where this place is, or I have to start driving around asking anyone who looks a bit magic-y about it."

"Fab plan, Morgan. Really low profile." He got up and trotted back to the kitchen door.

"You're really not going to help me."

"I *am* helping you, but I'm not walking through the jungle to get to the car. Let's go out the front door like civilized people."

I pulled my phone from my pocket and checked it. "Now? It's almost midnight."

"It's not the sort of place that closes." Ruiner vanished into the kitchen, and after a moment, I followed him, not without a distrustful look at the kitchen floor. I hoped there wasn't a body when we got back. I didn't much like the idea of randomly recurring bodies.

MANCHESTER'S AN OLD CITY, and a big one, cut through with canals and railways, the old, soot-stained buildings and narrow streets that sprout out of its industrial centre speared with the shiny slabs of new high-rises and office blocks, and starting to show signs of regeneration, but it still rests deep in its ancient bones of steel and steam. It's not far to greener spaces, though, hills that rise fierce and steep out of villages that have been all but swallowed by the city's sprawl, reaching for the tan flanks of the moors, and through it all run the rivers and locks that built the north's faded wealth, now left to fishermen and joggers and the long, low silhouettes of the canal boats.

I'd expected this club of Ruiner's to be in the industrial parks that ringed the city, perhaps, or jammed between the nightclubs and bars of the city centre, inhabiting the seedier corners of its heart. Instead, he directed me out of town to where the jumble of run-together villages started to thin out, wilted at the edges with neglect. The streets were patched with potholes, shop windows boarded up, and the plexiglass of bus shelters crazed with cracks. There was something deeply alive about the area, though, full of furtive movement and low-slung cars even as the morning crept into its small hours, unseen denizens hurrying off on their own missions. My old Volvo was far too dowdy and respectable for this place.

"Down there," Ruiner said. He had his paws on the dashboard and pointed his snout towards a skinny lane that dived between two buildings, one a working man's club with a peeling wooden sign, the other a second-hand furniture shop with a tired-looked lounge suite in the window.

"Are you sure?" I asked. "It looks like a dead end."

"I'm sure."

It wasn't like I could plug *magical illicit gambling dens Manchester* into Google Maps, so I just indicated, taking the turn in a wide swoop so I could aim directly down the alley. That was a grand name for it. It was barely wide enough for us to fit, and I winced, expecting a painful scrape from the wing mirrors, but we slid through without touching, the engine burbling roughly between the stained brick of the walls. A pile of old rubbish bags rustled threateningly as we passed.

I nudged a jumble of broken wood that might've been the remains of a communal outhouse, sending a plank clattering to the grimy cobbles. There were no lights down here, just the headlights reflecting in strange ways on the stone, so that I couldn't see more than a metre or so ahead, no matter if I had them on high beams or low. I slowed, peering over the wheel, and just as I was wondering how rusty my reversing skills were, the walls fell away.

And I do mean fell away. They were there, then they seemed to collapse on the edge of my vision, concertinaing back toward the world behind us. The road became two lanes, unrolling between fields full of rustling crops, and the sky opened up above us, thick with cloud but uncluttered with office blocks or towers. I checked the rearview mirror, both hands tight on the wheel, suddenly afraid I'd lost the way back. Far behind us were brick buildings, windows spotted with light, forming a wall that ran off in either direction to encircle the fields, vanishing into the darkness.

"What," I started, then just waved at the fields. There seemed to be far more corn than was reasonable, especially given that it was pretty much winter and there was nothing but husks to be seen. "What is this?"

"Darrowdale," Ruiner said.

"What the hell's Darrowdale? I thought we were going to the Oubliette?"

"The Oubliette's in Darrowdale."

"Right." I peered at a billboard as we passed it. *Impossible corn maze! You'll NEVER beat it!* The sign depicted five ears of corn pummelling a man with popcorn, which was all sorts of wrong. The road ran straight on, the corn forming a looming barrier to either side, preventing me from seeing anything beyond it.

Hog Roast! the next sign shouted. *Choose your own hog!* That sign had five men chasing a large pig around a table. The men had knives, and the pig was wearing a suit.

The sign after that promised an assault course and the best-ever laser tag. I caught glimpses of green and red neon flashing into the sky. Darrowdale was still open for business, evidently. I rolled my window down, letting in the damp, chilly air and some very dubious music that sounded like a techno version of "Cotton-Eye Joe."

Someone set off a rocket with a whoop of joy. I hoped the screech coming from the projectile itself as it arced over the road was good sound effects and not the trailing scream of panic it sounded like.

I braked as three men covered in feathers sprinted

across the road, pursued by half a dozen women who looked human enough, clad in shorts and horned head-dresses. They were armed with whips and leashes and were cheering loudly. I decided I didn't want any further details on that particular activity.

"What *is* this place?"

"Hollowbeck's not the only hidden village," Ruiner said. "There's quite a few around, apparently. I found Darrowdale first."

"How?"

"Leads and contacts," he said, his voice quiet. He hadn't moved from his braced position against the dashboard, gaze shifting restlessly from the road to the sprawling buildings revealed as the corn gave way to fields of long grass. Clouds of smoke rose from a chunky, windowless brick house whose sign proclaimed it to be *Greg's Smoked Meats & Crematorium*.

"Oh no," I said, wrinkling my nose.

"Probably a gimmick," he said, but without much conviction.

"Seriously, Ruiner, how did you find out about this place?"

"I told you I got mixed up with some dodgy sorts," he said. "I thought magic could be handy, and Darrowdale's not that hard to get into once you know about it. Everything's for sale around here."

"Do you still have debts here?"

"I'm a cat. Cats don't have debts."

I groaned. "Oh, bloody hell, Ruiner. I can't bail you *and* Jason out. This is ridiculous!"

"Relax. No one's going to recognize me."

"You can't know that!"

"You're just a witch, and I'm just your familiar. We have a poke around, see if we can find out where the

Muppet's being held, or at least by who, then we can make a plan."

I resisted the urge to bang my head against the steering wheel. Probably, he was right. People being turned into cats seemed to be a relatively rare phenomenon, even in the magical world. And no one would expect Ruiner to walk back in if he *did* owe someone money. Maybe it really would be fine.

But, as I watched someone roll across the road ahead of us in a giant hamster wheel that was actually on fire, I wasn't sure how. After all, Hollowbeck had proved dangerous enough. This place had all the magic and none of the charm from what I'd seen so far. I didn't see any way it could actually be fine at all.

We continued on, nevertheless. With each passing step I grew more and more certain this was a bad idea. Buildings sprouted up and clustered together as we got closer to town, tidy bungalows with gaudy, glowing butterflies stuck to the walls and lurching Gothic mansions sporting an excess of gables and towers, complete with bats flitting above the roofs. Huge dogs prowled the gardens, and topiary in twisted shapes turned to watch us pass, and houses built in glass and metal reflected our headlights, dazzling me. I spotted a woman dragging a complaining, pony-sized goat in a tutu down the street, and a man with a skirt of writhing tentacles got them tangled in his bicycle and tumbled off, swearing loudly. Gargoyles crept down the vaulted spires of a church that announced on a board out the front, *Free Curses for Cupcakes* (I wasn't sure if that meant they'd give you curses to put in your cupcakes or would trade curses for cupcakes. It was a bit unclear), and in the joined gardens of a row of terraced houses, three women and two men practiced naked yoga, ignoring a pack of llamas who were spitting over the fence at them.

I looked at Ruiner. "This place is weird."

"You thought Hollowbeck was weird, too."

"That mailbox just ate a dog," I said, pointing at an enraged elderly man tugging desperately on a leash emerging from the mailbox's mouth.

"The risks of magical towns."

The risks of magical towns without Theodore and Isabella to keep an eye on things, I thought, with an unexpected wave of homesickness, even though Hollowbeck wasn't home, and I hadn't even been there long enough to pine for it. I was suddenly sure that while Hollowbeck had no jail, this place wouldn't either, but not for the same reasons. I thought the reasons here likely had to do with the screaming rockets and human hamster wheel on the way into town. And possibly the feathered men, but that might've been more a recreational thing.

"I don't like it," I said to Ruiner.

"You wanted to come."

"I want to find Jason."

"So here we are."

I sighed and leaned over the wheel as I skirted a gathering of nine cats sitting in the middle of an intersection in a circle with a single sock in the center. They all turned their heads to watch us pass, their eyes flat and expressionless. Ruiner sank down a little out of sight, and I said, "It's not safe, is it?"

"No," he said simply. "We need to find out what we can and get out again as quick as possible."

I nodded. "Deal. Where do we start?"

He just pointed his snout onwards, and we slid deeper into Darrowdale's strange and furtive heart, the air hot and damp and redolent of violence.

NINE

Same but different

DARROWDALE *WAS* WEIRD. THERE WAS NO GETTING AROUND that. It was weird even by Hollowbeck standards, which was saying something. Yet it was also strangely similar, from the jumble of architectural styles (I spotted a house built entirely of woven palm fronds as if it was on some tropical isle, and across the street, a scale replica of the Parthenon with some windows punched into it haphazardly), to the questionable choice of animal companions, not all of which were entirely *right*. I spotted a pigeon with six wings and two heads splashing about in a bird bath, both heads fighting for ownership of a wedge of cheese, a small pony sporting pale, graceful wings that kept knocking its owner's hat off as they walked down the street, and a very large, very black dog with three heads.

"Is that...?" I said to Ruiner, letting the car slow to a crawl as we passed the yard the dog was restlessly patrolling.

"Of course, it's not bloody Cerberus. He's mythical. Mind the cars."

I jerked my attention back to the road before I could

scrape one of the parked cars. I did *not* want to upset any of the residents around here. I kept my eyes on the sparse traffic and tried not to be distracted by displaced light-houses, backyard coven meetings, or a swarm of flying squid.

It didn't take long before the houses gave way to shops, delivering us onto the main street. Darrowdale evidently shared Hollowbeck's range of nocturnal inhabi-tants, as everything was still open. We passed a health spa of some sort, a rather graphic sign in the window extolling the virtues of spider-bite facials, a swollen-faced woman giving a cheery thumbs up in the photo, and a shop that promised it sold only organic poisons. There was also a milkshake bar, brightly lit and staffed by men in roller-skates in hot pants, and another that seemed to sell nothing but pipes and things to put in pipes. I doubted it was all tobacco.

We didn't have spider-bite facials or a milkshake bar in Hollowbeck, not that I felt that was any great loss. What we did have, facing each other across the main street, was a Cosy Cauldron, a Bewitching Brews, a Mystic Munchies, and three dress shops, one that favoured gothic witchiness, one leaning into a more Stevie Nicks aesthetic, and a third that couldn't seem to make up its mind if its ideal customer was a tourist in search of a tacky T-shirt, or the floral and twin-set-wearing Upstanding Ladies.

And Darrowdale had exactly the same.

The main street was lit by orange streetlights that flickered and buzzed, casting jumping shadows about the place. A handful of nighttime residents scurried in and out of shops, lugging tote bags and dragging reluctant chil-dren or recalcitrant familiars behind them. The coffee shop here was called Bewitching Boos, which I had to admit was a pretty decent name. There appeared to be a drinking competition going on inside. A large-bellied man visible through the big front window was lying on the floor while a woman with short-cropped grey hair poured what looked to be an entire jug of cold brew down a funnel into his mouth. A handful of people were looking on, clapping and cheering. Across the street, at the pet shop next door to what was called the *Crafty* Cauldron but had an identical front to my own shop, two women were fighting over the last bag of dog biscuits on display while a third quietly stole away with the disputed loot under one arm.

A massive food fight was underway inside Monster Munch, which at least made the name appropriate (the name also made me wonder about trademark issues — and crave a pack of pickled onion crisps). A plate of lasagne smashed into the inside of the front window, narrowly missing two well-dressed women sitting at the table. One leaped up, grabbed her plate of lamb shanks, and hurled it toward the lasagne thrower while her friend simply shook her head and took a sip from a glass of wine. The door flew open, and a man in chef's whites bolted out, his apron torn in two places and smeared with sauce, and something the size of a spaniel but with far too many legs and very large claws shot after him. The chef swerved right, sprinting down the street without a look back, and a woman leaned out the door and yelled, "Sod off, then! Can never get the bloody staff!"

The man didn't stop, and the crab thing clicked its claws in a satisfied manner and sidled into the dress shop next door. A scream went up from inside, and a moment later, the crab shot back out again, pursued by a large woman wearing Dr Martens she evidently wasn't afraid to use.

"Morgan?" Ruiner said.

"Yes?" I said, still watching the crab. I didn't want it having a go at the tyres.

"Do you think you should maybe park somewhere? I'm not sure sitting in the middle of the street with the engine running is the most subtle approach."

"Oh. Right." I drove on a little, pulling into a space between two flickering streetlights where we didn't feel too obvious. There was a tea shop next to us, but it was boarded up, plants growing out of the gaps between the boards on the windows. I wasn't sure what tea plants looked like, but I'd have put money on these being them. I switched the engine off and looked at Ruiner. "Are all magical towns like this?"

"You know as much as me. I've only seen here and Hollowbeck too."

"But it's ... it's almost identical," I pointed out. "Do they have to be like that? Is it just the way magical towns work? Or did one copy the other on purpose?"

"I suppose it's a bit weird," Ruiner said.

"You *suppose?* Even the dress shops are the same!" I pointed at the three of them, cozied up next to each other just like in Hollowbeck, although I had to admit more PVC and interesting accessories were going on than was usual in even the gothic shop in Hollowbeck.

"Well, it might look the same, but it's not," he said, sounding far too serious for my brother. "We have to be careful here, Morgan."

"I know. We might get chased by land crabs." The creature was sitting in the middle of the road, making a sudden, claw-clicking dash at a passing scooter, which swerved violently.

"Trust me, the land crabs are not the problem." He looked at me critically. "Do you have a hat or something?"

"No. Why would I have a hat?"

"Put your hood up, then. And stash that bloody book."

"I'm not leaving it in the car." I pulled my hood up over my hair. The sweatshirt was too big for me, and my face was well hidden in the shadows. Jackie looked up at me, beady eyes catching the light as she put one paw on the satchel.

"It might be safer here," Ruiner said. "Who's going to bother breaking into this wreck?"

We both looked dubiously at my poor old car, but Jackie hissed, baring her teeth. Her feelings on the matter were clear, and I tended to defer to her on anything grimoire-related. "No, I'm not leaving it."

"Fine. Hide your bag under your coat or something, then."

I examined my brother. His tail twitched restlessly, and his ears flicked one way and the other as if desperate to catch the slightest noise. His gaze was fixed on the street. "Are you alright?"

He put a paw on the passenger door. "Come *on*. Are we doing this or what?"

"What do you know about this place, really?"

"I know you don't make eye contact with anyone who whispers to you out of alleys. You don't take any food or drink anyone offers you for free. You don't show your teeth to the bartender and never turn your back on the dealer."

"What, ever?"

"Not when you're playing, anyway."

I frowned. "How do you know all this?"

Ruiner sighed, sinking back into a sitting position. "Do you want to interrogate me or find out where the Muppet is?"

"Both."

"The more we hang about here, the more chance we have of being noticed."

"You didn't know this much about Hollowbeck."

Ruiner looked up at me, pupils huge in the low light. "Which town d'you think I'm more suited to?"

I held his gaze for a moment, considering, then looked back at the street as a pack of kids on bikes spun past, clutching bags of crisps and whooping delightedly. A man ran after them, waving an axe with altogether too much meaning. "I'll tell your dads!" he bellowed as he stumbled to a stop, and they vanished into the night, trailing laughter.

"Not long ago, I would've said here," I told Ruiner, still watching the street. "Now I'm not so sure. I don't think it's your style anymore."

He was silent for so long that I finally looked at him. He was watching me and immediately wrinkled his snout, showing his teeth. "That sort of ooshy-gooshy *niceness* is why we're in bloody Darrowdale, chasing a waste of space book thief and waiting to get eaten by land crabs."

"Is there anything else I should know?" I asked. "You know, other than not showing the dealer my teeth?"

"Don't show the *bartender* your teeth," he corrected me. "And don't eat or drink anything you haven't paid for. Nothing."

"Got it." I opened the door and got out, slinging my satchel on before pulling Jason's jacket over the top. I zipped it up without difficulty and dropped my phone into one of the pockets, more out of habit than anything else. I supposed I could get a new SIM or see about sorting out a pay-as-you-go tomorrow.

Ruiner followed me out, leaping to the bonnet of the car and then to my shoulder while I looked warily at a pretty woman lounging in the door of the pet shop. She wasn't wearing much despite the cold and had what appeared to be an entire leg of lamb in one hand. She bit into it, tearing a chunk off and chewing it noisily while the juices ran down her hand.

"No eye contact," Ruiner whispered.

"She's not in an alley. Or hissing at me."

"It's just generally good advice. Think of the whole town as being populated by rabid dogs, and you'll be fine."

"Wow. This is sounding better and better."

"We can still get back in the car and go."

It was deeply tempting. The air felt different, thick and humid, and too hot for the jacket and hoody. I lifted my hair off my neck, thinking of Hollowbeck's perfect, early-winter days, crisp, clear, and full of the scents of woodsmoke and frost. I could be curled into the big attic bed at Petunia's, listing to the frogs in the walls, full of Tanya's cocktails and Petunia's ginger cake, with my biggest concern a plague of bunnies.

Only it wouldn't be my biggest concern because I'd still know Jason was missing, and there was no one to help him but me. I shoved my hands into the coat pockets, lowering my head so the hood fell further over my forehead, and headed across the street, avoiding a pink ball that bounced down it, pursued by directionless laughter. I had to do this. Jason was every bit as useless as Ruiner said, but that only made it worse. After all, he wouldn't have had anyone to warn him about bartenders with teeth fetishes.

~

RUINER WHISPERED DIRECTIONS TO ME, perched on my shoulder and trying to look like any old witch's cat. It wasn't hard to follow them as we went straight to what would've been the Witching Hour in Hollowbeck. Here, it was called the Witch's Howl, sandwiched between a store that advertised instant loans and another that claimed it sold aquariums. The loan shop had a sign in the barred window that read *Second & Third-Born Accepted!*, and another on the door that added, *Organs Welcome!* The aquarium shop was devoid of signs, but as we passed, a man crept out furtively, looking each way before scurrying off with a plastic bag containing a goldfish in each hand. Given his nervousness, I wondered if they were some sort of flesh-eating goldfish or if Darrowdale had a goldfish ban in place.

No one was at the door of the Witch's Howl, although I'd half expected a bouncer who'd want fingernails as an entry fee or something. I slipped inside with my head still down and my heart going too fast, emerging into a long, low-ceiled bar vibrating with the pound of too-loud music, scented with spilled beer, sweat, and fear. It was busy, the stools at the bar taken and the booths along the walls — set up just as they were in the Witching Hour, but in deep red, plastic-y fabric rather than warm green cloth — packed with drinkers. Two servers in white muscle shirts moved smoothly behind the bar, eyes glittering in the red neon that lit the shelves behind them, and a woman in the same top swept through the room with empty glasses stacked in towers in her arms. Her gaze passed over me indifferently, and I shrank away as she brushed past me to the bar.

"What now?" I whispered, trying not to move my lips too much.

"Upstairs," Ruiner hissed, and I walked past the bar as casually as I could, trying to both look as if I belonged here and as invisible as possible. It was a tricky balance, and I'm pretty sure I failed on all points.

The stairs were in the same place as they were in

Tanya's bar, but these ones were sticky underfoot, the walls scratched and stained, and the rope banister so discoloured I pressed my hands to my chest to stop myself touching it even accidentally. The music from downstairs vanished as we turned the corner of the staircase as if we'd passed through a door. The walls went from dirty white to smooth, glossy black, the light a dim, directionless red. There was a plain black door at the top, bearing an ornate gold frame that surrounded small, tasteful text picked out in gold leaf. *Oubliette*.

"Now what?" I whispered to Ruiner, stopping in front of the door. There was no *open* sign, no bell, or even a handle.

"Now knock."

"Knock, how?"

"With your hand? On the door?"

I hissed impatiently. "You know what I mean. Is there a secret knock or something?"

"Yes, try the Macarena."

I rolled my eyes, which was rather lost between the dim light and the hood, then knocked sharply. The door opened almost instantly, and I stared into the icy eyes of a pale man who should've been playing professional basketball, given his height. He looked me up and down and said, "Toilets are downstairs." He started to push the door shut again.

"Wait!" I said, and he stopped, narrowing his eyes at me. "I'm not looking for the toilets."

"No? RSPCA then, maybe?" he asked, nodding at Ruiner, who, to his credit, didn't respond, although I felt his claws tighten on my jacket.

"I'm here to play," I said, looking past him into the room beyond, where the roof terrace should've been. Instead, it had the low, smoky lights and rich wood tones of some Prohibition dive, right down to a woman crooning into a microphone on the stage in the corner and bartenders in open-necked white shirts and red waistcoats.

"Yeah? What's your stake? The cat?" He wasn't quite smiling, but there was a smirk in his voice.

I looked at him properly for the first time, still keeping my face as hidden as I could. "None of your bloody business unless you're dealing me in, is it?"

There was a long, wary pause as he regarded me with an evaluating gaze, and I was sure he was going to turf me straight down the stairs, then he laughed softly and said, "Well, you sound like you should be here, even if you don't smell like it. On your head, be it. Welcome to the Oubliette, little witch. May you win what you deserve."

He stepped back, waving me in, and I took a first, cautious step into the Oubliette, already knowing it was a mistake.

But some mistakes can't be avoided.

TEN

May you win what you deserve

I HALF-EXPECTED THE ROOM TO BE CHOKED WITH cigarette smoke, as if we really were in some speakeasy in the 20s. Instead, the air inside was cooler and drier than outside, an undertone of eucalyptus and old wood almost smothering the mingled scents of alcohol and nervous sweat. The low lighting had an unchanging mellowness, gleaming on the glasses and smoothing the varnished edges of the gaming tables, and the carpet's subtle, tasteful swirl of patterns made me think we should be in Monte Carlo or somewhere like that, not upstairs of a neon-lit bar in a town hidden deep within the old soul of Manchester.

There were three steps down from the bar and entry area to the floor that held the tables, and I paused at the top of them, trying to act as confident as my bluff to the doorman while I scanned the room. It was long and deep, an open hall with no dividers, the ceiling high and invisible beyond the lights. The twenty or so tables were all occupied, players leaning over card games and roulette wheels and...

"Are those snails?" I murmured to Ruiner.

"Sure. Snail races, fudge-eating contests, hair plaiting competitions — anything they can bet on."

I examined the tables uncertainly. At the closest, half a dozen snails with numbers neatly painted on their shells were slowly slinking around a circular ring, people alternately begging, cheering, and pleading. Another table held four hamsters which were gobbling mini carrots, little snouts twitching pinkly.

"Chew, damn you!" a woman in a three-piece suit screamed. "Stuff those cheeks!"

"More!" a man yelled next to her. "You can fit *more,* you rodent!"

"Wow," I said. A woman in a glittering silver dress that exactly matched her eyes gave me a sideways look as she passed.

"Oh, yah," she said, her accent so upper class I almost curtsied instinctively. "Wait till they bring out the dogs."

"The dogs?" I asked, my stomach turning over.

"Most sausages eaten without vomiting. Or it might be pies. Depends on what the butcher's got." She shrugged fluidly, her eyes shining in the soft light. I was almost certain the colour wasn't from contact lenses.

"Oh." A sausage-eating contest was rather better than I'd imagined.

"Then they have a treadmill race," the woman added. "Sometimes they vomit *and* race all at once. Those are the best ones."

Still not as bad as I'd imagined, but also gross. Treadmills and dog vomit sounded like a bad combo. I managed to keep my shudder mostly under control, nodded at her, and started a circuit of the room, trying to appear as if I were merely deciding where to drop a load of cash. Looking around, I wasn't sure why the doorman had almost turned me away. Sure, there were women dressed as elegantly as the one who'd spoken to me, and men in smart twinsets or sharply cut suits, and there were tuxedos and cocktail dresses and kilts, but I also saw someone in nothing but a pair of Lycra bike shorts and a gorilla mask, another person in beekeeper's gear, and at least two people in dressing gowns. The dress code was evidently expansive, and my jeans and hoody combo simply wasn't that bad. Of course, he could've sniffed out my limited funds somehow. That would make sense.

A man in the bartenders' white shirt and waistcoat attire came past, offering me a tray holding a few bottles of beer (*Goblin's Grog*, the labels read), a tumbler of what looked like whisky, and a couple of glasses of champagne.

"Complimentary," he said, giving me a dazzling grin. The dentist in Darrowdale must be doing a good trade. As was the gym. I eyed his shoulders as I reached for a beer, figuring it was the least I deserved.

"Nothing you don't pay for!" Ruiner hissed, his voice a little muffled by the fact that the hood was in the way, but also more than loud enough, considering he'd jammed his snout into my ear. At the same moment, Jackie bit my other ear, and I jerked my hand back with a yelp.

The waiter looked at me curiously, one dark eyebrow quirking up.

"Not for me," I said. "Need to keep a clear head for all the … dog betting and stuff."

"As you prefer," he said, and strolled away again.

I watched his shoulders go regretfully, then murmured to Ruiner, "Now what? I'm not playing. We can't afford it."

"Bloody hell, no," Ruiner said. "No playing *anything*. Just walk around. Let me see if I spot anyone I know. And keep your hands off the bloody drinks."

I put my hands in my coat pockets just in case and

resumed my determinedly casual strolling. No one paid any attention to us, all intent on the tables. I stopped to watch a dealer with long, twisted fingers and nails that were much more like talons spin a roulette wheel.

"Final bets, my friends," she said, lisping slightly. Her teeth were *off*, not too long or too sharp exactly, but just not *right*, as if they didn't fit her mouth properly. She was wearing the same shirt and waistcoat combo as the bar staff, the creases on the shirt crisp and clean, and the red brocade of the waistcoat gleaming luxuriantly.

"All in on red," a stocky man with sweat on his bald head said, sliding a pile of chips forward. He wiped his mouth with the back of his hand, eyes on the ball rather than the dealer.

The dealer just nodded without speaking, and we watched the ball bounce and spin, the table an oasis of silence amid the cheers and shouts rising from others. With a final judder, the ball bounced into black eight.

"House wins," the dealer said, sweeping the chips towards her. The bald man didn't reply, just pushed himself away from the table and started for the door. He made it about two steps before stopping. He looked around the room as if searching for help, his gaze passing over me with a haunted anxiety drawing heavy lines in his features. He turned back, fumbling in his pockets.

"One more," he said. "This'll be the one, I know it."

"What do you have?" the dealer asked, holding her hand out. The centre of her palm glittered with pale scales.

He looked at what he'd taken from his pocket, then held it out to her. "My car?"

She examined it, then beckoned to a large man standing not far from me against the wall, wearing the same well-cut grey suit as the doorman. She handed the key to him, then looked back at the player. "He'll check," she said, and looked around the table. "Any others?"

"That can't be legal," I whispered to Ruiner. "Just taking someone's car."

"Of course not," he said. "Where d' you think we are? Brighton bingo halls?"

It was a fair point. I imagined Darrowdale had its own laws, even more so than Hollowbeck did. We moved on to where a game of blackjack was under way, the dealer distributing cards with unnerving speed. A woman sitting opposite him was counting her chips, fingers shaking. She slurped from a glass next to her and said in a small, strangled voice, "All in."

"You don't have enough," the dealer said, not looking at her.

The woman tugged at her hair, a nervous little gesture, and said, "I'll pay."

The dealer stopped dealing and looked at her. "Another slice?"

"One more. I can afford it." She leaned forward, bowing her head, and I almost jumped to pull her away as the dealer, a tall man with smooth dark skin and sorrowful eyes, produced a scalpel from under the table somewhere. He flourished it across the cards, then sent the blade in a complicated little flick around the nape of the woman's neck. I caught a whisper on the edge of hearing, deeper or higher than the buzz of the room and setting my teeth on edge, and he swirled a silk handkerchief along the edge of the blade. He folded the cloth neatly and dropped it into a wooden box sitting beside him on the table.

"Done. You're running out, though, Nina. You'll have none left if you keep this up."

"I know. But my luck's on the turn, I can feel it. I'll win it all back. I *will*."

"May you win what you deserve," the dealer said gravely, which wasn't any sort of agreement. Nina gave a shaky, almost grateful smile and picked her cards up, swaying slightly on her chair. She was paler than she had been and kept swallowing hard, as if about to throw up.

"It's her soul," Ruiner whispered, before I could ask. "She's betting pieces of her soul."

I wanted to ask how that was even possible, but the question seemed pointless. It was possible here, was all, in this sly, hungry version of Tanya's pretty bar, and as I looked around the other tables I realised Nina wasn't alone in her pale desperation. There were others too, tapping fingers and shuffling feet, checking cards compulsively or kneeling before tables of spinning cups, hands clasped over their heads as they watched the dealer reveal the coin beneath, all of them looking faded and unreal at the edges.

"What happens to the bits of soul?" I asked.

"We collect them," a voice said next to me, and I jerked around to find a tall, slim woman in a grey suit and red heels standing next to me. Her lipstick matched her shoes, and her well-coiffed hair was almost as pale as her skin, which bordered on translucent.

I blinked at her, wondering if she was a ghost, then said, "Collect them how?"

"Oh, you know." She waved vaguely, her nails the same bright red shade. "With a butterfly net."

"Really?"

"No. Now are you playing, or are you simply *looking*, little witch? Enquiring minds want to know."

"I think it's a bit rich for my taste," I said, and she smiled. She had very even teeth, and her whole face was worryingly symmetrical, like someone's idea of a human. "Who are you?"

"That should be my question. Players aren't too fond

of tourists. Games of chance are private things, to be shared only with those who understand the cost."

I looked around. "I suppose it must get a bit fraught when people are giving up their souls."

"The worst are those who gamble off their children's future," the woman said, clicking her tongue disapprovingly.

"Their savings, you mean?"

"No. Their potential. Their talents." She leaned close to me, her gaze on a table in the corner. "Watch. He's just bet his youngest son's musical abilities on a roll of the dice."

I shrank away from her slightly. There seemed to be a faint chill emanating from her, a frost rising from her skin and mixing with the sharp, crisp scent of some herbal perfume. Her colourless hair was up, but a curl tumbled across her check with artistic elegance, and her eyes were sharp and still, her pupils pinpricks fixed intensely on the player. I managed to look away from her just as the man pushed back from the table, hands clasped to his head.

"And *boom*," the woman said softly. "No Royal Academy of Music scholarship for young Niall. No school choir, no lamenting guitar to charm a lover, not even a desire to dance wildly as the dawn comes up on a beach in Ibiza. All gone."

"That's awful," I said. There was a horrible pressure at the back of my throat, threatening tears.

"Little Niall never even knew such things were a possibility. Never will. He'll take up rugby instead. Or chess." She shrugged. "No one forced his father to play."

"But it's not right. There's laws against letting people gamble when they can't afford it." Even if those laws hardly extended to things like souls and musical abilities.

She smiled at me, still standing a little too close.

"Maybe out in the big wide world, little witch. Not in Darrowdale. I should know."

I wrinkled my nose slightly. This was just my luck. "You're police?"

"Inspector Lise Oddvarson. And you are?"

"Morgan." I looked away, trying to keep my face hidden and thinking that Hollowbeck might only have a sergeant, but Theodore would never allow this. I could hardly say *ooh, Hollowbeck's better*, though. It was bad enough I'd attracted the attention of the police after being in town for a sum total of about ten minutes, especially with a dead body lurking about somewhere, just waiting to make a reappearance.

"So if you're not playing, why are you here, Morgan?" Lise asked me, her gaze flicking to Ruiner. "You and your ... cat." She sounded dubious about the last word, as if she could tell he wasn't quite a cat at all.

"Tourists, like you said," I said. "I heard Darrowdale was the place to come for a good night out."

She laughed softly, a surprisingly warm sound. "I'm not sure you're prepared for a Darrowdale night out, little witch. Although I could show you around if you wanted." She raised a hand and I flinched away, making her laugh again. She brandished a card at me, pinched between two long fingers. "If you need to contact me for anything. And don't worry. I only bite if you ask nicely." She thought about it. "Or if you've been a really bad girl. Goodnight, Morgan. May you win what you deserve."

I took the card automatically and she put her hands in the pockets of her trousers, strolling away with a perfectly straight back and a prowling gait that made me think of big cats, all smooth muscle and hidden claws and eyes that see everything.

"Let's go," Ruiner said, his voice barely audible over a

sudden clamour from a table in which frogs were leaping wildly after crickets.

"She didn't say we had to."

"No. But I think we've drawn more than enough attention to ourselves for one night, don't you? And I haven't seen anyone we can talk to here."

I looked at the card. It read *Inspector Lise Oddvarson, Darrowdale Police*, in small black type on heavy white card. There was a phone number below it, and nothing else. No logo, no address. I turned it over, but the back was blank, too.

"A police inspector who collect souls?"

"Someone's got to do it. Let's go, Morgan. More people are going to notice we're not playing."

I glanced around the room, adjusting my hood to keep my face deeper in shadow. He was right. The waiter was speaking to the bartender as he reloaded his tray with drinks, both of them looking our way. The bartender narrowed his eyes, then picked up a cocktail shaker and started mixing mint and ice into it in what looked like the start of a mojito. My mouth watered like one of Pavlov's dogs, and I looked away with difficulty. I couldn't see the doorman, but the man who'd gone to check on the player's car keys had come back and was standing uncomfortably close to us, making me wonder if he'd heard us talking.

"This was a mistake," Ruiner said. "No one comes in here and doesn't play. Let's *go*."

And this time I didn't argue. It felt like we'd been here both too long and barely any time at all, the minutes stretched and twisted. I was tired, and anxiety was scratching at my chest, and all around the room people were betting scraps of their lives — and their *children's* lives — on a spin of the dice or a flip of the cards. Or on how many crickets a bloody frog could eat. Somehow that was even worse. The *triviality* of it. My stomach turned over, and I shoved my hands into the pockets of my borrowed coat, pushing my way through the crowd more brusquely than was necessary as I headed for the door.

Both my brother and my ex had been playing at these tables. That made my stomach even sicker.

ELEVEN

Nothing for free

"THOUGHT YOU WERE HERE TO PLAY," THE DOORMAN called after me as I hurried past him, pulling the door open and rushing out. I ignored him, his snort of laughter following me as I clattered back down the stairs, rounding the turn into a rush of heat and pounding music that was deeply comforting. The place simmered with alcohol and excess, but at least it felt like the worst thing you might lose was a tooth or your wallet, depending how the night went.

I paused before emerging from the stairwell, leaning against the wall despite my previous misgivings about the cleaning standards of the Witch's Howl. The hot, thick air was making me dizzy, or the strange, stretched time in the Oubliette was. I took a couple of deep breaths, ears stuffy with noise, then slipped into the crush of bodies filling the bar. It was busier than when we'd arrived, and someone was doing some sort of interpretive dance on one of the tables while two of the bartenders carried a short-haired woman past me to the door, holding a leg and an arm each. She wasn't resisting, just singing a Celine Dion song at the top of her voice, which seemed like reasonable grounds for being removed, to be honest.

I followed the yodeling cry of, "My heart will go on and *ohhhhnnnn...*" to the door, keeping my head down. With the crowd in here, I didn't feel quite as obvious as I had upstairs, but there were so many people who *could* be looking at me without my noticing. I wondered if this was how an antelope felt running the gauntlet of a waterhole. Probably not. They presumably had lots of other antelopes to hide behind, and I felt as if I were wearing a sign that read *eat me, I'm a tourist*.

But no one stopped me, or even moved to talk to me, and a moment later we were back out on the street, watching the bartenders depositing the still singing woman in a plastic chair next to the door. She promptly got up and twirled down the street, arms outstretched.

"Near! Far! Where-*eeehver* you *aaaare—*"

"Hope she moves onto some Pink next," one of the bartenders said as he walked past me, heading back inside. "Getting bloody sick of Celine."

"Nah," the other said. "She did Pink in the summer. Be Streisand next, I reckon."

"Oh, sod that."

They vanished back into the Witch's Howl without giving me a second glance, and I shifted the strap of my satchel, the weight of the book digging it into my shoulder uncomfortably. The air was still sticky, but after the chill, threatening atmosphere of the Oubliette, it didn't seem so bad. I turned towards the car, following the diva fan.

The unsteady streetlights cast shadows that were deep enough to make me feel a little less antelope-like, and I relaxed a bit. Town wasn't busy, but people were still coming and going from the shops and other businesses, and someone had trapped the crab under a large rubbish bin in the middle of the road. About five people were standing around it, all arguing about what to do next. I kept my head down as I passed them, then hesitated, looking toward Bewitching Boos.

"Don't," Ruiner said. He was still balancing on my shoulder, which did make it easier to talk, but was also annoying. I wasn't my brother's transport human.

"Buying a coffee should be fine, right? You just said not to take free stuff."

"We should just get out of here. Sort your caffeine addiction out later."

"Get out of here and go where? We don't have anywhere to stay, and I'm not sure I want to try whatever the equivalent of Petunia's guesthouse is." There'd probably be giant, poisonous toads in the walls rather than frogs.

"We go back to Hollowbeck."

"You know I'm not doing that until I know Jason's safe."

He sighed, very heavily for someone who wasn't even having to get his paws dirty. "Well, gee, if only we knew a place that was safely out of Darrowdale but close enough that we could get back easily."

"I know— wait. No."

"It's that or sleep in the car, and I think someone nicking the wheels would be the least of our worries around here."

"There was a *dead body* in the kitchen, Ruiner."

"Not when we left."

"That's even worse! Someone's running around scattering dead bodies about the place, and I *touched* it! It's got my fingerprints on it, and who knows where it is!"

"Well, not on the kitchen floor anymore, which seems like a good sign if we want to sleep there."

I veered toward the coffeeshop.

"What're you doing?" Ruiner demanded.

"I need coffee before I can even think about this." I hurried down the pavement to Bewitching Boos, the scent of freshly brewed coffee drifting out of the shop to meet us. Two women in camouflage gear with stripes painted on their cheekbones were sitting at one of tables outside, digging into large ice cream sundaes heaped with nuts and cream, and at the table next to them a man lapped coffee out of his cup like a cat, while an actual cat sat next to him, looking on with its ears back and snout wrinkled.

Having decided that the large guns lying next to the women were for paintballs (a theory the splatters of luminous yellow and orange on their clothes seemed to support), I threaded my way past the tables and pushed through the door, shivering with a weird sense of dislocation as I did so. Boos was set up in an identical manner to Brews, with a wooden counter and high stools, a couple of small tables and chairs, and a coffee roaster lurking off to the left. Instead of industrial matte black paint and dark metal, though, all that darkness lifted by the warm rich tones of the wood, Boos favoured shiny chrome and glossy black paint, everything so reflective it made my eyes hurt. The countertop was a pale, gleaming wood, the light bouncing off it, and I squinted around the shop.

The drinking competition had evidently ended a while ago, as the only person present was a big, bearded man mopping spilled coffee off the floor and bopping to some tune I didn't recognise, but which at least wasn't Celine Dion. He didn't look up as I came in, just said, "Wet floor, mind yourself."

"Thanks." I took a stool at the counter while he finished what he was doing, then disappeared out the back with the bucket. Ruiner jumped to the stool next to me.

"Be careful," he hissed.

I nodded. I had full intentions of that, but I also had full intentions of caffeinating myself. It had been a long day and longer night, and when I took my phone out to check the time I wasn't surprised to see it was almost four in the morning. Time seemed to have got a little elastic in the Oubliette. My stomach rumbled, reminding me that a couple of chocolate Hobnobs did not constitute dinner.

The bearded man re-emerged, drying his hands on a cloth, and regarded me critically. His hair was tied back in a bun and he had a couple of silver butterflies clipped into his beard. "Caramel latte?" he suggested, and I made a face.

"Americano."

"Boring," he said, but he grinned as he said it, already setting a handle on the grinder. "Anything else?"

I peered at the cake stands. There were a couple of cupcakes topped with mountains of pink icing on one, and vast slabs of carrot cake on the other. "That one," I said, pointing at the carrot cake.

"Right you are." He served me up a slice while the coffee ran through and gave Ruiner a curious look. He found some lactose-free milk in the fridge and poured some into an espresso cup, setting it in front of him. Ruiner looked at it then at me, twitching his ears.

"How much for the milk?" I asked.

"On the house," he said, taking my mug from the machine and popping it on a saucer with a teaspoon before sliding it over the counter to me.

"I'd rather pay."

He gave me an amused look. "Do you think I'm going to steal your cat away?"

"No idea," I said truthfully. "And honestly, you probably wouldn't want him. But how much?"

"Throw 50p in for the milk, then," he said, and I slipped some money across the counter, the simple act of paying feeling unfamiliar after Hollowbeck. He passed me my change, then made himself a large glass of cold milk with caramel syrup, leaning against the far side of the counter to drink it. "You're new."

"Just passing through."

"Now there's a lie." He examined me over his glass. "You looking for someone?"

Ruiner gave me a sideways look, and I took a forkful of cake to give myself time to think. It was really good, moist and rich and flavourful, with a thick swathe of tangy icing on top. "Why would you think that?"

"Well, if you'd been losing in the Oubliette, you'd be after something stronger than coffee and cake, and you don't look lucky enough to be winning over there, either."

"Accurate," I said, pointing the fork at him, then putting it down to sniff the coffee. I made a little *hmm* of appreciation and took a sip. It tasted even better than it smelled, strong without being bitter, well-rounded and spiked with citrus notes. This could give James' coffee a run for its money.

The barista took another gulp of cold milk. "You also don't look like you're here for any of the team building. Not enough bruises."

"Team building?"

"Yeah." He nodded in the rough direction of the road out of town. "The laser tag and so on."

"Shooting people out of cannons?" I said doubtfully.

"I believe the official description is *adrenaline-pumping stress relief for your whole team*. Usually executive level groups. None of your shop floor lot here. Most of them even get back in one piece." He was grinning, and I couldn't tell if he was joking or not. Then again, the only job that hadn't forced me to go on some excruciatingly pointless team building day was the bookshop I'd briefly worked at between leaving Jason and falling into Hollowbeck, and that was because the entire team had been me and the distinctly creepy owner. For all I knew, the magical world had employee of the month and casual Fridays, just like everywhere else. Or maybe Darrowdale got regular businesses in here, selling them on some wildly extreme version of team building. That was actually pretty likely, when it came to high-level executives. Anything to one-up each other.

"Definitely not here for that," I said aloud, scraping the dregs of icing off the plate with my fork.

"So what *are* you here for?" the barista asked, arching bushy eyebrows at me. "We're not exactly tourist central."

I hesitated. He seemed alright. He hadn't tried to poison or drug me, which was an improvement on my first week in Hollowbeck, and the butterflies in his beard made me inclined to trust him. I unlocked my phone and scrolled through the photos until I found one of Jason, congratulating myself on being an adult and not deleting them all. Although, admittedly, that had partly been because I'd forgotten, and partly because, once I'd discovered magic existed, I'd been toying with the idea of seeing if I could curse him with adult acne. I zoomed in on Jason's face and held the phone out. "Have you seen him?"

The bearded man took the phone in one big hand and inspected the picture, frowning slightly. "Don't think so, no," he said. "Most people don't come to Darrowdale for the coffee, though."

"They should. It's excellent."

"Thanks," he said, grinning, and handed the phone back. "Why was he here? That might help you narrow down where to look."

"I'm not sure," I admitted. "I thought maybe he was playing at the Oubliette."

The barista sucked air over his teeth. "That's a tricky one."

"Yeah, I'm kind of thinking that."

"You should ask the town witch," he said. "She knows pretty much everything that happens in town. She'll be over there." He nodded towards the window, and I swivelled on my stool to look with a weary sort of resignation.

"You mean at the Cosy Cauldron?"

"Crafty Cauldron," he said, clearing my cake plate away and dropping a little square of shortbread biscuit onto my saucer. "But yeah."

Of course he did. Suddenly I just wanted out of Darrowdale. I was exhausted by it, by the almost-but-not-quite Hollowbeck-ness, by the unrelenting sense of threat, by feeling I was constantly being observed, by the thick, humid air. I wanted to be back in actual Hollowbeck, in my big bed under the eaves of Petunia's attic, listening to the frogs and the quiet excursions of the boarding house's other residents, or, failing that, out in the grey and dreary cold of the ordinary world. Anywhere but here.

I drained my coffee and got up, nodding at the barista. "Thanks."

"No problems. Pop in any time. I'll keep you some carrot cake."

"Thanks." I picked up the piece of shortbread as I turned to go, and had it halfway to my mouth when Ruiner leaped to my shoulder, slapping it out of my hand. It spun to the just-mopped floor and I swore, looking back at the barista apologetically. "Sorry, he's such a—"

The words died in my mouth as the barista glared at Ruiner, his eyes huge and black, the butterflies in his beard transformed into giant, clawed creatures with sharp-ened proboscises, scrabbling in the moving tendrils of his beard while their feelers pointed frantically at me. He hissed, baring a wall of needle teeth as he clutched the counter with clawed hands, puncturing the wood. Ruiner shot off my shoulder and bolted for the door, pouffed up to about twice his actual size, and I just stared, frozen in place.

"Get out," the barista snarled, his teeth stabbing his lips. He grabbed the butterflies as they launched themselves towards me. They twisted in his grip, clawing at his hands. "*Get out!*"

For some utterly inexplicable reason I saluted, then legged it after Ruiner, who was desperately clawing the door. I nudged him out of the way with one foot and hauled the door open, my shoulders hunched against attack, and we tumbled out onto the pavement. I scurried through the tables to the street, Ruiner sprinting ahead of me, and only once I was on the road itself did I risk a glance back. The barista was calmly clearing my mug, looking as friendly and non-toothy as he had when we'd arrived.

I swallowed hard and wiped my fingers on my jacket, just in case I had any shortbread crumbs on them, then turned and hurried towards the car, waiting until we were ensconced in its dubious safety to look at Ruiner and say, "What the hell was that?"

His tail was still doing the feather duster thing, and he looked at me with wide eyes. "I did tell you not to eat anything you didn't pay for."

"You did *not* say anything about attack butterfly clips. And the teeth! What was he?" I waved wildly at the coffeeshop.

"Fae of some sort. There's a bunch of different varieties, but you don't mess with any of them."

"Well, that's just great," I grumbled, coaxing the car into life. "The coffee was really good."

"Of course it was. It was Fae food."

I stared at him. "But you let me eat it! You said it was fine if I paid for it!"

"It is. Just Fae make really good food, obviously. Can't exactly tempt someone with a dried out Cornish pasty and some Rich Tea biscuits."

I rested my forehead on the wheel for a moment, eyes closed, then straightened up and put the car in reverse to pull out of the parking spot. "I have questions for you."

"Thought you might."

"I'm finding a takeaway first, though," I said. "A human one."

I turned the car towards the road out of town and hoped it'd let us go.

TWELVE

Gateway games

IT DIDN'T SEEM TO TAKE AS LONG TO GET BACK TO Jason's house — my old house — from Darrowdale as it had taken to get there. I found myself checking the rearview mirror compulsively, as if we might've been pursued by Lise or the barista or, for all I knew, the giant bloody crab. But no matter how many times I checked, no one appeared behind us except other cars tracing their own journeys through the nighttime streets. The whole trip was uneventful, in fact, even leaving Darrowdale. No flaming hamster wheel rolled over us as we left town, no one shot the car up with lasers or tried to drag us into the crematorium-slash-smokehouse, and the walls of the alley back to Manchester didn't slam shut in front of us, or on us. We either left unnoticed or were allowed to leave, and at that particular point I didn't even care which it was, just that we got out.

I'd been craving a decent curry, but by the time we made it back onto regular streets we were well into the morning, early delivery vans already taking over the streets. I had to settle for a breakfast deal from a fast-food chain, overcooked, unseasoned egg and flabby circles of bacon on a squishy bun with a cup of watery coffee, plus a side of extra bacon for Ruiner on the theory that it was marginally better than a breakfast patty. Even that paltry meal took a good bite out of our funds, which were rapidly vanishing, and I stopped at a cash machine to see if my bank might've somehow missed the fact I'd stopped getting wages months ago. The machine ate my card and told me in large, flashing letters to contact my branch manager, so that was the end of that little experiment.

Back at the house, we ate at the kitchen table, avoiding looking too closely at the spaghetti-splattered floor. The body hadn't come back, at least, so that was something.

"What's the next step?" I asked Ruiner, feeding Jackie a piece of soft apple from the little pack that had come with my breakfast deal. She looked unimpressed and investigated the solitary grape instead.

"Give up?" he suggested. "You tried."

"We barely tried at all. We went to the one place, and that was it." I pointed my breakfast sandwich at him. "You know far too much about Darrowdale. Where else might he go?"

"I don't know — maybe he's touring the historic houses?"

I scowled at him. "How did you know about the food? And the bartenders and teeth thing? And why didn't you tell me about Darrowdale before?"

"It's not exactly Club bloody Med, is it? I didn't think you'd have to go to Darrowdale for anything, so I didn't think it was worth mentioning." He licked his chops. "This bacon's terrible."

"I know." I took Lise's card from my pocket and set it on the table, looking at it thoughtfully. "Do you think—"

"No. She's not going to help you."

"Why not? He's a missing person who could be in her town."

"Lise works for the Oubliette more than she does the town. If Jason's got himself in trouble through a game, she's more likely to be involved than to be up for helping you."

I got up and looked in the fridge, discovering a can of Lilt that looked like it had been in there since I moved out. I took it back to the table. "How do you how all this?"

"The same way I knew about Hollowbeck. You move in magical circles, you pick stuff up."

"Darrowdale is nothing like Hollowbeck."

"Well, no, but also yes." He yawned and started cleaning himself.

"Can you not do that on the table?"

"Fine." He jumped to the floor and stalked through the door to the living room, calling as he went, "I still vote for leaving Jason to sort himself out. Darrowdale's not a good place to be poking around in."

I didn't answer. I just sat there drinking my Lilt and watching Jackie eat her fruit. She finished and squeaked at me, with I assumed meant she expected a better standard of food tomorrow.

"You and me both," I told her. I got up and cleared the table, checked the back door was locked, for whatever good that might do, then went into the living room and straightened things up enough that I could sleep on the sofa. There was no way I was sleeping in my old bed. Some things were just a step too far.

It wasn't until I was stretched out on the sofa with the satchel under my pillow that I thought to look at my phone, mostly to see if it needed charging. The email icon was bright with new messages, and I blinked at it, then realised Jason had probably never changed the wi-fi. It had connected automatically. I opened the app, ready to skim through, and stopped on the first message. *Hollowbeck Library.* I opened it.

Morgan, please come back. Isabella can't leave Hollowbeck and Theodore can, but he needs somewhere safe for the days, and they're both really worried. Starlight told us about the haunting. And if you won't come back, tell me where you are. I'll come and find you. Please.

It's Ben, by the way.

I looked at it for a while, feeling a smile in the corner of my lips. *It's Ben, by the way,* as if it'd be anyone else. I somehow doubted most of Hollowbeck were even aware that email existed. Finally I hit answer, and wrote, *I'm fine, still looking for Jason. He seems to be mixed up with some magical gambling club. No luck so far, but I'll keep looking tomorrow. Don't worry. It's Morgan, by the way.*

I debated putting an *x* at the end, and finally decided against it, going for a winking emoji instead. I hit send, found a charger, and ignored the other ninety thousand emails. They could wait.

I DIDN'T THINK I'd sleep, strung out on worry and stress, even with the warmth of the email to soothe my nerves a bit. I expected every car that went past to stop and drop a dead body on the doorstep, and I saw the barista's huge, glossy eyes every I closed my own. But at some point exhaustion must've won out, because I woke with a yelp to the doorbell ringing insistently across the room. The satchel was still under my pillow, and it had given me a crick in the neck that jabbed another yelp from me as I sat up. I tried to stretch it out as I got up and staggered across the room to the front door, still fully dressed and feeling like I'd been on an all-night bender.

I opened the door to an elderly woman wearing lime green slacks, a mint green cardigan, and neon green earrings. Her smile widened to about twice its original size when she saw me, which would've been gratifying if I'd had about five hours more sleep.

"Morgan! I thought that was your car!"

"Mrs. Mullen," I said, rubbing a hand over my face. "Lovely to see you." It had been inevitable, of course. If the police had surveillance half as effective as my old across-the-road neighbour, the whole country would grind to a halt.

"Are you back full time?" She was trying to peer around me, evidently hoping to have caught Jason and I reconciling, and I half-closed the door, blocking the gap with my body.

"Just house-sitting."

She tipped her head to one side. "Are you alright, dear? You look rather rough."

"Night shift. I've not slept much — not that it's not nice to see you, but I'm knackered. Is there anything I can help you with?"

"No, no. I was just rather hoping you were back for good. I've been keeping an eye on things since you left, you know. The class of people coming by has rather gone downhill." Her tone was reproving, and I nodded, rubbing my stinging eyes.

"Sorry to hear that."

"Yes, it didn't used to be so bad when you were here. Only the odd person, while you were at work. Now it's all the time!"

I squinted at her. The green combination was making me queasy. "While I was at work?"

"Oh, did you not know?" She leaned a little closer, eyes shining. "Sometimes women, sometimes men, and *some* of them were quite respectable, but others, well—"

I really wasn't interested in hearing about the women she'd seen coming around and was only telling me about now. And even if she had seen anything useful, how would I know? What was I going to say, *have you seen anyone who doesn't look human?* "Mrs. Mullen, it's been lovely seeing you, but I really am exhausted—"

"—and, of course, your brother was around a lot—"

I'd been starting to shut the door, and now I stopped. "My brother?"

"Yes, I always thought it odd he visited so much when you were out, and after you left. I haven't seen him for a while, though. Is he well? Such a nice boy."

I had my own opinions on how nice he was, and I went back to closing the door, mumbling an apology. She kept talking, leaning into the gap, and I garbled something about needing the loo then shut it firmly in her face. I didn't live here anymore — I could afford to be rude. I looked around for Ruiner. There was no sign of him in the living room, so I crept up the stairs, hoping he hadn't been listening.

I checked the spare room first, avoiding the floorboard at the top of the stairs that always creaked. It was empty, and I eased back into the hall then edged up to the door of the master bedroom. *There.* He was curled into the crumpled pile of the duvet, all four paws folded together and his chin resting on top of them.

I tip-toed carefully into the room, but just as I reached the bed a board creaked under my weight. I froze, caught mid-step with my hands raised like a cartoon villain. Ruiner's ears twitched and his eyes opened a crack. I held my breath, willing myself invisible, but his eyes snapped toward me, widening as he unfolded with fluid speed, going from asleep to full flight in an instant. I lunged forward, but he was already diving off the far side of the bed. I flung myself backwards, making it to the door half a stride ahead of him and slamming it shut. He spun and shot under the bed.

"Ruiner! Get out here!"

"What the hell's wrong with you? Did you eat that bloody shortbread after all?"

I dropped to my knees and peered under the bed. He was hunkered down in the exact centre among the dust bunnies, eyes wide.

"Come out."

"I won't. You just about belly-flopped on me like you're trying out for the WWF."

I scowled at him. "What were you doing visiting Jason while I was at work?"

"He was my brother-in-law."

"You hated him."

"Hate's a strong word."

"Fine, you *disliked* him."

"I was right to."

"That's beside the point," I said. "Why were you visiting someone you didn't even like, and why didn't you tell me?"

He eyed me carefully, then said, "He wanted help."

"So he went to *you?*"

He narrowed his eyes at me. "I was a successful entrepreneur."

"Have you said that so often you actually believe it?"

"No," he admitted, and we stared at each other, then he said, "Is there any bacon left?"

"No. And you couldn't have any even if there was. This whole place stinks."

"That was probably the milk."

"It was lactose-free." I rocked back on my heels as he emerged from under the bed, cobwebs adorning his ears. "Why were you talking to Jason? What did he need help with?"

He sighed. "Would you believe it wasn't my fault?"

"Not really."

"Well, it wasn't. It started because he got caught up in some games — *not mine* — and wanted help to get out of debt before you found out."

I rubbed the crick in my neck. "Multiple times?"

"He was not a great card player."

"So what happened once you got involved? What did you do?"

Ruiner looked at his paws, pressed neatly together on the carpet. "You don't just walk into the games at the Oubliette. You start at other clubs, regular human ones, and then someone invites you to something a little *different,* and one thing leads to another."

"Is that how you discovered the whole magic thing in the first place?"

"No. Anyhow, I'd seen Jason at some of these kind of gateway games. I knew he was going to get sucked in, and where it'd lead. I tried to get him out before he got in too deep, because I knew you'd be the one who'd end up paying."

I didn't answer straight away. Getting caught up in some get rich quick scheme had always been Jason's weakness. He'd invested in three different MLMs, bought an ice cream van in the middle of winter, sold dodgy imported cosmetics that caused severe allergic reactions, and almost been arrested for setting up a service to help people break into their own cars and houses, which had, predictably, ended up in him being employed by less than upstanding citizens. His judgement was almost as bad as my brother's, but it had never been as downright illegal.

"He doesn't gamble," I said to Ruiner, who arched his whiskers at me.

"Sure?"

Of course I wasn't sure. I couldn't be sure. But I *could* be sure that my brother did nothing *but* gamble, in one way or the other. "You got him into this," I said.

"I didn't."

"You want a bet? Then I'll place money on the fact that you did. Just another bloody Ruiner mess, trying to make some quick cash and thinking it'll never catch up with you. Only this time it's caught up with my sodding *ex*, and I still have to clean it up. *Still*." I got up I stomped downstairs, wondering if there was any chocolate in the house. There better be. It was going to be that or whisky.

RUINER CAME into the kitchen while I was eating stale cornflakes with milk. I'd thrown a good couple of spoonfuls of sugar on top of them, so they were soggy and sweet and cardboard-y all at once. They were terrible.

Ruiner jumped to the table and looked at me. "Any ham left, then?"

I got up without answering. I'd found sausages in the freezer that were unlikely to be any better for him than the bacon had been, but there wasn't a lot of choice. I took the plate out of the microwave where I'd been defrosting one and dropped it in front of him.

He sniffed it and looked at me. "The microwave? Really?"

"I didn't realise you were such a gourmand."

He nibbled one end of the sausage delicately then said,

"To be fair, they taste like they're half sawdust anyway. Don't think a pan would've saved them."

I didn't answer, just finished my cornflakes then went to make a cup of tea. Ruiner chewed stolidly through half the sausage, waiting for me to sit back down again. Only then did he say, "I really was trying to keep Jason out of trouble, Morgs."

I tapped my fingers on the mug, staring at a chip on its rim. I'd got the mug in Blackpool, when we'd gone for a day trip. It had been cold and windy, the whole place winter-drab, showing its peeling paint and cracked facades, the salt spinning off the sea and turning the air to mist. Jason had complained all day because he'd worn summer trainers and no socks, his jacket wasn't warm enough, and he'd somehow got sunburnt at the same time. But it had been as much of a holiday as we'd had that year — or as I'd had — because I'd had to use our savings to pay off a loan he'd taken out to turn our garden shed into an Airbnb. That had never quite eventuated because he'd bought a DIY kit online, and he and a mate had tried to put it up together, including the wiring, which had worked about as well as could be imagined.

"How long have you known about places like Hollowbeck and Darrowdale?" I asked my brother.

"A while," he admitted.

"How long had Jason known about them?"

"He didn't," he said, and I raised my eyebrows. "Not that I knew of, anyway. Like I said, he joined me for a couple of games—"

"You did not say that."

"Well, fine. He did. We needed an extra player, so I asked him if he wanted to step in. He was always asking about my games."

That much was true. Jason had far too much admiration for Ruiner's questionable lifestyle. "Were these those, what did you call them, *gateway* games?"

"No. I never got him into that."

"Ruiner—"

"I really didn't. And when I found out he'd tried to join a game without me, I warned him off. Told him it was way out of his league, and it seemed like he listened. I thought he actually quit playing after that. You know how he went from one thing to another all the time."

"Pot, kettle," I said, and rubbed my forehead. "But now it seems he's somehow caught up in them."

"Maybe. The only thing we have that points that way is the brand on the dead guy's wrist, though," Ruiner said. "It could be unrelated."

"Sure. But what are the odds of that, when he's calling me saying he needs help, and someone who's been banned from a magical gambling club is dead on his kitchen floor?"

Ruiner didn't answer immediately, and I waited for him to trot out his favourite refrain: *It's not my fault.* Instead he said, "What d'you want to do?"

I looked at him. "We have to go back to Darrowdale. Talk to the town witch and anyone else."

My brother sighed deeply, his furry sides heaving. "You really want to go back to Darrowdale?"

"No. But we can't just leave him there. You know what he's like. He'll have no idea what's going on, and he's probably making things worse the whole time." I got up and put my mug in the sink. "Honestly, it's pretty surprising you didn't like him. You have a lot in common."

"Hilarious."

"No, it's not."

He huffed, but didn't dispute it.

THIRTEEN

An exercise in attention-getting

A GOOD SEARCH OF THE HOUSE TURNED UP A COUPLE OF chocolate protein bars, which I pocketed in case of emergencies, and another forty quid. That was hardly going to buy Jason out of trouble, but at least meant we could put fuel in the car and get a bit of food. The sausages were already doing terrible things to Ruiner's digestive system, and the milk was almost gone. I could manage very happily without having stale, soggy cornflakes again, but if I had to drink tea without milk I'd start throwing things. Coffee would be another matter, of course, and highly preferably to tea with or without milk, but there wasn't so much as a jar of instant in the cupboards. That situation needed a remedy. A complete lack of caffeine would probably result in me storming the Oubliette single-handed or something.

My restored emails hadn't yielded anything interesting this morning. Ben hadn't replied, and while I found the email from Jason, all it said was the same thing. He needed my help. No indication on how, or where, so I had to assume he'd expected to be at the house to meet me, rather than the dead body. So Darrowdale was still our best option, which said a lot about just how limited those options were.

Darrowdale was somehow even harder to find in the daylight, the alley so painfully narrow and dull that it blended with the grimy stone of the buildings that hemmed it in. Even knowing it was there, I mistook it for a shadow and drove straight past with Ruiner yelling, "Left! *Left!*"

I found somewhere to do a U-turn and went back a little more carefully, the road quiet enough that I was able to do a wide turn again and aim directly at the gap (which still barely *looked* like a gap, and I spotted two women in hijabs watching, puzzled expressions on their faces as I apparently drove straight at a wall). I scraped one wing mirror on the way through, but given the state of the rest of the car, I wasn't about to panic over that. I just patted the dashboard and whispered, "Good girl," as we rumbled out the other end of the alley and the walls peeled off to either side. There was something off about the perspective, rendering them high and impossibly long, stretching on unbroken as far as I could see even in the daylight. I swear there were clouds curling lovingly around some of the more distant ones, and they looked to be capped with snow. I half-expected to see a dragon take flight from them.

I hadn't seen the welcome sign last night, and I'd rather not have seen it this morning. On the surface, it was benign enough — a family laughing and clutching ice creams. But the closer we got to it, the more the laughs looked like screams, and the more the ice cream looked ... well, like strawberries weren't what were giving it its visceral red colour. Something had also burned a hole through one of the mother's eyes, which hardly improved matters. *Live your dreams in Darrowdale!* the sign proclaimed. I definitely didn't want any of their dreams. That way lay madness, or at least an unnatural attraction to questionable ice cream.

The road through the fields to town was quiet, no laser tag teams crashing out of the corn or rockets going off. The buildings that had been glowing with neon and excitement last night looked all but derelict in the dull grey day, only plumes of smoke from the chimneys to suggest life. We passed a couple with plywood boarded over all the windows, and another with smoke stains painting half its facade. I could see more signs now, faded and punched through with holes, advertising things like *Catch-Your-Own Hog Roast* and *World's Best Corn Maze! You'll Never Get Out!* They emerged from the corn then were swallowed again as we passed, leaving us in a featureless corridor of plants. I wasn't a fan of it. Sure, it was out of season, so it made sense the plants were dead, but they seemed to move as the car passed, ripples of motion that weren't caused by our passage, and were too isolated to be the wind.

"See any creepy kids popping out anywhere?" Ruiner asked, sitting bolt upright on the passenger seat with his tail over his toes.

"That's helpful," I said, glancing at Jacqueline. She was perched on the satchel where it lay in the passenger footwell, and every time I looked at her she bared her teeth and chittered in outrage. I got the feeling she wasn't a huge fan of me taking the grimoire out of Hollowbeck, let alone bringing it here. But there was no way I was leaving it alone at Jason's.

We made it into town without any rockets being fired at us or overly happy ice cream-lovers chasing us down to indoctrinate us regarding the glory of the all-seeing soft serve. I did have to stop once, as a family of pigs stampeded across the road with a pack of geese in hot pursuit. One of the birds noticed us and started screaming at the car, wings beating the air wildly, and I had to drive around it before it tried smashing the windscreen in. It and three of its buddies charged after us down the road until we were far enough away that they evidently felt we'd learned our lesson.

"I prefer the plague of rabbits," I said to Ruiner.

"Yeah, I reckon I could take a bunny."

"I definitely could." I thought about it. "As long as it was just one, and not a plague. And they weren't too cute."

"Cuteness complicates any altercation."

Our parking spot just beyond the clutter of shops in the centre was still free, and I pulled into it, giving Bewitching Boos a longing look. It really had been good coffee. And the *cake*. My mouth watered at the thought. Evidently I was in baked goods withdrawal as well as caffeine withdrawal, but I wasn't going back in there. Instead, I slung the satchel across my body and pulled Jason's coat over it once again, then headed along the road to the Crafty Cauldron, head bent against a steady drizzle that had started up while we'd been driving. At least it had broken that strange, humid heat from the night before.

The shop had a couple of wheeled displays outside, just like we did in Hollowbeck, but along with the books these held potted plants instead of cheesy kitchen signs. One of the display windows showed off an artfully arranged selection of jewellery, silver and stones all glowing gently in the light from inside, while the one to the other side of the door was full of crystals and arty books, all of it set off by a backdrop of dark velvet. I wondered if I should take some photos for inspiration. The most notable thing in our display windows at the moment was either a sleeping ferret or a dismaying quantity of dead flies, which seemed to regenerate instantly, no matter how often we vacuumed.

I tried to push the door open, and it didn't budge. "Huh." I peered inside, but I couldn't see anyone, and there was no note on the door, not even a *Closed* sign.

"Well, at least you've got your shop hours in common," Ruiner said.

I glanced back at the street. "Careful. We're attracting enough attention without anyone hearing you talking."

Ruiner crouched, and launched himself to my shoulder, setting Jackie squeaking. "Oh, shut up," he muttered. "I'm not going to eat you."

She wriggled around to the other side of my neck and settled there. I could feel her whiskers tickling my ear, and I sighed. What had happened in my life that I'd become a climbing frame for animals?

"What now?" Ruiner asked.

"We'll have to try later," I said, fishing my phone out of my pocket and pulling up Jason's photo again. "But we can ask around if anyone else has seen him."

"That seems unnecessarily attention-seeking."

"Do you have any other ideas?"

He didn't answer, so I headed across the road to Monster Munch, wondering if they sold coffee. It was worth asking.

MONSTER MUNCH WAS OPEN, but the only people inside were a woman sharing a pot of tea and some biscuits with a parrot, and a young woman mopping the floor. She didn't recognise Jason, and looked so worried when I asked about coffee that I immediately told her not to bother.

"We've got coffee ice cream," she offered. "Or I could make you a really strong tea?"

"No, that's fine," I said, then had to ask, "You don't serve coffee at all? Not even after dinner?"

She shook her head, letting go of the mop with one hand to tuck hair back under her baseball cap. "Bewitching Boos does coffee."

"Yeah, I was just hoping to get one somewhere else."

She stared at me, going back to clutching the mop with both hands, as if it might keep her upright. "Bewitching Boos does coffee."

We looked at each other, then I nodded. "Got it. Thank you."

She slumped with relief as I headed back out the door, and as I walked to the dress shop, I murmured to Ruiner, "It's the *only* place that does coffee?"

"Maybe he's a bit territorial."

That was a fun thought. I wound my way through the racks of leather and lace to the counter, where a thin man was painstakingly stitching teeth onto a plaid miniskirt. I hoped they were plastic, but one still had a filling in it.

He looked at me over his glasses, gaze travelling over my borrowed coat and old jeans, then said, "Souvenir T-shirts are next door at Jeannie's."

"Thanks." I showed him my phone. "Have you seen him?"

"No." He barely glanced at it before going back to his stitching.

"Are you sure? Can you take another look?"

"Yes, and no."

I took a deep breath. "Look, he's a friend of mine, and I think he might be in trouble—"

"Doubly no, then." He held a tooth up to the light,

inspecting it. "Would you say this is more chiffon or parchment?"

"What?"

"The colour."

"No idea."

"You're not much help, then." He selected a different tooth, and I managed not to tell him I felt the same. Instead, I left before he could start eyeing up the shades of my teeth.

Jeannie was equally as helpful, although in an entirely different way. She rushed around the shop, presenting me with one thing after another.

"Scarf spun from badger hair!"

"No thanks. Can you just—"

"Coasters depicting the pillaging of the village in 1523!"

"No. Look, I have this photo—"

"Earrings paw-made by squirrels!"

"No. I — wait, what?"

"Squirrels." She shook a set of earrings at me. They didn't look like they'd been made by *anything*, two unmatched conglomerations of fragmented white shell and dead leaves and fur.

"How do squirrels make them?"

"Well…" She hesitated. "I mean, *technically* the owls make them after they've eaten the squirrels, but they *contain* squirrels, so…"

"Those aren't shells, are they?"

"No?"

I decided to try the third dress shop, on the off chance that the third time was the charm, but found it packed with middle-aged men and women, all of them head-banging wildly to the pounding beat and screaming lyrics of a scantily clad trio who'd set up a makeshift stage at the shop counter. They all had hefty horns of varying lengths, tails of varying hairiness, and so many piercings and tattoos I wasn't quite sure what was clothing and what was skin.

I retreated back onto the pavement, ears ringing even from my short foray into the impromptu mosh pit, and looked around, hands on my hips. The street was quiet, the few passersby keeping their eyes on their feet as they hurried between Bewitching Boos and the grocery shop and the various little businesses the little town somehow supported.

After a moment I tugged my coat closer and pulled my hood up. No one was *obviously* paying attention to me, but they were still paying attention. The claustrophobic sense of being observed was back, and if anything it had intensified. I hated to think Ruiner was right about anything, but maybe asking questions and waving Jason's photo about hadn't been my best move.

I crossed the street to try the door to the Crafty Cauldron again, but it was still locked. I knocked hopefully, but no one emerged from the shelves inside except for a snake that dropped abruptly from above the door and hung there, peering out at us with its sleek body swinging gently. Jackie squawked and dived inside my coat, scrabbling down my hoody until I felt her curl onto the top of the satchel.

"It's okay," I said, but it wasn't. Not because of the snake, but because I was still no further forward. I opened my coat so I could get to the bag, unzipping it to let Jackie crawl in with the grimoire. She squeaked at me gratefully.

"Room for a small one?" Ruiner asked. He was all pouffed out again, and I was happy the coat was heavy. He'd have shredded my shoulder otherwise.

"You're fine," I said. "It's probably not even dangerous."

The snake stuck its tongue out at me.

"Shall we not find out?" Ruiner said.

"Well, we can't get in anyway." I wandered over to the displays, picking up a book to read the back. They couldn't have gone far, to leave everything set up, unless Darrowdale was even more law-abiding than Hollowbeck. Or just not inclined to steal books.

I looked around thoughtfully, then did my coat back up again and started down the road, working on the assumption that if everything else was a slightly distorted reflection of Hollowbeck so far, the town layout would be too.

"Where're we going?" Ruiner asked, but the tone of his voice suggested he'd already guessed.

"The one place we might get some decent info. The library."

"Oh, sodding *hell*," he said.

RATHER THAN HOLLOWBECK'S COLONNADED & ivy-clad town hall with its elegant brick and well-spaced windows, nestling amid peacock-patrolled lawns and lush flowerbeds, the Darrowdale town hall was a hard-angled, sleek monolith of glass and steel. It loomed out of extravagantly wild gardens like a microwave jammed into the earth on a diagonal, gravel paths cutting through the trees and bushes to connect it to the road. I thought it might've been intended to look like a pyramid, a smaller version of the Louvre, but set amid the greenery it more closely resembled a melting greenhouse, and the large Town Hall sign on a stretch of lawn in front of it felt like it was having to do too much work to explain itself.

The library was next to the hall, sporting just as much glass and metal and impractical angles. In contrast to the hall, which looked like it got a regular scrub and a liberal application of Windex, the library was being swallowed by the undergrowth around it. Where it emerged from the greenery it exposed crazed glass panels, or ones that had been replaced with corrugated iron or plywood. A sign on the door suggested, rather hopefully, that there would be a fund-raising sale of old library books on the weekend, and another sign advised that performing blood sacrifices on library grounds was strictly prohibited. In smaller print, it helpfully suggested that a photocopier and laminating machine were available for a small fee.

I pointed that sign out to Ruiner, who hadn't moved from my shoulder.

"That's promising," he said.

"Is it?"

"Well, no one's going to sacrifice us while we're inside, are they?"

"I suppose that's a positive." I pulled the door open and stepped into the cool, faintly damp interior, scented with a gentle undercurrent of must and old paper. A quiet hum drifted from somewhere, a dehumidifier or an extractor, perhaps, and in the distance someone was singing a very off-key version of "Faith." Unsurprisingly, the layout wasn't dissimilar to Hollowbeck's library, with a mezzanine floor above the main lobby area, and a circular check-in desk right in front of us as I walked down the stairs from the doors to the sunken main floor. Even with the patched roof, all the glass let a dull grey light and the constant sound of the rain in, and all the plants pushing against the sloping walls made me feel like I was in a large yet oddly claustrophobic greenhouse.

I stopped in front of the desk and looked around dubiously. Overhead lights hung from metal frames above the lobby, and dotted the underside of the mezzanine floor, shedding a warm yellow glow. Quite a few of them were dead, while others flickered uneasily, as if they hadn't quite made their mind up whether to cling to life any longer or not. There was no one in sight, but an old-fashioned round bell sat on the check-in desk, gleaming invitingly. I stepped up to it, one hand hovering over the shiny metal.

"Well?" Ruiner hissed when I didn't ring it.

"This feels weird," I whispered.

"I thought libraries were your happy place."

"I mean, usually, but—" I was cut off by a scream from somewhere in the stacks, and I staggered back from the desk in fright.

"Nope," Ruiner said. "No, absolutely not. Let's *go*."

The scream rang out again, bouncing off the glass and setting the books rattling anxiously, and I turned towards it, my heart surging in my chest.

"*No*," Ruiner said again.

I took a step towards the scream, and now I could feel my brother's claws even through the coat. "What're you *doing?*"

"They might be hurt," I pointed out, taking another hesitant step deeper into the library. "We can't just leave them if they need help."

"We absolutely can. Do you really want to wander around the spooky library in the spooky town, following the frankly terrifying screams?"

Another cry went up as he spoke, some mix of rage and fright, and while my answer to Ruiner's question was actually, *no, I really don't want to*, I hurried towards the sound, Ruiner wobbling on my shoulder and cursing as we went.

"If you get eaten by a library ghost, it's totally not my fault."

FOURTEEN

It's alright if you fit

I DIDN'T THINK GHOSTS WERE CAUSING THE SCREAMS —
or were capable of eating me, for that matter — but that
didn't slow my pounding heart as I ventured into the
dimmer spaces under the mezzanine floor. The faltering
lighting rendered the stacks thick with shadows, and the
musty scent grew stronger the further I went from the door,
rising around me like a physical presence. I almost thought
I could feel the dust motes sliding over my skin and
sticking to my hair, setting up shudders that started in my
belly.

Another scream, and I adjusted course towards it,
skirting a children's section with far too many clowns on
the walls, along with weird toothy dinosaurs that looked
like they'd be on me as soon as my back was turned.
Beyond it I discovered a section where the shelves were
filled with old, heavy leather tomes, some of them with
split spines and the lettering worn completely away, others
held together so roughly with parcel tape that Ben
would've needed a little lie down and one of his own
calming teas.

This time when the scream came, I let out a little shriek of my own and Ruiner dived off my shoulder with a squawk, because the cry had risen from the next aisle over. I edged around the end of the shelving, heart beating far too fast and spots swimming in my vision, while Ruiner hissed something behind me that could only have been dire warnings or complaints that if I died he'd have to find someone else to cart him around. I ignored him and braced myself for the worst as I peered into the narrow channel between the high shelves.

The scene was calamitous, at least for the books. The middle three shelves on each side of the aisle had been swept clear, as if someone had rushed along in a rage, tumbling them to the floor. Gaps yawned on other shelves where more books had been displaced, all of them old volumes that should've been handled with the respect their age deserved. They were jumbled carelessly on the floor, and I took half a step towards them, one hand pressed to my chest, before I noticed the movement. Not movement among the books, but *in* them. They were vibrating with heat and indignation, the tremors setting them sliding across one another with the whispering sound of snakes passing each other in a nest, and as I watched one of them tumbled off the pile. Rather than stopping at the bottom it kept going, flopping end for end as it made a break for freedom. On the shelves the remaining books were trembling in their effort to either stay put or join the great escape. Ink smeared the shelves, as if the wounded books had been bleeding on them, and as I hesitated, a chunky book shuffled towards me. It was open, pages down, and hunched itself up then slid open again to move, caterpillar-like. The title was picked out in silver print on its dark blue cover: *How to Raise Echidnas & Other Mystical Beasts*, which raised some questions about either my knowledge of echidnas or the author's.

New movement caught my eye, and a hand with an inkwell tattoo on it clawed out of the pile of books, plucking ineffectually at them. A couple snapped at it, one landing a painful-sounding blow on the hand's knuckles, and a muffled yelp emerged from the pile.

I skirted the creeping echidna book and approached the pile-up warily, ignoring Ruiner hissing, asking me if death by books had always been my life goal. I tried nudging a couple of the volumes on the edge of the jumble with my trainer. None of them snapped at my ankles or threw themselves at my head, so I started pushing them aside, gingerly at first then with increasing enthusiasm as they mostly left me alone other than a few slaps to my calves. I didn't quite dare to bend down and use my hands, as that felt like trying my luck a bit too much, so I just kept sliding them away as gently as I could with my foot, offering silent apologies to the protective spirits of book-shops and libraries everywhere. Ruiner sat at a safe distance behind me, occasionally shouting that a book was creeping up to me on one of the shelves, but otherwise offering no assistance whatsoever.

I uncovered a second arm, pinned to the floor by three open books with their spines up, then found a chest, then finally the head of a man about my own age, his glasses knocked askew & his coppery hair rumpled by the attack. He peered at me shortsightedly, straining against the books' grip on his arm.

"Thank you *so* much," he said. "I thought I was going to be stuck here till Monday."

"What happens Monday?" I asked, helping him pry his arm loose while the books fussed and muttered around us.

"The cleaner comes in."

"Right." We heaved together, and the books finally tore free of the floor with a horrendous ripping sound, leaving shredded pages behind them. I made a regretful little noise, and the man (who I assumed was the librarian) snatched up one of the damaged books and shook it at the others.

"You see?" he shouted. "You see what happens? Can't you just behave yourselves?"

The books muttered back unhappily.

"This happen a lot, does it?" I asked.

"Only when I try to clear a few out. I'm meant to be having a library sale this weekend. They're all going to go to a good home. But no. Can't talk any sense to the damn things." He shoved the books off his legs, revealing a few more volumes straining to pin him to the ground. They didn't have as good a grip as the ones on his arms had had, though, and with both of us pulling, he was soon free. He stood up, shaking his legs out and rubbing a bruise on his cheek gingerly. He looked at me, grinned, and held a hand out. "Connall," he said. "Thanks for this. Most people scarper when they hear things getting hairy."

"Morgan," I replied, shaking his hand, and looked at the mess. "And honestly, I didn't think libraries could get this hairy."

He shrugged, examining his glasses and bending one leg back into shape carefully. "Just a regular Friday, really."

I wondered what an irregular one looked like. "Do you need help clearing up?"

"Oh, no." He tried his glasses again, and gave a grunt of approval. "No good going near them until they've calmed down a bit. I'll have to cordon them off for a few days."

"Right." I shifted the bag under my coat, where the grimoire was far hotter that it should have been. I hoped

Jackie wasn't cooking. "Shouldn't you have the dangerous books locked away or something?"

"All books are dangerous," he said, giving me a broad, white-toothed grin. "You can't start locking them up just for being what they are."

I didn't have an argument for that, but before I could point out that being buried under books for an entire weekend was the kind of incident that suggested *some* action might need to be taken, Ruiner screeched. it was altogether too human for a cat yowl, but Connall didn't show any sign of noticing anything weird about it. Cats make strange noises, I guess.

Both of us spun toward him, and I saw a woman — or woman-like figure — crouched on top of one of the stacks, knees high around her ears and long teeth bared. She had Ruiner in both hands, and looked very much as if she was about to turn him into lunch.

"Effie! Put the kitty down," Connall ordered. She snarled at him, and licked Ruiner with a long, pointed tongue. Ruiner squawked.

"Please put him down," I said. "He's my — mine."

She chattered her teeth at me. She had an awful lot of them, and they were all very sharp.

"Effie, we do not eat the library patrons. We've talked about this." Connall had his hands on his hips.

She brandished Ruiner at him.

"Just because he's a cat doesn't mean he's not a book lover. One can't make these assumptions."

Effie looked at him, licking her lips with her over-long tongue. I wondered how she didn't shred it on her teeth.

"No ice cream if you eat the cat," Connall said. "No ice cream for a *year*."

She hissed, a guttural sound that made me duck instinctively, and when I looked back at her she was grinning in delight. She flicked her tongue at me and I gave a watery smile.

"Cat," Connall said, walking over to stand under her with his arms outstretched. "Now."

She narrowed her eyes at him, apparently considering her options, then with no warning she flung Ruiner at me and vanished into the shadows. My brother slammed into me with all paws outstretched, gouging my neck, and I grabbed him, clutching him to my chest as I stumbled under the impact. I caught my heel on a book and went down hard, thinking for one horrified moment I'd be buried in a book mountain until Monday as the tomes chattered excitedly around me, then Connall had my arm and was hauling me upright again.

"Up-si-daisy," he said. "No playing in the books."

"Up-si-daisy?" I demanded.

"I don't get many visitors," he said, giving me that grin again, and I found myself grinning back. "Want a cuppa?"

"Coffee?" I asked hopefully.

"I can do that. I have a machine. From *outside*." He winked, and Ruiner growled.

I glanced down at my brother, still clutched in my arms, and sighed. "Can I buy a coffee off you?"

"No, why — oh." His grin widened. "Did you meet Jim?"

"Butterflies in his beard, scary teeth?"

"That's him. But you're fine here. I'm not Fae."

"That's exactly what you'd say if you were Fae."

He laughed. "Fine. Coffee and biscuits for a pound, how's that?"

"Bargain," I said, and we picked our way out of the morass of books, into the quiet, whispering depths of the library.

THE STAFFROOM WAS in a slightly different spot to the one in the Hollowbeck library, and while that one was untidy, this was a dumping groud. Books were packed in boxes and plastic tubs, piled on cabinets and stacked on the floor, some of them looking relatively harmless, others melting the tubs around them or sending papery vines clambering up the walls. A couple of chairs with shattered legs leaned against one wall, sporting teeth marks and suspiciously shredded upholstery, and a jumble of clothing spilled out of a half-open cabinet. I hoped it was all lost property and not items left over from either Effie or the books' activities. Connall moved a crate full of lightbulbs off a chair and waved for me to sit down. I looked at the lightbulbs, then at him, rising my eyebrows.

"They blow out all the time," he said. "I have to buy in bulk. I think the books don't like it when it's too bright, but I can't let the place get too dark. Things get a bit weird when it's too dark."

"Only when it's too dark?" I asked, pushing a box along the table to give myself some more room. Inky tentacles snapped out of it and I yelped.

"Fair point," he said, giving the box a disinterested look. Maybe yelping library patrons were just business as usual around here. "Milk and sugar?"

"No thanks." I sat down, eyeing the book in the box. The tentacles had withdrawn, but the whole thing looked a little warped and water damaged. *A History of Deep-Sea Civilisation* was printed in silver on the front, along with a line drawing of a fish-man with a trident. I checked under the table to make sure my feet weren't too near anything that looked like it might bite and undid my coat but didn't take it off. Jackie poked her head out of the satchel and gave me a look that felt very disapproving.

I was facing the door, so I saw it creak open, and Effie crawled in over the lintel like a large, jeans-clad gecko. Ruiner hissed, flattening himself to my shoulder. I could feel his heart pounding where his belly was pressed against me. He'd refused to get down since Effie had let him go, and I didn't blame him. If I was snack-sized for a hungry library ... *something*, I wouldn't want to be left alone either.

Effie crept across the wall, keeping her eyes on my brother. They were a pretty, pale hazel, huge in her skinny face, and she licked her lips.

"Um," I said, as Ruiner dived off my shoulder onto my lap.

Connall turned around and followed my gaze. "Effie, stop stalking them," he said. She hissed, and he gave me an apologetic look. "Sorry. She gets a bit overexcited."

"Right." I kept my eyes on her as she climbed up to the ceiling and started a slow, deliberate trek across it. She had bare brown feet below her jeans, and was wearing a long-sleeved T-shirt with a cartoon duck clutching a knife on it. *Duck this*, it said. "Is she ... what is she? Sorry, is that rude?"

Connall glanced at her as he set a mug and a packet of Jaffa Cakes on the table in front of me. "Not rude. She's an other, you can ask what you like."

Effie's head swivelled towards him, and she bared her teeth.

"An other?"

"A non-humanoid. You know, things that are more animal. Not like vampires and werewolves, which you can have an actual conversation with."

I watched Effie as she glared at Connall, her lips pulled back from her sharp teeth. "I think she understands you."

"In a way?" He shrugged. "I read up a bit, and I think she's a ghoul. I give her a frozen chicken a couple of times a week, and she makes sure no one breaks in."

Effie had reached the ceiling above me, and we stared at each other. She reached a hand down, pointing, and I looked at Ruiner, then back at her. "Sorry, no," I said, and she hissed. I took a Jaffa Cake from the pack and offered it to her. "Do you like chocolate?"

She tipped her head inquiringly, then plucked the biscuit from my outstretched hand. She put it in her pocket, nodded, and scuttled back across the ceiling and out the door with disorientating speed. Ruiner shuddered, his fur pouffed up wildly.

"Don't feed the wildlife," Connall said. "You'll only encourage her."

I shrugged and I dug into my pockets for the change I'd looted from Jason's bedside table. I found a pound coin and slid it across to Connall, who lifted it to the light and examined it.

"Looks legal," he said. "Payment accepted. No freebies here." He pocketed it and sat down opposite me, slapping away a book that was scurrying across the table on thousands of minuscule legs, like a weirdly shaped millipede. "Book lice," he explained. "They get all twitchy."

I watched the book scuttle off and said, "This is all normal, then?"

Connall smiled at me over his mug. He had very blue eyes. "First time in Darrowdale?"

"Yes."

"Not your first magical town, though. You're nervous but not freaking out."

"No. I've been in Hollowbeck for a bit."

"Hollowbeck?" He leaned over the table, both hands clasped around his mug. "Is it as nice as everyone says?"

"Well, no one's tried to eat my cat in the library. So far, anyway."

He laughed. "I suppose that's a good sign. I heard it was all toffee apples growing on the trees and champagne on tap, that sort of thing."

I blinked at him. "Seriously? You think it's like Oz or something?"

"It has kangaroos? Wait, does Oz have champagne on tap? Wouldn't they have Foster's or something?"

"Not Oz as in Australia. Oz as in — oh." I stopped as he grinned at me. "Funny."

"So you Hollowbeck-ers do think the rest of us are a bit on the slow side."

"I've only been there a few months, so I'm not a *Hollowbeck-er,* and why would anyone think that?"

He took a mouthful of coffee and winkled a Jaffa Cake out of the pack. "You must fit the Hollowbeck mould, then."

"What're you talking about?" I didn't like the mocking edge to his voice.

He didn't answer straight away, just dunked his Jaffa Cake and ate it thoughtfully, then finally said, "You didn't ask anyone there about Darrowdale before you came?"

"No," I said. Ruiner was digging his claws into my leg warningly. "It was a kind of spur of the moment thing."

He scratched his chin and nodded. "Okay, that makes sense. They'd probably have told you to stay away from such a dump."

"It doesn't seem that bad."

He gave me an amused look. "Other than the library trying to eat your cat."

"Well, there's that. Is a risky library visit the only issue Holllowbeck has with Darrowdale?"

Connall examined his coffee, then looked up at me. "I've never been to Hollowbeck, so this is mostly hearsay. Some of it's going to be exaggeration, Darrowdale getting all tetchy, but not all of it is. Hollowbeck gets rid of those that don't fit."

"*Fit?*"

"Yeah. Those who don't match the Hollowbeck vibe or whatever." He offered me the Jaffa Cakes, and I took one automatically, still frowning.

"That doesn't seem right."

"Of course it doesn't. If you fit, you're not going to think there's anything wrong with the system."

I thought about it while I nibbled the Jaffa Cake. "So Darrowdale hates Hollowbeck?"

"Not fans, at least."

"Why does it look so much like Hollowbeck, then, if people hate it so much?"

Connall shrugged. "Half the population came from there. I guess it makes them feel less homesick."

"Why not go back?"

"Because of the fit. They stepped a little out of line, and boom. Out on their ears. Exiled."

Exiled. I knew one person who'd been exiled, and she hadn't stepped a little out of line. She'd been so keen to be town witch she'd killed Norma, and tried to kill both Starlight and me when we figured it out. Being exiled had seemed like a pretty lenient sentence for Edith, really.

I looked at my coffee, the biscuit suddenly too sweet and too cloying. *Exiled. The town witch.* It couldn't be. Could it?

"Oh, sodding hell," I whispered.

FIFTEEN

Fancy seeing you here

"MORGAN? ARE YOU ALRIGHT?" FROM THE TONE OF Connall's voice, and the way Ruiner was pointedly nudging my arm, he'd already asked me more than once.

"What? No. I mean, yes."

"Lost you there for a moment."

"Just thinking about the whole exile thing. That's pretty wild."

He shrugged, taking another biscuit. "Everything's a bit wild in magical towns, I think."

"Have you been to a lot?"

"Not that many. Anyhow — what're you doing in Darrowdale if you've not been turfed out?"

Ruiner abandoned my arm in favour of digging his claws into my jeans again, and I breathed out slowly, still wondering about town witches. Asking specifically seemed like a good way to raise half a dozen alarm bells, though. "Just finding out where I fit, I guess. A friend of mine used to come here sometimes. Might still do."

"Oh? Hoping to find them?"

"I'd like to." I took my phone out and showed Jason's photo to Connall.

He peered at it for a moment, then shook his head. "Don't know him. But people who visit Darrowdale aren't usually after library books. You should ask at the Crafty Cauldron. The town witch usually knows everyone who's coming and going."

"Good to know." I pocketed the phone, trying to ignore the twist in my stomach. It had been a good thing the shop was shut. What if we'd just walked straight into Edith? Not that I *knew* she'd be town witch, of course. Presumably there had already been a town witch when she arrived, so maybe she wasn't one at all. Maybe I was jumping to conclusions based on nothing but panic. Like coming here. I'd been silly to think I'd find Jason's trail at a library, of all places. And if my main reason had been to be soothed by the books, that hadn't worked so well either. "Do you like living here?"

"Sure," he said, scraping some words that were spilling out of a dictionary off the table and trapping them back inside it. "I mean, head librarian jobs are really hard to come by, so I'm pretty lucky. But also it's pretty cool. Where else do you have to chase books back to their sections?" He grinned at me, wide and infectious, and I found a smile somewhere in return.

"Does that cancel out the risk of being held hostage by books for the weekend?"

"Mostly." He pointed at my mug. "Want another?"

"No thanks." I got up, Ruiner jumping back to my shoulder with far too much familiarity. "I should go. Poke around a bit more."

"Sure. Let me know if you need a local guide. I close up at six."

"Thanks."

Connall led us back through the dimly lit stacks to the main lobby, where he picked some yellow and black caution tape up off the desk and waggled it at me. "I'd better seal off those books."

"Better do." I pointed vaguely upwards. "Who's singing?"

He cocked his head as if hearing it for the first time. The singer had moved on from "Faith" to "Manic Monday," the sound faint, as if they'd drifted deeper into the building. "Oh, that's Effie," he said. "As long as she's singing, you know it's safe."

"What if she's not singing?"

"Then she tries to eat someone," he said, with a nod at Ruiner. "Good luck finding your friend."

"Thanks," I said, and watched him vanish into the stacks, a stocky man with an easy grace to him, the fragmented light sliding off his red hair and turning it gold at the ends.

"Can we go?" Ruiner whispered. "One almost-eaten experience is sufficient."

"He said it's safe while she's singing."

"Maybe. But she's singing closer," he replied, and I frowned. He was right. I headed for the doors, pushing out into the grey drizzle of a town full of exiles, at least one of which might have a not insignificant bone to pick with me. All I hoped was that she wasn't the town witch. Although, to be honest, any sort of witch was going to be a problem, given my current skill level.

We needed to find Jason and get out before anything else caught up with us.

"CAN YOU GET DOWN?" I asked Ruiner as I started down the path, pulling my hood up as much to hide from lurking witches as to fend off the rain. "You're getting heavy."

"I'm positively svelte. And I don't trust something else not to eat me. Half of these plants are probably carnivorous."

I glanced warily at the flowerbeds edging the paths, which were full of tall, sharp-leaved ferns and dark, glossy leaves sporting ragged-edged blooms, with strange vines and pitchers crawling between them. I was no gardener, but nothing looked even vaguely familiar. The rain pattering through the foliage gave the plants whispering voices, and some of them moved in a breeze I couldn't feel. "Everything can't be dangerous. People live here."

"People live in Australia too. Everything wants to kill them there."

I didn't have an argument for that, so I let him stay where he was. I was halfway to the road when I heard a door closing. I turned to peer back at the library, wondering if Connall had thought of something useful, but there was no one behind us. I stood on my tiptoes to see over the taller plants that separated us from the path that led to the town hall, and sure enough, there was someone walking briskly down it, gravel crunching. It was a woman, tall and slim, her hair bundled into one of those annoyingly effortless buns at the back of her head, the sort that always made me look like I'd lost a fight with a hedge when I tried them.

I watched her approach the junction where she'd join our path, a curl of misgiving unfolding in my stomach. There was something familiar about her, something in the way she moved or in that sweep of thick dark hair, but from this angle I couldn't see her face. Then a curve in the path turned her just enough towards us that I saw her profile, and I caught my breath so loudly her head jerked up. I dropped straight into a crouch behind the plants, smacking my knee painfully on the rocky border of the flowerbed, and the woman called, "Who's there?"

There was a cool sharpness to the words, and if I'd doubted what I was seeing before, I couldn't doubt the familiarity of that voice. I looked around desperately, wondering whether to sprint for the library or dive into the undoubtedly dangerous foliage, while the crunch of gravel turned towards us.

"Is that...?" Ruiner hissed.

"Yes," I whispered back.

It was Grace. Grace was in Darrowdale, and there was no way that could be a coincidence. Evidently I'd been worrying about the wrong bloody witch.

"I *told* you," Ruiner muttered in my ear.

"This is not the time." I was still hesitating, the library too far away but the undergrowth looking too *anticipatory*. Away from the witch and into the compost bin came to mind, assuming the compost bin was carnivorous.

"I know you're there," Grace called, and I just about stood up simply to get it over with, except she hadn't used my name. Maybe it was a universal sort of *you*, and we still had a chance, but it was running out rapidly. Grace's boots crunched deliberately on the gravel, her stride measured and firm. "There's no point hiding."

I was going to have to bluff it out. I put my shoulders back, starting to rise from my crouch, and a cool hand landed on my head, pushing me down again. I swallowed a squawk of surprise, and Effie skittered past us, skidding on the gravel and leaping into Grace's path before she could turn the corner.

"Oh, bloody hell, Effie — was that you sneaking about?"

I couldn't see the ghoul, but I heard her hiss, and the scrape of gravel under her hands and feet as she scampered about.

"You shouldn't be out here," Grace said. "Back to the library. *Back!*"

More crunching gravel, this time receding in the direction of the town hall.

"Oh, suit yourself. Bloody librarians and their pets." Grace started walking again and I stiffened, but her footsteps moved off. She'd resumed her course towards the road, and after a moment I stood up cautiously, ready to dive back into cover if necessary, but she was walking towards town with an easy, elegant stride.

"What's she doing here?" I asked Ruiner.

"I could hazard a pretty good guess. But shall we make ourselves scarce while we can?"

I looked around for Effie, wanting to thank her, but there was no sign of the ghoul, so I pulled my hood into place a little more securely and headed for the street.

"What're you doing?" Ruiner asked, as I trailed after Grace. "What if she turns around? Take a different route, you muppet."

"I want to know what she's doing."

"Probably looking for us, so she can turn us into newts."

"Newts?"

"Or whatever. She's looking for us. It's the only reason for her to be here."

"Maybe," I said. "Or maybe she's looking for Jason too. To help."

"Really? So that's why you dived into the flowerbed? Because you think she's here to *help?*"

I didn't answer. He didn't need to know he was right.

Ruiner huffed. "She's after us. Or rather you, and the damn book."

"We don't know that. And we've got no other leads, so I'm going to follow her and see what she's doing."

"*Leads*. You're not Miss bloody Marple."

"No. But unless we want actual police starting to ask questions when Jason stays missing and we've been seen at his house, I'm going to have to start acting like it."

Ruiner growled. "This is getting way too complicated. Grace in Darrowdale? Maybe Edith too? Both witches we know would love to get their hands on your grimoire. This is way above your witchy level."

"Thanks for the vote of confidence."

"Am I wrong?"

I didn't bother answering, just slowed down a little so I could keep my distance from Grace and tried to look casual. Just some witch out for a stroll in the rain with her cat and her rat. It would've been easier to blend in if there'd been more people on the streets, but apparently Friday lunchtime was graveyard shift in Darrowdale.

But we'd been allotted some small sliver of luck, at least. Grace didn't look around, just walked at that same easy pace until she turned onto the main street and headed for the Crafty Cauldron.

I wasn't surprised, but my heart still sank as I watched her push through the door into the shop. I picked up my pace immediately, hurrying down the pavement on the opposite side of the road before crossing over and diving into the alley that ran down the side of the building.

"Where're you going?" Ruiner asked.

"See if we can hear anything," I replied, picking my way down the paved lane. There were no downstairs windows to worry about here, but I tried to keep close to the wall so that no one looking from upstairs could see us. I paused at the corner, looking into the back patio and wondering if I dared creep up to one of the windows that overlooked it.

"Would this be a good time to remind you that being caught sneaking around out here is unlikely to go well for either of us?"

"I'm aware of this." I couldn't be certain the layout of the shop was identical, even if the odds seemed good. There were too many windows overlooking the patio, both upstairs and downstairs, and not enough cover to reach any of them, not even a potted plant decorating the flagstones. I grabbed Ruiner, lifting him off my shoulder and holding him in front of me.

His eyes widened as he dangled in my grip. "No."

"You're right. I'm going to get caught."

"But Grace knows I'm a cat. So does Edith."

"So be quick and cat-like, and make sure no one sees you." I set him on the ground facing the shop and gave him a little push. "Off you go."

"I'm not getting zapped by a bloody witch."

"You're already a cat. What else are they going to do?"

"Turn me into an ugly cat," he suggested. "Or an earthworm or something. Send your rat."

"She can't tell me what she sees. Hurry up, can't you?"

He glared at me over his shoulder. "This is pushing sibling affection too far."

"So's having to hold you on my lap because you're afraid of a ghoul. You're thirty-four, Ruiner."

"I'm snack-sized," he replied, but jumped easily over the low wooden fence and loped across the patio towards the shop, a grey shadow on grey paving stones. I drew back out of sight, concealed from the road by the bins. It wasn't a pleasant place to wait, not least because the magical waste bin (orange here, rather than Hollowbeck's soothing lavender), was creaking and shifting as something inside tried to get out. But as a hiding place it felt secure enough, and when I peeked around the corner, I could see Ruiner slipping along the wall of the building, ears back as he peered up at the windows.

He checked the first one, which would've been above the sink in the Cosy Cauldron, dismissed it, and edged past the door to the one on the other side. That was apparently no good either, but at the next he put his paws up on the wall, straining to see in. He couldn't quite make it, and he glanced back at me. I spread my hands and shrugged. From here, I couldn't tell if anyone was inside. He looked back at the window, then crouched slightly and jumped to the sill. I caught my breath, waiting for a yell or a scream, but there was nothing. Ruiner sat down, mostly looking at the sky, but occasionally stealing little peeks inside.

I saw the moment he spotted something. He froze, staring into the room, then started to ease off the windowsill. I think maybe he thought that if he moved slowly enough, he might evade detection completely. But then he abruptly threw himself to the ground and bolted, ears back, heading for the small path that ran along the back of the little yard, dividing it from the one belonging to the house opposite. He vaulted the fence as the sash window slammed up, and a woman leaned out. She hurled something after Ruiner, and it smashed into the fence, sending up a snap of blue light and leaving a scorch mark behind, but Ruiner was already gone.

"Dammit," the woman said. "Almost had him."

Grace appeared at the window, her expression disinterested. "Never mind. We can grab him later."

"I suppose."

Grace vanished back inside and the woman looked

carefully each way across the yard, then slid the window back down and drew the curtains.

I leaned back against the wall, pressing into it, my legs suddenly shaky. The last thing I wanted to do was sit down here among all the rubbish and spilled magic, but I wasn't at all sure I could stay upright. It had been Edith. I hadn't quite believed it could be, but it was. She *was* the town witch. Edith who had tried to burn us alive, Edith who'd tried to break my brother's neck. Edith here in Darrowdale, with Grace, where I was almost certain Jason had gone missing.

I put my hands on my knees, gulping the damp, smelly air and wishing I could run to the town hall to find Isabella, or know that Theodore would be waiting to help as soon as dark fell. Wished I could go to the library where Ben would offer me tea and gentle, bookish silence, or that I could simply go and get a coffee without being worried someone was going to steal me away for a thousand years.

"Morgan?" Ruiner said. He'd crept back down the alley and was looking at me with wide blue eyes. "Did you see?"

"Evidently," I said, my hands still on my knees.

"Right." He looked around. "We need to go."

"Where?"

"Out of Darrowdale. We know what we're dealing with now, and it's too much."

"We can't," I said. I desperately didn't want to be here anymore, but we still needed to find Jason. Figure out a way to storm the Crafty Cauldron or something, although the very thought made me hiccough with laughter.

Ruiner squinted at me. "Are you alright?"

"No."

"Then let's go."

"We can't," I said again. "We can't just leave Jason."

"And you can't take on those two on your own."

I nodded. He was right about that, at least. "So, what — do you know where I can rent a witch hunter or something?"

He snorted. "No. But let's get out of here, at least. Go back to the house and come up with a proper plan, rather than hiding in an alley. Call bloody Book Boy and see if he can get Theodore out here."

I blinked at him. "They'll just want me to go back to Hollowbeck."

"They'll be right, but when you say no they'll probably also help, because you're *their* town witch, and that's worth something. Plus at least one of them fancies you, which is gross."

I gave another little hiccough of laugher, but it was marginally less bordering on hysterical this time. I wasn't sure it was a great course of action, but it was something. I straightened up and led the way back to the street, hesitating at the corner of the alley. I couldn't see anyone, but of course Edith and Grace could be standing just inside the shop door and I wouldn't know. I fished the car keys out of my pocket and said, "I guess we just run for it."

Ruiner didn't reply, and I started to turn, looking for him. "Ru—?"

I was cut short as someone grabbed me, jerking me back into the alley. I tried to cry out, but there was a hand over my mouth, and I caught a whiff of a soft, floral scent as someone dropped a cloth over my eyes. I just had time to think, *oh, bollocks*, then the alley was gone and all was silence.

SIXTEEN

Many ways to get in trouble

IT WAS QUIET, DEEPLY SO, A LUSH, WARM SILENCE THAT invited rainy days and books and introspection, or at the most some murmured, thoughtful conversation. Or maybe simply daydreaming, a hot drink to hand and cake waiting on a side table while one watched the rain that would no doubt be running softly down some deep-silled, elegantly curtained window. The sort of window that would have a well-cushioned seat under it, and a reading lamp, and a soft blanket waiting to be snuggled into. There would probably also be a cat. Or preferably a dog. I was going off cats.

I was captivated with the thought of it, of just reading or napping, of listening to the pervasive stillness and letting it fill the world, scented with cut flowers and smoke from a wood fire, as well as the whiff of someone with dubious personal hygiene. I hoped it wasn't me.

Wait.

I pressed my face into the cushion, trying to keep hold of that gentle, captured moment, but the smell had ruined it. There was a suggestion of boiled eggs about it, and I lifted my head with some difficulty. It felt too big, ungainly on my neck, and I sniffed, finding I'd been drooling in my sleep. I wiped my chin, surprised I could move my arms, then remembered why I was surprised.

My eyes snapped open, and I winced at the sudden assault of light, although the room was as mellowly lit as the one in my dreams had been. I was lying mostly on my right side, like someone had put me in the recovery position, and seemed to be on an old-fashioned sofa with an elaborately carved wooden frame and what I strongly suspected was embroidered silk upholstery. Whatever it was, it was far too fancy for me to be drooling on.

I squinted at as much of the room as I could see without moving, trying to find something familiar, but I'd never seen anything like it outside of movies featuring old school men's clubs in fancy London postcodes. There didn't seem to be any windows, or overhead lights, just standing lamps and smaller ones perched on more old, dark wooden furniture, sideboards and bureaus and side tables. I couldn't have said exactly what any of them were, other than expensive, all of it.

There was a coffee table directly in front of me that probably weighed more than my car, and a sofa beyond it that looked like it matched the one I was drooling on. That sofa was empty, as was the large leather armchair that bracketed the end of the table towards my feet. The chair near my head was occupied, though. I could see well-made boots & finely tailored trousers from where I lay, and I licked my lips, wondering if I should be considering making a run for it. Probably not, given I didn't know where the door was.

I shifted my head as subtly as I could and spotted Ruiner sitting bolt upright on the far arm of the sofa, his eyes on whoever was in the chair. His pupils were wide, his tail twitching softy, and he glanced at me, then back at the occupant of the chair. I licked my lips again, preparing myself to get up, and the legs moved. I listened to the sound of water glugging into a glass, then a long-fingered hand with an oddly copper sheen to it, as if it had been dipped in a little too much bronzing powder, appeared in my vision.

The hand was holding a tumbler that I assume had to be cut crystal, given the rest of the place. It looked a bit like the cheap glasses my mum had bought because she swore they were exact replicas of the royal family's ones. The hand was wearing a signet ring on its middle finger, the stone a deep black with an ammonite emerging from the depths.

"Water?" A deep voice asked. The voice had warm curves to it, a softness that didn't match the glass or the furniture. I'd expected either clipped and upper-class military, or the lazy drawl of someone too rich to bother enunciating properly.

"Thanks," I said, and pushed myself halfway up, shutting my eyes again as I waited for a wave of dizziness to subside. "How much?"

The ring-wearer chuckled, a sound that was all chattering brooks and warm breezes. "On the house."

"Sorry if I don't entirely believe you." I made it all the way to sitting, swinging my legs off the sofa and opening my eyes. The room still swam a little, and I tried not to look too longingly at the water. My mouth was sticky and tasted as if I'd been chewing on a pigeon's wing. Or what I imagined that would taste like, anyway. Dusty and oily all at once, and a little dirty.

The hand tipped the glass from one side to the other gently, setting the water sloshing against the sides.

"Dealer's word. Drink up. You're probably a little dehydrated."

I wiped my mouth, grimacing. Yes, I'd definitely been drooling. "How much?"

I finally looked at our host properly, and he gazed back at me just as openly. Everything about him was long and thin. Graceful hands, long legs, an angular face with a long thin nose and cheekbones that made Theodore's seem almost ordinary. His skin had that same strange, burnished hue, his eyes so dark they looked pupil-less. His hair was dark too, cropped short and styled with wax or something, glossy and fixed firmly in place. He wore an open-necked shirt under his immaculately tailored suit, and a pale blue pocket square poked out of his breast pocket. He looked like he should smell of cognac and cigars, but instead I got that whiff of something nasty again — overripe eggs or clogged drains.

"Answer some questions," he said.

"What?"

"Answer some questions. That is the price of the water."

"What questions?"

"The ones I ask."

I frowned. "I'm not agreeing unless I know what the questions are. You might ask me for my bank details or something." For all the good that would do him.

He smiled, revealing straight white teeth. "What would you pay, then?"

"I think I've still got a few pounds in my bag," I offered.

"What about a *look* in your bag? The one your rat's so carefully guarding."

I twisted, scrabbling to find my satchel with panic rising like bile in my throat, and his smile widened into a grin. The bag was still there, though, slung across my body and wedged between me and the back of the sofa. No one had even taken my jacket off, although they'd opened it. Jackie squeaked indignantly, pushing her head out of the bag to glare at me. I really wasn't improving her opinion of me, but at least I still had the book. That had to count in my favour.

The man held up his hand, and I could see a dressing on one long finger. "She's a ferocious guardian."

I looked at Ruiner, who twitched his ears urgently. I didn't know what that meant. We really should've worked out some sort of code, but it was a bit late now.

"What do you want?" I asked our host.

"Answers."

"Why not just ask, then? Why grab me off the street? Bit bloody excessive, that."

He inclined his head gracefully, his hair unmoving, and set the glass in front of me. "All refreshments are entirely free," he said. "Call it an apology for the inconvenience."

"*Payment* for the inconvenience?" I demanded.

"If you like."

I picked the glass up, looking at Ruiner again. He didn't try to knock the glass out of my hand, so I assumed it was a fair deal. I gulped the water, cool and fresh, washing the stickiness from my mouth. I could've scoffed the whole thing in one go but managed to stop myself and set it back on the table, wishing I had a coaster. The table looked too expensive for water rings.

"What am I doing here?" I asked. "And who are you?"

"I could ask you the same things." He leaned back in his chair, fingers steepled in front of him.

"I'm a tourist," I offered, and he snorted, which hardly matched his aesthetic.

"I'm sure you are. Just wandering around, taking in the

sights, shooting a few selfies with your cat and your rat and your mysterious bag?"

"Yes. And you abducted me. I should report you to the police."

"To the Darrowdale police? I don't think you'd have much luck there. And the outside police are not ... equipped for such things, wouldn't you say?"

I scowled at him. "You snatched me off the street! That's kidnapping. You can't just get away with it."

He nodded thoughtfully, as if considering my words, then said, "How's your brother?"

"Excuse me?"

"Rainier Winters. Your brother." He didn't say it like a question, and I managed not to look at Ruiner.

"Ruiner," I said aloud.

The man blinked. "I'm sorry?"

"I call him Ruiner. And based on that, I assume he's off somewhere ruining things. It's his lifestyle of choice."

The man gave a startled chuckle. "Ruiner. I see. Yes, that seems fitting."

I didn't have to look at my brother to be able to feel him bristling. Hopefully he'd be smart enough not to give himself away. "Who are you? How do you know my brother?"

The man uncrossed his long legs, leaning forward in the chair as he straightened his sleeves, then extended one hand to me. "I am The Dealer."

I stared at his hand, hearing the capitals in *The Dealer*, then took it hesitantly. His palm was smooth and hot, the skin faintly textured against mine in the way I imagined a lizard's skin might be, and as he folded his fingers over mine, I could feel them baking with internal heat. I caught a whiff of that scent again, something volcanic and elemental, and said, "Morgan," in a much smaller voice than I'd intended.

"I know," he replied. "I've been watching for your brother to return. I didn't expect it'd be you instead."

I sighed and reclaimed my hand, leaning back in the sofa and folding my arms. "How much does he owe you?"

The Dealer laughed softly and took a bottle from a drink tray set on a side table next to his chair. It matched the tumblers, the liquid inside amber and full of light. He unstoppered it and poured some into another glass, the scent of whisky rising peaty and dank in the silence. And it really was silence. I could feel the pressure against my ears, hear the passage of blood in my veins.

The Dealer offered me the tumbler. "For the inconvenience, Morgan. A glass of water is not much payment. My people were overly enthusiastic in their methods."

"They drugged me," I pointed out, taking the glass.

"A necessary precaution against a witch, in their minds."

"I'm not much of a witch."

"No? You have not one but two familiars, and you carry a book of power with you. That's very witch-like." He raised a second glass to me in an unspoken toast and took a sip.

I copied him, the whisky strong and warm, clearing the last of the staleness from my throat. "I thought you didn't know what was in my bag."

"One does not have to see such things to recognise them."

That felt an awful lot like he'd *smelled* it, sniffed it out like a dog with a bone, and I braced myself against a shiver. "Why are you looking for my brother? And why grab me?"

"Again, I apologise for the technique." That softness in

his voice was warm as the whisky, speaking of deep valleys and harshly cut mountains, long coastlines and the twisted hills of hard-farmed land, and the desolation of old, deep, and hungry mines, full of ghosts and whispers.

I blinked and stared suspiciously at the whisky, then looked back at him. "The technique's beside the point," I said, trying to keep my own tones sharp. "What do you want?"

He rolled the glass in his hand, the sharp facets reflecting the light and setting fire to the contents. "I wish to talk to your brother."

"About what? Maybe I can give him a message."

"Are you sure you want to know, little witch? I hadn't thought this was your world. Your brother certainly suggested it wasn't."

My brother suggested that? That meant he'd been discussing me with this ... with The Dealer, whatever he was. And he'd hardly run over here on his little kitty feet, so he'd been having these discussions *before*. My name, somehow, had come up in this strange and frightening town before I even knew magic existed, and now here I was, dragged along in his wake.

I swallowed my anger, not without difficulty, and said, "You're right, it's not my world, not really. But if Ruiner's in trouble, I'm the one who always has to get him out of it. So tell me."

He regarded me, head tilted slightly to one side, those cheekbones looking like something ships could wreck themselves on. "Tell me why you're in Darrowdale first."

"You grabbed me. You owe me an explanation."

"No. I have already compensated you with whisky and water, and the promise that all you consume here has already been paid for." He grinned, exposing those neat white teeth again, too straight and too even. "Now we begin anew. Why are you here?"

I sighed and looked at Ruiner. He stared at me blankly, not giving any indication that he had an opinion on the matter, but his whiskers were trembling, which could be fear of The Dealer, or fear of what I was going to do to him when we got out of here. Both were justified, in my mind. I turned back to the Dealer, who was still smiling at me. "Fine. I'm looking for my ex-husband. I found a ... a receipt from the Oubliette at his place, but I can't find him." I pawed my phone out of my pocket. "I've got a photo here."

The Dealer leaned forward to look at the phone, and I could feel the heat rising from him along with that mineral scent. "No."

"No?"

"No, he did not play here."

"But—"

He raised his free hand elegantly, the other still holding his glass. "I know everyone who plays at my club. And I think you are mistaken about the receipt."

I made a small noise that I hoped could be read as *I'm not*, or *oh really?* depending on what was going to be most believable.

"Firstly, we do not have *receipts*."

"Oh."

"Also, I have seen him before. He wanted to join some of my games. He was not welcome. My games are expensive, and I insist people understand the cost."

"I thought the whole point would be taking people's money."

He made a thoughtful noise. "And other things. But that was not the issue. The issue was if he *understood* what it could cost him. And he did not. I think he was not capable of that."

I sighed. "That does sounds like Jason. But I still think he's here, in town."

"Here, perhaps, but not playing."

"He sent a message saying he was in trouble."

The Dealer shrugged, smooth and liquid. "There are many ways to get in trouble in Darrowdale. But there are no games other than mine. I do not allow it."

I wondered just how all-seeing The Dealer really was. Being able to keep a lid on everything even in an ordinary town seemed unlikely, let alone in a magical one. But I just said, "I suppose I'll have to keep looking, then. You haven't seen him recently?"

"No. I can look for you, though. It'll be much quicker and safer than you doing it."

"And what'll that cost me?"

He grinned, wide and hungry. "Now you, Morgan Winters, understand that things have a cost. You would be welcome to play."

"Thanks, but I'll pass. How much to find Jason, though?"

"Just your book. If you're not much of a witch, you hardly need it, do you?"

"No," I said. "Absolutely not."

"Oh, well, then." He waved dismissively, as if it were all the same to him, and set his tumbler on the table before leaning back in his chair again. "But I do owe you an answer to your question, of course. Your brother's business. *Our* business."

"What was it?"

"Well—"

He was cut off by my brother, who leaped to the table,

skidding along it to knock The Dealer's whisky glass to the floor with a furious hiss.

"Bloody hell," I started, and The Dealer laughed, talking over me.

"Hello, Ruiner. An interesting transformation, my friend."

"Sodding hell," my brother muttered, and stuck a paw in my whisky, his ears back.

The whole keeping a low profile thing was going super well.

SEVENTEEN

The clams are nice

I WATCHED MY BROTHER LICK WHISKY OFF HIS PAW, HIS ears back and his whiskers quivering. He hadn't acknowledged The Dealer yet, and The Dealer had that look people get when they really want to pet the cat but know it's a bad idea.

"What the hell?" I said to my brother. "Here I am covering for you, pretending I don't even know where you are, then you're just like, *Heeeere's Ruiner!*" I shook my hands in the air to either side of my face. The Dealer gave one of those weirdly inelegant snorts again. I had the feeling we were providing him with more entertainment than his games usually did, but whether that worked in our favour or not I wasn't sure.

"He knew already," Ruiner said, sitting down and putting his paw in my whisky again.

"I did," The Dealer agreed, his warm voice even smoother and more rounded, if that were possible. I could feel it curling in the pit of my belly, and not in an unpleasant way. He glanced at me with a smile twitching the corners of his lips, as if entirely aware of the effect he

185

was having. "Anyone can see that this is not a regular cat. And your brother always did have rather beautiful eyes. A feature you share."

I rescued my whisky glass from Ruiner, horrified to find I was blushing. I kept my eyes on my brother, scowling at him. "I can't even drink this now."

"It tastes awful anyway," he said.

"That's because you have cat tastebuds."

He yawned, giving me a good view of his cat taste-buds, then retched. "Ugh. I don't think it agrees with me."

"Shocking," I said, looking at my whisky sadly. It wasn't my usual drink of choice, but with human tastebuds it had been pretty good. And much needed, given the general ... well, given everything.

The Dealer poured another glass and handed it to me, relieving me of the first one. "I think we shall get rid of this, now he's had his feet in it."

"My feet are perfectly clean," Ruiner said. "And adorable. Look how fluffy they are." He lifted one back leg and stretched it out in front of him, spreading his toes for inspection. The toe pads were pink, and he was quite right. His feline feet were very fluffy and adorable.

"Quite," The Dealer said, his expression as grave as if Ruiner had marched in and declared the club was bank-rupt. "But I would not even drink from a glass which had had my own feet in it. I assume you can't drink whisky right now."

"Can," Ruiner said immediately.

"Can't," I said. "I have no idea what it'll do to a cat body, but given the effects milk has, I'd say it'll probably kill you. And you even said it tasted awful."

He bared his teeth at me and I shrugged, taking a sip from my new glass and giving an exaggerated sigh of pleasure.

"A little water shall have to do," The Dealer said, topping up another tumbler and setting it in front of Ruiner. I blinked at it. I could've sworn he'd only had two glasses when we started, one for me and one for him. But I was getting distracted by the wrong things again.

I looked at Ruiner. "What's this business, then? Is it more debts?"

"It's not important," he said.

"On the contrary," The Dealer said. "It's very important indeed. I've been waiting for you to turn up, but I see now why no one's been able to find you."

I stared at Ruiner, who didn't look at me, just stared at The Dealer with his tail twitching. His whiskers had stopped trembling, but that tail always gave him away.

"It's nothing to do with Morgan," he said. "We're just looking for her useless bloody lump of an ex."

"I want to know about this business," I said.

"No, Morgan, you don't." Ruiner's voice was flat and oddly serious, and he still had his eyes on The Dealer. "It's my thing."

"As you say," The Dealer said, swirling his whisky and taking a slow sip. He shifted his gaze to me. "But this ex of yours..." He waved his free hand vaguely.

"Jason."

"Jason. As I said, I can find him for you."

"The book isn't an option," I said.

"And we're not doing any deals," Ruiner added.

"Any *more* deals," The Dealer said, and gave that alarmingly perfect smile again.

"Your business is a deal?" I asked my brother. "The one with Norma wasn't enough?"

He glared at me, his tail cranking up speed.

"Another deal?" The Dealer said. "And with someone

else? I'm *wounded*." He pressed a hand to his chest, dark eyes shining.

Ruiner ignored the dig, if that's what it was. "This really doesn't have anything to do with Morgan."

"I appreciate that, and your sister has no need to be involved," The Dealer replied. "But you vanished on me. Not even a note. That is not … *respectful* behaviour, Ruiner. Not what I expect from those I do business with."

"It's Rainier."

"I prefer your sister's version."

Ruiner sighed. "I vanished because I was a little busy trying to sort out the whole cat situation."

"*Hmm*. Yes. It's quite the enchantment. But you and I shall have a chat, nonetheless." He got up, the movement languid and graceful, and extended a hand to me, palm-up. I looked at it, drained my glass, and set it on his palm. He blinked, then burst out laughing. "Thank you." He set the glass on the table as I got up, and smiled at me, "If you are hungry, I can recommend the *spaghetti alle vongole*. The clams are very fresh." He gestured towards the door, not dismissive, but expectant. He was used to having his directions followed.

"I'm not leaving without Ruiner," I said, not moving.

"We won't be long, will we?" The Dealer said to my brother.

His furry flanks heaved with a sigh. "We won't. It's fine, Morgs. It's just … stuff. My stuff."

"Your *stuff* always ends up becoming my problem. Usually an expensive one, at that."

"I might observe that you have a pattern," The Dealer said. "Given the whole ex-husband situation."

"Well, thank you, Dr Phil," I said, although he wasn't wrong. He looked puzzled, and I folded my arms. "Ruiner?"

"No," he said. "I'm not talking with you here. She can't stay," he added to The Dealer, who shrugged.

"My people only brought her here because they were looking for you. Not that it hasn't been a pleasure, Morgan."

His voice was giving me goosebumps of the good sort, and I scowled. "You could've talked while I was unconscious if you were that worried, Ruiner."

"I didn't know if he knew it was me. I kind of hoped he couldn't tell."

"And I was intrigued to see how long he would carry on the pretence," The Dealer said. "Evidently only until he thought you might become privy to his secrets." He winked at me.

"It's not about secrets," Ruiner said. "Please, Morgs. This is one thing I don't want you to get tangled up in. It really is my stuff."

I held his gaze for a long time, the tension in my jaw radiating down into my shoulders. Whatever this was, it *would* end up being my problem. It always worked that way with Ruiner. He'd never fallen into anything that he hadn't come running to me to get him out of again, not since we were small and he'd convinced almost every one of the other kids on our street to give him their best toys in exchange for magic carpets. The magic carpets in question had been Mum's placemats, pilfered from the dining room, and, when the kids complained, Ruiner had simply declared they evidently weren't smart enough to work them properly. The entire street had been on the verge of all-out war by the time I got everything back to their original owners.

So no, Ruiner had never got himself out of his own problems. That I knew of, I allowed. I hadn't known about any of this side of his life, any more than I'd known Jason was involved in dodgy gambling rings. And I still couldn't help feeling Ruiner had to be responsible for that, one way or the other. But standing around arguing about things wasn't getting us anywhere. If Edith had recognised Ruiner — and assuming she was Jason's captor, which was an assumption I was willing to jump to, given how much she'd wanted the grimoire — we didn't have much time to spare.

"Fine," I said aloud, adjusting my bag and checking on Jackie, who hissed at me. "I'll be waiting outside."

"Do ask my men if you'd like anything to eat or drink," The Dealer said. "Compensation."

I didn't answer, just crossed the heavy old carpets to the door, my footsteps swallowed by the thick red pile. The door was a double one, each heavy wooden side taller and broader than a regular door. The handles were old black iron, and I put my hand on one, looking back at Ruiner. The Dealer stood next to him, his fathomless eyes fixed on me.

He placed one hand on his chest and bowed his head just slightly. "A pleasure, Morgan. I hope to see you again soon."

"Not bloody likely," Ruiner said, and I let myself out, their eyes still on me until I closed the door with a soft snick of the latch. I stood there, one hand flat to the wood, and wondered if I should try eavesdropping. But I had an idea that I wouldn't be able to hear anything, even if it had been just a cheap flimsy door I was dealing with. Plus there were two rather large men bracketing the doors who would probably object to it. One was bald and the other had short, fair hair, and while neither of them were hugely bulky, they both had the sort of shoulders that suggested they could remove me from the premises single-handedly.

"Um, hi?" I said, and they both looked at me expectantly. It was like being eyed up by two German Shepherds, and I couldn't tell if they thought I was a chew toy or their handler. "He said I could have food or drink?"

They glanced at each other, and the bald one nodded very slightly. The fair one looked at me and smiled, which made me suddenly sure I was the chew toy. But all he said was, "Of course. Let's get you sorted."

He stepped forward, beckoning me to follow him, and I turned to find we were on some sort of mezzanine. I'd been so intent on what Ruiner and The Dealer might be up to that I hadn't even looked at my surroundings. In front of the doors was a lounge which was inhabiting an entirely different century to The Dealer's room. A couple of big, modern leather sofas and a chunky wooden coffee table took up most of the floorspace, magazines scattered on the table and the light coming from a couple of standing column lamps. Beyond the sofas was a wooden railing that marked the edge of the mezzanine, built to be just the right height for leaning on. Its top was wide enough to act as a bar, with a little lip at the outer edge to stop anything plunging over and down to whatever lay below, and a row of sleek, padded stools were pulled up to it.

A murmur of noise rose from below, not loud, but full of intent, and the doorman paused between the sofas and the stools. "Where would you prefer?"

"Stool?" I said.

"Good choice," he replied, like a maître d' who'd just sold the most expensive bottle of wine off the menu. A very ripped maître d', too. He pulled a stool out for me, and I climbed onto it, setting the satchel on my lap. The doorman twiddled his fingers at Jackie when she poked her head out and said, "What can I get you?"

"Coffee?" I asked hopefully. Surely if anyone else could sell coffee in Darrowdale, The Dealer could.

"Sure. Anything else?"

I considered it. I didn't know how long I'd been out — or what time had been doing while we'd been in here, since it had certainly got a bit wonky last night in the Oubliette, and the odds were it worked the same here — but I was hungry. "I heard the *spaghetti alle vongole* was good."

"With the coffee?"

"Yes," I said, frowning at him.

"Then that's what I'll get." He gave me a smile that was nowhere near as disarming as his boss', and which left me with the distinct impression that he was going to tell half the kitchen about the weird woman who wanted pasta with clams and coffee *together*. I didn't care. I was getting coffee.

He turned away, and I started to settle myself in the stool, then jolted upright. "Wait!"

"Yes?" He turned back, and I could almost see him expecting me to ask for something different to drink.

"This is paid for, right? Compensation for the abduction, The Dealer said."

He winked at me. "You're safe. It's all covered." He headed across the floor at an easy pace towards a door at the other end of the mezzanine. I watched him go, checked on his impassive buddy, then peered over the railing to the main floor below.

As I'd suspected, we were upstairs from the Oubliette. The gaming floor was as busy now as it had been last night, lit by lights strung below the level of the mezzanine. They faced down, and with the dimmer lighting above, it was no wonder I'd had no idea this was up here. My balcony perch gave a perfect view of the bar and the gaming tables, cards flipping and dice clattering, squirrels battling to get into puzzles and three people engaged in what looked to be a soup-eating contest without the help of their hands or utensils. The noise was oddly muted but clear, like the volume had been turned down on a TV. Someone was sobbing quietly next to large jar of what looked to be earthworms, and a woman with a smile so wide it looked like a rictus was clawing up chips, hugging them to her chest like scraps of her heart. At the roulette table just beyond her, a man was holding a potted palm in each hand, his lips moving in supplication as the wheel spun.

I leaned back on the stool a little, looking away from the players and at the bar instead. That felt safer, less voyeuristic. I didn't want to watch people's hopes collapse amid the crisp cards and battling hermit crabs. Instead I watched the servers come and go, the bartenders' steady dance of glasses and bottles and trays, hypnotic and reassuringly *normal*. Bartenders were no different here than they were anywhere else. I kept watching even as The Dealer's bouncer reappeared with my food and my coffee, which didn't go at all well together, but individually they were both excellent, for as much attention as I paid. Most of my attention was on the bar below, and, more specifically, on one of the bar staff who'd just arrived, and vanished into a back room.

They'd reappeared, minus hat and coat, and I was still watching them when Ruiner jumped onto the next stool and looked at me. "Save me any?"

"Yeah." I pushed the plate toward him, the leftover clams already pulled from their shells and piled neatly on the side of the plate, waiting for him.

"Really? What, are they no good?"

"I'm just a much nicer sister than you deserve. Hurry up and eat them. I want to get out of here."

"Fair enough." He all but inhaled the shellfish as I got up.

The doorman was already coming to meet me. "Can I get you anything else?"

"No, we'd just like to go."

"Of course. I'll escort you out." He stepped back, inclining his head towards the end of the mezzanine.

"I'm pretty sure we won't get lost, Tweedle-fit," Ruiner said around a mouthful of clams, and I flicked his ear. "What? If his boss knows about me, he probably does too."

"Whenever you're ready," the doorman said, not seeming at all surprised by the talking cat. I took a last look at the bar then headed along the mezzanine, and a moment later Ruiner trotted to join me, licking his chops.

"Could've given me a moment," he complained. "I didn't even get to lick the plate."

"Too much garlic. It's not good for you."

"Still."

The doorman avoided the gaming floor completely, leading us into a hallway and down a set of back stairs that deposited us in the alley behind the Witch's Howl. "Sorry for any inconvenience," he said to me.

"Thanks for lunch," I replied, and headed for the street. Either the Oubliette really had done its time shift thing again, or my little nap had been longer than expected. The light was low already, made even more so by the rain. Despite that, though, everything felt too bright and too sharp, and I was having trouble breathing properly.

"Morgan?" Ruiner said.

"Not yet." I kept going, turning left when the alley opened onto the street, leaving town behind us and heading into quieter areas. I went two blocks before I stopped in the shelter of an almost leafless tree, then crouched down to look at my brother.

"Look, I know," he started, and I cut him off with a shake of my head.

"I know how to find Jason."

"What? You mean Edith?"

"I don't think so. One of the bar staff just came in, and he was wearing Jason's lucky hat. Either The Dealer's lying about him never being allowed to play, or there really are other games going on. They know where Jason is."

"Oh, *bollocks*," Ruiner said, which seemed like a bit of an understatement.

EIGHTEEN

I wouldn't mind biting someone

OF COURSE JASON HAD A LUCKY HAT. PEOPLE LIKE JASON always have lucky hats, and they always think it makes them look cool and suave, and not like someone who's going to call every female he encounters *babe,* and insist that a pat on the bum is just being friendly, and honestly, men can't do *anything* these days, it's political correctness gone mad. I was confused yet again as to how I'd apparently ignored all these things before. They were less red flags than flashing red neon signs. Had Jason really been a bum-patter? Of bums other than mine? Well, and his younger model, obviously, which probably indicated that yes, there had been other bums patted along the way.

"That was his lucky hat?" Ruiner was asking. "I thought he was getting a bald spot."

"No, he said it made him feel more confident. I'm pretty sure he used to wear it to job interviews."

"That explains a lot," Ruiner said, as if he'd ever bothered to go to a job interview in his life.

"We have to follow that barman," I said. "He could lead us to wherever they're holding Jason."

Ruiner wrinkled his snout, fangs hanging out. "It could also have nothing to do with Jason being missing. Maybe he just left his hat behind. Or there was some off-the-books game, and the barman won it there. There could be any number of explanations."

"Including that he stole it from Jason when they kidnapped him."

"Sure, but if The Dealer really took him, d'you think he'd let his staff take trophies? He strike you like that kind of person?"

"No," I admitted. "But maybe he didn't know."

"Trust me, he'd know." Ruiner shuddered as he said it, and glanced over his shoulder, back in the direction of the club. "The more likely answer is that Jason got himself kicked out and the barman took the hat. Remember the brand the dead guy had, the one barring him from the Oubliette? Maybe Jason's got himself one of those too. Or, you know, it's just the same type of hat. You couldn't see it *that* well from up there."

"I don't imagine too many hats have pink flamingos on sticks stuck in the band."

"Okay, pretty distinctive. But I still think it's more likely Jason tried to sneak in and got himself a permanent ban."

"That does seem more his style," I admitted. "But what if the barman *does* have something to do with it? What if he's working with Edith on the side or something? Or Grace and Edith together, and it really is all about the grimoire? Maybe The Dealer already knew Jason was your ex-brother-in-law, and when he tried to come to the club but got banned the barman got wind of it. He's being paid by Edith to keep an eye out for anything related to us, so he tells her. She gets him to nab Jason by tempting him into an illicit game or something, and *bam*. Now she's got him strung up in a dungeon, without his lucky hat, and she's going to start cutting his fingers off or something if we don't get a move on."

Ruiner looked at me for a long moment, then said, "What's it like living in your head? Was it always like this, or have you read so many books it's addled you?"

"Is it any weirder than the fact that we're in a valley *inside* Manchester that I guarantee you isn't on any map? And a barista tried to eat my soul?"

"Fae don't eat souls. They just enslave you for a few hundred years."

"*So* much better."

Ruiner sighed. "We're just guessing on all of this. We've got no idea what's really going on."

"Only one way to figure it out. We follow Hat Guy. Unless you'd rather follow Edith, but she's already spotted you, and the odds are Hat Guy can't zap us with any spells."

"You're talking about following someone you suspect of being a kidnapper, Morgan. Maybe a murderer, if he was responsible for the dead body."

I checked the street for eavesdroppers, sighing. He was right, but what other option did we have? I looked back at him and shrugged. "Still think it's better than following someone we know has already tried to kill us once."

He squinted at me. "I'm not comfortable with this. I'm the reckless one, remember? You're meant to be the sensible one. Weren't you going to call Ben?"

"Oh." I pulled my phone out and checked it. "Oddly enough, no signal."

"Not much of a magical town if you can still call an Uber. We were leaving, remember?"

"We might lose Hat Guy."

"Oh *no*."

I pocketed the phone again, looking around. "You're right about us needing help, though. Let's do both."

"What?"

"You keep an eye on the club and see if Hat Guy comes out. You can hide better than me, anyway."

"You're *leaving* me here?" He sounded outraged.

"Not in Darrowdale. Just on this spot. I'm going to go to the library and see if they've got a phone."

"You and your bloody libraries. What if Hat Guy leaves and you're not back? What if he's driving?"

"You'll figure something out." I waved him toward the club. "Go on."

"I'd really like to go back to our normal roles."

"This is what you get for dragging me into your messes."

"This is Jason's mess." But he was already loping away, keeping to the shelter of the walls, and I watched him go for a moment. He was right. I was acting more like him than he was. But I'd tried to do everything right, for everyone, for so long, and what had it got me? A divorce, an empty bank account, and being yanked out of the world I knew to become the owner of a book I was completely unqualified to handle. Honestly, it was past time I tried a different approach. Not that channelling Ruiner was ever going to be the *best* approach, but I supposed I had to start somewhere.

I pulled my hood up again and headed for the library, opening the satchel as I walked to check on Jackie, curled along the spine of the books. I was still carting around the bloody comportment thing the Upstanding Lady had given me, too. No wonder my shoulder was hurting.

"Alright?" I asked Jackie, and she twitched her snout at me. I was a little surprised she hadn't traded me in already, to be honest. Even if I'd technically claimed the grimoire and it therefore couldn't just be taken from me, I had a sneaking suspicion that Jackie was old enough and smart enough to circumvent all that and take the book off to a better witch. That she hadn't done so was either a vote of confidence in me or an indicator that pickings were slim in the witch department. I tried not to think too much about which option was the most likely.

The library looked derelict in the drizzle, blackened lines of mould showing along the metal framing, heavy streaks of muck running down the panes, and the makeshift plywood panels dark with damp. The lights were on inside, though, and I eased my way through the door warily. Effie was singing in the distance, "Sweet Dreams" by the sound of things, and as the door snicked shut behind me, she stopped. The library fell into silence, broken only by the ceaseless whisper of the rain murmuring its secrets, and an ominous rusting coming from the stacks.

"Hello?" I tried, and the word seemed overly loud, rattling across the floor to bounce against the walls. The rustling stopped, and I swear the rain held its breath, waiting to see what would happen.

Then the library exploded with movement. Connall came sprinting out of the stacks with his arms full of books and his hair looking like someone had been using it to clean cobwebs. Effie dived off the mezzanine, landed on the main desk, and somersaulted to the floor directly into Connall's path. He tripped over her with a yell, the books flying out of his arms and skidding across the floor. Effie screeched, skittering sideways on all fours, and deep in the shadowy reaches of the library something papery and Leviathan lurched across an aisle and vanished into the stacks on the other side, setting off a flood of bats who poured into the lobby area, screaming and chittering.

A splintery crash rang out from somewhere in the depths of the building, and Effie scampered up to me, rising to her feet and putting both hands on my shoulders. She was a good head shorter than me, her eyes wide and dark, and she grinned, showing me her impressive collection of sharp teeth.

"Hi," I said, and she cocked her head questioningly. "He's not here."

Her shoulders slumped, and she touched my cheek with one hand, her skin even colder than mine. I wasn't sure if that was her begging me to produce Ruiner, or simply being friendly, but I dug in my coat pocket and found one of the chocolate protein bars. I offered it to her and she grabbed it eagerly, then ducked away as Connall swung a book at the back of her head. I yelped, jerking backwards and banging into the door, and he spun around, hurling the book at Effie. She dodged it easily, hissing.

"Stop attacking the bloody customers!" he bellowed. He was red-faced and sweating, and one shoulder of his shirt was torn.

"She wasn't attacking me," I said, more sharply than I'd intended. "She was looking for Ruiner. My cat."

"Oh, so she could have a little cuddle?" he demanded, then took a breath. He grabbed one of his dropped books off the floor in his tattooed hand and brandished it warningly at Effie, then gave me an embarrassed grin. "Sorry. She bit Mrs. Evans this morning. I'm a bit nervous she's got a taste for it now."

I looked at the books scattered on the ground. The one he'd thrown at the ghoul was vomiting pages everywhere, covered in heavy ink sketches and row after row of numbers, and some of them seemed to be trying to make a break for it back to the stacks, leaving their cover behind. "Maybe Mrs. Evans deserved it."

"I doubt that. But Effie can't help it, I suppose. Ghouls bite, cats scratch, and rats get into filth."

Jackie stuck her head out of the satchel and looked at him, then at me. I'm not sure which of us she was most disapproving of.

"Most things'll bite if you provoke them enough," I said. "I've been tempted myself at times." Like now.

"But you haven't *done* it," he pointed out, and clapped his hands at Effie. "Go on! Go!"

I was about to tell him to leave her alone, then remembered I was here to ask a favour. It's not like there were many other places I could go for a phone. "I can see it's not ideal for her to bite library customers."

"It's not," he said, and winced as something crashed in the far reaches of the stacks, where I could see a bunch of the lights had gone out.

"What is that?"

"Not entirely sure. I've not got close enough to tell." He considered it. "Not sure I want to, either."

"Right." The bats were still wheeling about the lobby, leathery wings working furiously, and I watched Effie snatch one out of the air. I braced myself for her to shove it in her mouth and start munching, Ozzy Osbourne style, but she just petted it gently, making little soothing sounds, until it cuddled into her neck, clinging to her hair with its sharp little claws.

"You probably didn't come to talk about the stack monsters, though," Connall said, running his hands back through his hair and grimacing when they came away covered in cobwebs. "What's up? After another cuppa?"

"Not right now. Does your phone work?"

"Sometimes," he said, and waved at the front desk. "Help yourself."

I crossed to it as he set about collecting his books,

digging in the side pocket of the satchel as I went. There was a jumble of stuff in there, a couple of interesting pebbles, some nuts for Jackie, and, more importantly, my Hollowbeck library card, which had as its logo a frog reading a pile of books while a snail looked on suspiciously. I always suspected Petunia had something to do with that.

The library phone wasn't as ancient as the one in the Cosy Cauldron, but it was still a wired one. I picked up the handset warily, bracing myself for the voices. There was nothing but a regular dial tone though, and I turned my library card over to find the number on the back. I poked the old buttons of the phone, and as I did the chatter started, setting my skin crawling. The voices repeated the numbers at first, calling them back at me in nonsensical order, then as I put the last digit in the chorus started.

"Hollow ...*beck!* Hollow ... *beck!* Hollowbeck li ... brary! Li ... brary! Hollowbeck library! Hollowbeck library!*"

I tried to clamp down on the shudder traversing my spine, holding the handset a little away from my ear, as if I felt a finger might pop out and poke me. Nothing did, though, and the voices kept yelling until there was a click of connection and they cut off abruptly.

"Hello? Ben?"

Nothing but silence, yet it didn't feel like a dead line.

"Hello? Is anyone there?"

I almost thought I heard someone catch their breath, as if they were preparing to speak, and I both wanted them to and didn't. What if the voices had connected me to something that *shouldn't* be spoken to? Something that had slept until I'd woken it? Something dangerous? I wanted to put the phone down, but I couldn't seem to move.

A whisper drifted down the line. There were no words

to it, just a sense of *something* being there, something listening and waiting and — the phone was removed neatly from my hand. I jerked away, startled. Effie was crouched on top of the desk, and she looked at me with solemn eyes, then put the phone to her own ear, head inclined as she listened. She didn't speak. I leaned close enough to her that I could hear that near-silence continuing on the other end, then Effie sighed, long and low. I couldn't tell if what I heard from the handset was an answering sigh, or just an echo. I held out my hand, eyebrows raised, wanting to hang up and try again, and she looked at me with the phone still clamped to her ear and the four bats decorating her hair eyeing me warily.

"Effie! Bloody hell—" Connall reached over the counter, grabbing for the phone, and Effie shot from her crouch into a vertical leap, phone still clutched in one hand. The cable tore out of the wall and she vanished across the mezzanine with it clattering after her. I looked at Connall, and he grimaced. "Sorry."

"Have you got another phone?"

"No. She'll bring it back, though. Hopefully." He rocked on his heels, tucking his hands into his pockets. "Coffee while you wait?"

"Internet?" I asked hopefully.

"No, it's been down since last Wednesday. It only works about three days a month." He sighed. "Is Hollowbeck better than this?"

"Not for internet and phones," I said truthfully. "No monsters in the stacks, though. That I know of, at least."

"That must be nice." He peered up into the mezzanine. "I can go and look for her, if you want?"

"She's not singing," I pointed out.

"No," he agreed. "But if you need me to…"

I would have liked him to, to be honest, but the odds of

the phone working any better the second time around were slim, and I didn't want to give him any reason to throw more things at Effie. I shook my head. "It's fine. There was no answer anyway." Besides, my brother was out there stalking our best lead, and the longer I waited around, the more likely it was that Hat Guy would be on the move. "Thanks, though."

"No problems," he said. "Come back and have a coffee when you have more time."

"Absolutely." I headed for the doors, pulling my hood up again as I stepped back out into the drizzly day. I stood under the shelter of the building's overhang for a moment, unsettled and anxious. I supposed monsters in the stacks and aggressive books and library ghouls would do that to you. But they seemed less creepy and more simply a product of books left too long in magical towns. Something else was irritating me, and I had an idea there was some connection I was missing. Something else or more or different I should be doing to find Jason and get us out of here.

But I couldn't figure out what it was, so all we could do was the best we could with what we had. I walked out into the rain and went to stalk a kidnapper, which was a course of action that really had me considering my use of the word *best*.

NINETEEN

Many versions of truth

I WAS STROLLING DOWN THE PAVEMENT IN THE RAIN towards the Witch's Howl, trying to look casual, when a hiss caught my attention. I discovered Ruiner under a parked car, his blue eyes narrow as he stared out at me.

"What're you doing?" he demanded.

"Looking for you."

"You're way too obvious. You can't just stand there talking to me."

"*You're* talking to *me*. You could've just come out."

"It's wet out there."

"Well, what'm I supposed to do if we want to talk? Crawl under there with you?"

"No. Go and get the bloody car so we can both stay dry."

"Your wish is my command." I stalked off, making sure to keep my head down. There was no one on the door of the Witch's Howl, but Ruiner was right. Anyone could be watching. Not that the talking cat thing was much of a secret anymore, at least in the Oubliette, but there was no point being more obvious than we needed to.

The car was still where we'd left it, which was finally something in our favour. I was careful not to look at the Crafty Cauldron as I unlocked the door and peeled my jacket off. No one shouted or launched any magical attacks at me, and a moment later I was safely ensconced in the chilly interior, shivering as water ran down my neck from my hair. I removed a reluctant Jackie from the satchel, setting her on the passenger seat in the folds of my coat so I could tuck the bag out of the way under my own seat. Then it was onto the ritual of persuading the engine into life, which seemed a bit more precarious every time I did it. It was a delicate dance of revs, enthusiastic key-turning, and a little bouncing up and down in my seat for encouragement. It wasn't elegant but it did work, and she'd just caught, roaring into complaining life, when someone knocked on my window. I swore, stalling the car as I jerked back in the seat, and Jackie dived off the passenger seat and vanished.

"Thanks for the support," I muttered, and wound the window down, looking out at the smiling face of Lise. She had a multi-coloured umbrella resting against her shoulder, fingers long and slim on the handle. I supposed that meant she wasn't a vampire, then. Unless the thick late afternoon clouds were enough of a UV filter, which I supposed was possible. The day was so grey and the oncoming dusk so mournful that the town felt like it had forgotten what sunshine was. "Hi," I said, as brightly and innocently as I could.

"Hello, little witch. What are you doing back in town?"

"Exploring," I said. "I heard the food at Monster Munch is extraordinary."

She grinned, that weirdly creepy, too perfect, too symmetrical grin. "It certainly has been described as such, among other things. But that's not why you're here, is it?"

"Well, partly. Food, architecture. A bit of shopping. Just a tourist doing tourist things." I laughed, the sound high and false in my ears.

"I see. And do those tourist things include spying on local shopkeepers?"

"Of course not," I said, trying to make it sound as if I thought the idea was ridiculous.

Lise didn't answer at once, just stood there with one hip cocked elegantly, the rain pattering softly on the umbrella and her pale eyes fixed on me. She was motionless, carved from marble, and I tried to keep an enquiring smile on my face and not shift around in my seat too much. I had a feeling I was all but radiating guilt, though.

"Harassment," she said finally.

"I'm sorry?" I didn't have to fake my astonishment.

"You've been reported for harassment."

"*How?*"

Lise twirled the umbrella gently, spinning drops off the edge. "One of our residents is newly arrived from Hollowbeck, where she was a respected businesswoman, until the new town witch and her cat attacked her. Law enforcement took the new witch's side, and poor Edith was ousted. We were happy to welcome her here, as we do so many of Hollowbeck's displaced. Our borders are always open to those Hollowbeck finds *wanting*." She said it with a touch of distaste, and I stared at her, aware my mouth was open. She raised her eyebrows, waiting for me to respond.

I finally remembered how to talk and spluttered, "That is *not* what happened. She tried to kill me, and my friend, *and* my ... my cat. And she killed the old town witch!"

"Every story has its sides. And maybe Hollowbeck favours the cute little witch, but here we favour the truth."

"Not if you believe that, you don't."

She smiled slightly. "Your truth may not be her truth. And as she is one of ours now, her truth is what matters."

"I'm pretty sure the law doesn't work that way."

"Oh, it does. Even in your precious Hollowbeck." Her smile widened. "Of course, I wasn't sure you were who Edith claimed you to be, but you've rather told me, haven't you?"

I huffed a breath out, deflating in my seat. I could hardly deny it. "I wasn't harassing her. I didn't even know she was here until we — I saw her this morning."

Lise nodded. "Maybe you didn't know, yet here you are. And what did Edith find on her windowsill? Only your strange cat, who, I hear, is maybe not such a cat after all. And that, little witch, is stalking and harassment."

I took a deep breath. "My ex-husband is missing."

"Isn't that the intention when one makes them ex?"

"No — I mean, yes, actually, good point, but he's missing in the general sense."

"And that's the reason for your cat to be on Edith's windowsill?"

"We were checking everywhere in town?" I offered, somewhat weakly.

"So he's a peeping tomcat?"

I was starting to get the feeling Lise was enjoying playing with me, not unlike a cat herself. "We were asking around. Can I show you a photo? Maybe you've seen him."

"I'm sure we can discuss that later," she said, and stepped back from the door. "Get out of the car."

"No, I can't, I have to find him."

"Get out of the car," she repeated, and while I couldn't have sworn that I saw anything change, something did anyway, every angle of her abruptly sharper and more clear cut, as if she'd been assembled from shards of glass and they'd suddenly all shifted, jagged ends out.

For one wild moment, I considered just driving off, squealing out of the parking space and heading for Darrowdale's narrow gateway as fast as the old car could manage, but there were at least three things wrong with that plan. Firstly, even if I could get it started again, my car hadn't had the ability to squeal off anywhere in about two decades. Secondly, Ruiner was still staking out the club, and I could hardly leave him behind. And finally, I had a sneaking suspicion that the gateway would simply clamp closed as I reached it, either forcing me to a stop before I could get out, or pinning us between the walls to await Lise's arrival, or — and this felt the most likely — smashing the car between the sheer cliffs of brick like a sandwich in a panini grill.

I didn't fancy any of those options, so I got out, grabbing my coat from the passenger seat as I went. I pulled it on as the rain set about soaking me with great enthusiasm.

"Your cat?" Lise asked.

"Not here."

She frowned and leaned down to peer into the car, but there was nothing to see. Jackie would be hunkered down with the grimoire, and all I could hope was that I could get back before anyone got close enough that she'd have to defend it. I locked the door and slipped the key into my pocket, and Lise nodded.

"Off we go," she said, pointing down the street, and I turned, pulling my hood up to fend off the worst of the rain. I was shivering, but it wasn't really the cold or the damp that was doing it. In the space of five minutes our little party had been split into three, every single one of us was at risk, and I had no idea how I was going to reunite us. Lise had as much as said she had no intentions of listening to my side of the story.

"Morgan?" someone said, and Lise put a hand on my shoulder, as if to hold me in place. Connall was standing on the pavement in a dark green anorak, frowning at us. "What's going on?"

"I'm being arrested," I said.

"Detained," Lise said. "What do you want?" Her voice was cool, unfriendly, and Connall ignored her, looking at me.

"Are you okay? Can I do anything?"

"Go back to your books, Connall," Lise said, and started walking, propelling me ahead of her with her hand still resting on my shoulder.

"Morgan! Can I call anyone? Tell me what to do!"

Great. I had one potential rescuer, and he needed written instructions. I just gave him a despairing shrug and let myself be escorted away, leaving him standing on the street, rain running down his anorak and spattering his glasses.

Darrowdale evidently had no use for police vans or cars. Instead, Lise escorted me along the street in a walk of shame past all the businesses and shops, customers and workers alike emerging onto the street to watch.

I glanced at the Crafty Cauldron as we drew level with it, a compulsive little peek. Edith was in the doorway, leaning against the frame. She backed inside when I saw her, and I stumbled, almost falling off the kerb. Lise caught my arm. "Careful," she said. I wanted to ask her what the point in being careful was, when she was just about to do Edith's job for her.

"What's she done?" Jim called from the doorway of Bewitching Boos. He had a tea towel flung over his shoulder, and his beard decorations were lizards today.

"Unconfirmed. Innocent till proven guilty and all that," Lise said.

He didn't reply, watching me go with a frown stitching his brows together. I had the uncharitable thought that I hoped they stuck that way.

We walked the length of the main street before Lise guided me towards the town hall. A woman from the grocery shop threw a couple of squishy tomatoes at me, which seemed a bit unfair. I hadn't even been into her shop. They fell short, at least, but I didn't much like the sentiment behind it. I wondered what Ruiner would do when I didn't come back. Hopefully he'd get some help, but who knew how long that'd take. He couldn't exactly drive himself back to Hollowbeck.

By the time we pushed through a big set of glass double doors into the coldly lit atrium of the town hall, my hood was so soaked I may as well have just emptied a bucket over my own head. My trainers squelched noisily as we crossed the marble tiles, echoing against the walls, and I stopped in the centre of the entrance foyer, looking around. It was a grand room, stretching up two storeys, a jagged modern chandelier hanging in the centre and setting a wash of clear light to reflect off the tiles. Stairs wound up either side of the foyer to the floor above, and the walls were a stark, smooth white, immaculately kept. Big, arty black and white photos of the town in heavy frames hung on the walls. There were no people in them, just empty landscapes and silent buildings.

"Keep going," Lise said, nodding towards the back of the foyer. Broad hallways opened off to either side, their front walls formed by the glass exterior of the building and the back walls the same smooth white as the foyer. They held flush doors with metal signs on them, too small for me to read from here. But we weren't going down the halls anyway. Instead, Lise guided me towards some older, more utilitarian doors that lined the back of the foyer. One was marked *Toilets,* another *Staff Only,* and the third said simply, *Inspector L. Oddvarson.*

She unlocked it using a little keypad and ushered me into a sleek office with a desk set under the window at the back, two chairs facing it. I started for them, but she grabbed my arm and swung me toward a door to my right. It was unlabelled but had a small glass pane set into the top, reinforced with wire. There was another keypad lock, and she tapped in the number then opened the door. "In you go."

"No, wait," I started, stopping on the threshold, but she shoved me in the back. There was no hostility in the movement, just a simple, businesslike efficiency, and I stumbled into a room no bigger than a store cupboard. It was equipped with a plastic bench bolted to the floor against one wall, and a bucket sitting rather ominously against the other.

Lise didn't wait around to ask any questions, or to answer them. She just closed the door again and I heard the click of the lock resetting, leaving me in silence. I looked around the room with a numb sort of disbelief. I couldn't even really call it a cell. It was just a box to put people while they figured out what to do with them. I touched my pockets, as if there'd be something that could help me in there, but the only thing I came up with was the phone, which was as useless as it had been earlier. I supposed I could throw it at someone, or stab them with my car key, but given Lise hadn't even bothered to check my pockets, she evidently wasn't worried about me having any sort of success with such tactics.

I sat down on the bench, wondering what was going to

happen now. Would Lise hand me over to Edith? Burn me at the stake? Throw me in a dungeon somewhere? I couldn't even seem to dredge up the appropriate degree of horror, though I knew I should. The whole situation was a disaster, but it was also just so surreal and ridiculous I couldn't quite believe it was actually happening. All the wild situations I'd had to bail Ruiner out of, and I'd never ended up arrested.

I supposed there had to be a first for everything.

I WAS STILL SITTING on the bench, thinking of all the times Ruiner *should* have been arrested but had either charmed his way out of it or been dragged out of it by me, and wondering how I'd managed to be the one who got locked up, when the whispers started. I froze, looking around the room wildly. There was no window for someone to be standing outside of, no cupboard for anyone to hide in. There was just the bucket, the bench, and me, and now the whispers washing around me like a tide coming in too fast to outrun.

I started to get up, thinking I'd run to the door and beg Lise to let me out before the voices could drown me, but they were already here, swirling around me, flooding my ears and my thoughts, pinning me in place with their whispered almost words. I pressed both hands to my ears, aware I was adding to their chorus with my own. "No, oh no, oh stop, *stop—*" They were awful, the voices, insidious and ceaseless, and all I could think of was Starlight saying, *a haunting.*

The voices were so all-consuming, even more claustrophobic in the tiny room than they had been on the street, that I almost missed the fact my phone was vibrating in my pocket. I dropped my hands, groping for it, and fumbled it out. Just as before, the screen was blank except for the phone icon, and I hit it so hard I was surprised at some level that the screen didn't crack. Last time answering had made the voices stop. *Please, please*.

The line connected, and the voices *did* stop. I gave a little whimper of relief and put the phone to my ear. "Hello?" I whispered.

"It's the answerphone again," Jason said, apparently to someone else. He was clearer this time than he had been in Hollowbeck, and I wondered if that meant he was closer. Or more ghostly.

"Jason?"

"Yeah, yeah, okay," he said, still talking to someone else. He didn't sound very ghostly. He just sounded impatient. "Morgs, if you can hear me, you need to hurry, okay? They're running out of patience. I need help *now*." There was a pause, as if he was listening to whoever was with him. "And you can't tell anyone, okay? You have to come to—"

The keypad beeped on the door, and the phone went instantly dead. No whisper of the ghosts, no creepy *boop-boop-boop*. The phone simply cut off, and I sat there with it still to my ear as Lise opened the door. We stared at each other.

"Mobiles don't work here," she said.

"Um, yeah," I said. "Guided meditation. For the stress. I downloaded it." I lowered the phone slowly and put it back in my pocket. Come where? Where was I meant to go? And how was I meant to get out of here to go there?

Lise gave me a dubious look, but didn't move to take the phone. "The mayor wants a word."

"Sure." I got up, straightening the front of my soggy

jacket, and braced myself for a ghost, which had to be the minimum. Probably they'd be something scarier, a poltergeist or a banshee or something like that. Darrowdale was really into one-upping Hollowbeck.

Lise stepped back, and Grace walked in.

TWENTY

Run, little witch, run

"WHAT'RE YOU DOING HERE?" I BLURTED BEFORE SHE could speak, and she blinked at me.

"I'm the mayor?" She said it almost in a question, as if confused as to why I'd ask.

"Funny, you never mentioned that before."

"Well, no. I've never met you before."

"What?" We stared at each other, while I tried to figure out why she'd bother with such a blatant lie. Was it some ploy to throw me off balance? A really extreme form of gaslighting? Or — and this was a stretch, but one never knew — was she actually here to help, and just pretending not to know me? But Lise had closed the door again, so surely she didn't need the pretence, plus she was the *mayor*. How the hell had she managed that?

"Ah," mayor-Grace said suddenly, her face clearing. "You've met my sister."

"Your sister?"

"Grace. My twin."

"Your *twin?*"

She sighed slightly, as if exasperated by my inability to

do anything but parrot her words back at her. To be fair, I was exasperated by it too. But a twin? What sort of *Parent Trap* shenanigans were these?

"Identical twins. I'm Faith."

Surely they couldn't be *that* identical. The same wash of warm brown hair, the same sickeningly perfect skin, the same elegant stance and cute little nose. The world couldn't support two such winners of the genetic lottery, surely.

"You're identical twins? Really?"

"Last time I checked. What're you doing in Darrowdale?"

"I didn't know Grace had a twin. I didn't even know she had a *sister*."

"Besties, are you?" she asked, leaning against the wall and crossing her arms.

"No," I admitted. "But..." I'd been going to say it was something she'd have mentioned, but I supposed it wasn't. Most of our conversations had been limited to me begging Grace to help me fix various grimoire-related incidents, and her gentle suggestions that it might not be in the right hands with me. I decided to leave the twinsies thing alone for now and try another tack. "Why have I been arrested?"

"Arrested's a bit harsh. Detained. Briefly."

"Fine. Why've I been *detained briefly?*"

She put her head to one side. "Did you come here for Edith?"

"No. Why would I do that?"

"You attacked her in Hollowbeck, and now here you are, with your cat spying on her. It certainly seems like you're following her."

I shook my head. "I don't know what she told you, but *she* attacked *me* in Hollowbeck. She tried to break my cat's neck. I have zero desire to see her again, ever."

"So what was your cat doing?"

"Who knows what cats do? He probably thought it looked like our shop back home and was scrounging for treats."

Faith raised one eyebrow. "What's your reason for being in Darrowdale, then?"

"Tourist. I wanted to see what other magical towns were like."

"And you decided on Darrowdale? That seems like a poor choice. It's where Hollowbeck sends all its rejects. You must've known Edith would be here."

"I had no idea that's how it worked," I said truthfully. And then, because I really was curious, I added, "Does everyone here come from Hollowbeck originally?"

"Not everyone. Some people were never meant for Hollowbeck's tweeness." Her mouth twisted in a small moue of distaste. "They were born here, or stumbled here and found their place."

"And you? Since your sister's in Hollowbeck?"

"My sister's welcome to it." She straightened up, flicking some hair over her shoulder. It rippled gently, looking as though her stylist had just dropped it in place. "Come on. Why are you really here?"

"Curious. Like you say, Hollowbeck can be pretty twee."

She didn't speak for a while, just watched me, and I watched her back, wondering if Jason was stashed in another cell-slash-cleaning cupboard elsewhere in the hall. Or if there were stairs to a dungeon lurking in some dimly lit corner somewhere. It seemed likely in this place.

"You need to leave," Faith said, her flinty expression revealing nothing.

"Sorry?"

"You're not welcome in Darrowdale. You'll leave, and you won't come back. The borders will be closed to you."

I blinked at her. "That's it?"

She raised an eyebrow. "What did you expect, a ducking stool?"

"I mean, maybe."

Faith waved dismissively. "Edith isn't interested in pressing charges, she just doesn't want to be worried about you jumping her—"

"Not bloody likely," I started, and Faith gave me a small frown. "I mean, great. Good."

"Yes. And I don't particularly want your pet police officer charging in here with his fangs hanging out, so I'd rather not deal with you."

"He's not—" I gave up. I shouldn't be arguing about the fact that I wasn't getting the ducking stool. "Okay."

"You should count yourself lucky," Faith said. "Hollowbeck's rarely so lenient with anyone from Darrowdale."

"I don't believe that," I said. "Isabella's lovely."

"Sure she is. As long as you're a good little citizen." She grinned at me, showing familiar and charmingly crooked teeth, and I tried to see something that wasn't Grace in her. The dusting of freckles forming different constellations, her hair a little shorter or a little longer, her eyes one shade darker or lighter. I couldn't, though. She wasn't even a mirror image of Grace. She *was* Grace, and I couldn't make sense of it.

"Lise will take you back to your car." Faith knocked on the door and the handle turned immediately, revealing Lise standing just beyond the threshold.

"Well?" she said.

"Escort her out of town," Faith said, and glanced back at me. "No coming back, or it will be the ducking stool."

"Got it," I said, and Faith nodded. She left, her heeled boots clicking softy on the tiles.

"Come on," Lise said. "Need the loo before we go?"

"Yes," I said immediately. "I can't believe you left me in here for so long without offering."

"There was a bucket."

"Ew."

She grinned and led me out into the entrance hall, pulling her office door closed behind her. "Go on," she said, pointing at the toilet doors. "Hurry up."

"I'll try, but I had shellfish for lunch. It feels a bit urgent."

She grimaced. "That's detail I could've done without."

"Just explaining the situation."

I headed into the loos, the door swinging softly shut behind me. Three cubicles faced a double sink with a big mirror above it, and everything was spotlessly clear. I could smell jasmine and a whiff of soap, and there wasn't even a water spot on the mirror. Things were better kept in here than they were on the exterior, apparently.

But none of that really interested me. What *did* interest me was the frosted glass window set high in the back wall, which was almost exactly Morgan-sized. Or I hoped it was, anyway. I pulled my jacket off and grabbed the sill, trying to lift myself up enough to peer over it. Unfortunately I couldn't remember the last time I'd been to the gym, and I was a hundred percent certain I'd never done a pull-up even when I had been going, so I couldn't get high enough to see out.

I looked around, spotting a bin by the sinks. It was just a plastic swing-top thing, but I pulled the lid off and upended it under the window, stepping onto it gingerly. The plastic bent a little under my weight but held, and I found myself looking into a wall formed by one of the unidentifiable plants, growing straight up past the window. Huge white blooms speckled it, accompanied by equally large thorns, but if all it did was give me a few scratches I'd count myself lucky. It was a better option than going with Lise. Even if she really did just escort me out of town, and not to some tar pit, I'd then be stuck outside while Ruiner and, presumably, Jason, were stuck *inside*.

Plus the tar pit seemed a better fit for the town. Or being fired out of a cannon for the entertainment of the masses.

I threw the jacket at the bush, hoping it'd protect me from the worst of the thorns, then heaved myself up. Even with the bin to help it was a graceless effort, and when I managed to get myself up I almost overbalanced and pitched head-first into the garden. I hung there, belly on the sill, trying to work at how to get my legs up so I could go feet-first, and Lise shouted from beyond the door, "Are you alright in there?"

"That was *not* catch of the day," I yelled back, and gave up on finding an elegant solution. I let go of the sill, put my hands out to catch myself, and slithered into the sodden undergrowth, hoping that when I inevitably got bitten by something it wasn't venomous.

The mutant rosebush didn't bite me as I collapsed to the ground between it and the wall, but it wouldn't relinquish Jason's jacket, either. I struggled briefly to free it, but when I heard Lise call out again, I scrabbled the car key and my phone out of the coat pockets and abandoned it. At least it had protected me from the worst of the thorns when I landed, although I could've done with a bit more protection as I clawed my way out of the flowerbed. Thorns snagged my hoody and ripped my sleeve, and one hooked my jeans so firmly I almost face-planted into the dirt. Another gouged my hand, pulling a little yelp out of me, and just as I thought I was free I was jerked to a stop. The bloody plant seemed to have grabbed a fistful of my hair, and as I battled to free myself Lise shouted, "That's enough now. Let's get moving."

"I'm on the way," I yelled in the general direction of the window. "But unless you want vomit-scented car seats..."

"Bloody hell. Did you eat at the corner shop? No one eats at the corner shop. Let alone *seafood* at the corner shop."

"*Urk*," I said, as convincingly as I could, and ripped myself away from the bush. It felt like I left a good clump of my scalp behind along with my hair, but my yelp of pain must've worked in my favour, because Lise didn't tell me to hurry again.

I scuttled out of the flowerbed, dodging a cactus with spines as long as my hands and jumping a gaping flower that snapped at me hungrily as I passed. I wondered briefly what sort of specialty training the gardeners around here had — and how long they lasted. But then I was on the gravelled path, pulling the hood up over my head to hide both my face and the mess of my hair. I was out.

The sunset had crept in while I was kicking my heels in the mop room, the sun itself lost behind the heavy clouds and the streetlights already visible on the road beyond the hall. They didn't reach this far, though, and the gardens were deep and wild, the fading daylight and some strange luminosity in the plants themselves the only illumination.

"Don't like this," I whispered, scurrying down the nearest path, then immediately wished I hadn't spoken, because a soft whisper came back from the plants that felt too much like an answer. There was no wind back here to cause it, just the steady, melting drizzle.

"*Little witch.*" It wasn't a shout, just a low voice that seemed to uncurl right by my ear, breathing down my spine. "*Don't make me come after you.*"

Every hair on my arms made a concerted effort to desert me, and I had to swallow a scream. I spun around, expecting to feel one of those pale, long-fingered hands creeping up my arm towards my neck. No hand, and no Lise, and I spun around again, searching for her as a whisper of laughter caressed my cheek. I had the sudden, knee-weakening thought that it was pointless to run, that I should just sit down and wait for her. Then at least I'd know what the hell she was, and wouldn't that be better? To just face her, rather than be run down like an animal?

And I might've simply given up right there, but the whispering bushes seemed to take up the call, passing it between them across the garden, *little witch, little witch, little witch*, and the small, terrified animal that runs things in these situations took over. My big, thinking, *homo sapiens* brain was absolutely going to get my soul sucked out through my ear or something, so it was summarily demoted.

I bolted into the garden, gravel crunching under my trainers at what felt like an impossible volume. A grassy area loomed to my left and I veered into it, a smooth expanse that was probably meant for garden parties or croquet games, but which was currently playing host to some truly disturbing wicker sculptures. I glimpsed the library on the far side of it, light glowing through the roof like a beacon, and I had no idea if it was a safe haven or not, but at least it was cover. Lise was going to be on me any second. I put my head down and willed my startled legs to go faster.

Air rushed behind me, a vast intake of breath or the sound of something moving through at the pace of a thun-

dering train, and my hood blew off my head with the wind
of its passage. My legs suddenly remembered what a sprint
was, and that intellectually curious part of my brain that
was still considering if disembodied whispers and ghostly
freight trains were possible sat itself down and shut the
hell up. I charged straight for the library, hurdling a curva-
ceous stone bench and swerving around a wicker thing that
looked like the lovechild of an octopus and a badger.

That raging wind blasted past me again, whipping my
wet hair into my face painfully, but I didn't slow. I reached
the path on the far side of the green, almost slipping on the
loose surface and swallowing a scream but keeping my
balance. I aimed myself at the library doors and put everything I had into a final sprint.

This time, the wind was so close it made me think of
that beach by the airfield in the Caribbean where people
get blown over by the jet blast. It must feel like this. Its
passage buffeted me sideways as if someone had shoved
me, and I staggered off the path, one foot sinking into the
damp mulch of the flowerbeds and sending me off balance.
I went to one knee but popped straight up again, not
wasting time looking around for my attacker. The library
was so close. Another ten metres and I'd be inside, in with
the bats and the stack monsters, but at least not out here
with Lise, or whatever she'd set on me, and I'd be safe in
the library, libraries were safe place, or at least saf*er,*
and—

My rabbiting thoughts were cut off by a blow to my
back that sent me stumbling forward three or four paces,
doing big, cartoonish strides as I tried not to fall. For one
moment I thought I'd manage it, that I'd recover myself
and keep going, then my foot hooked some unseen
obstruction and I went down hard, hands outstretched, the
gravel shredding my palms and shoving the sleeves of my

hoody up as it attacked my arms. I crashed full-length to the ground, still sliding forwards, and wound up sprawled full-length on the path with the breath all but knocked out of me. I managed to roll over as I came to a stop, raising my bleeding hands as if I'd be able to fend off attack. The garden sang with threat and gravel scattered under swift feet, and I had a moment to think, *I should've gone for the ducking stool*, before hands closed on my shoulders.

I'd been caught.

TWENTY-ONE

Physics always applies

I LOOKED UP, EXPECTING TO SEE LISE'S TRANSLUCENT SKIN and horrifyingly even teeth, but instead there were a lot of *very* sharp, very uneven teeth, and big eyes narrowed with either concern or hunger, I wasn't sure which. Before I could react, Effie scooted backwards towards the library, dragging me with her so fast I could feel the back of my hoody disintegrating under me.

"No! Drop it! *Drop it!* Bad ghoul!" Lise shouted, and I craned my neck to see her loping down the path, moving with that same languid, big-cat grace I'd seen the night before. "It's not for you!"

Effie hissed and let go of my shoulders, then bounded over me, crouching on the path between me and Lise.

"Go back," Lise said, slowing her approach and pointing at the library. "Get back *now!* You're a *very bad ghoul*."

I clambered to my feet a little unsteadily, everything stinging. I seemed to have sacrificed a lot of skin to the path. I glanced at the library, the doors tantalizingly close, then back at Effie.

"Don't make me do it," Lise said, her voice slipping into something low and intimate, smooth as a razor at the throat.

Effie hissed, dropping deeper into her crouch, her hair hanging in lank, damp locks around her face, not backing down.

"Bloody ghouls. Always a problem," Lise said, her voice back to normal, and then she simply *blurred*, the movement so fast as to be all but unseen, there then not. Effie leaped straight up, flipping as she went, as if trying to vault over Lise. Lise remerged from whatever impossible plane of movement she'd been in right next to Effie, sending her spinning sideways into the bushes. Effie's snarl turned into a screech of pain as she crashed into one of the thorny plants, and Lise turned to me, a smile widening on her face before she blurred into a single smudge of movement.

I had no time to prepare, no time to think about what was happening at all, but that little, instinctive critter with its relentless commitment to survival was still in charge. I just dropped to my knees and snatched up a handful of gravel, hurling it straight at Darrowdale's oncoming, super-speedy police inspector. It wasn't a hard throw, not from my angle. And it was just *gravel*. The most it would've done to anyone moving at regular speed would've been to provoke them into yelling at me for being a git. It probably wouldn't've even stung unless I'd been lucky enough to hit them in the eye or something.

Lise wasn't coming at anything like normal speed, though. She was moving so fast the pressure wave of her approach made my ears pop. And I guess physics applies just as much to magical creatures as it does to anyone else — or some aspects of physics do, anyway.

I'd thrown the gravel high, and Lise met it face-first,

although I glimpsed one of her hands moving up to fend it off. But her hands weren't as quick as her momentum, and she took a solid hit to the forehead from one particularly well-aimed (or, rather, luckily thrown) stone. She stopped so hard the gravel kicked up under her feet, spraying over me like someone had skidded their bike to a stop at my feet. I yelped, covering my own face with both arms, and when I cautiously lowered them, Lise was prone on the ground, arms spreadeagled. I stood up, staring at her. Her hands were bleeding where she'd managed to stop most of the stones, one finger twisted back at an unnatural angle, and there was a hefty graze on her cheek. But the most impressive was the chunk of gravel embedded in her forehead, just above her eyes & right between them. It gave her a sort of cyclops look with her actual eyes closed.

I took a hesitant step towards Lise, straining to see in the low light. Her eyelids fluttered slightly, and now I could see her chest moving. Okay, that was good. I hadn't killed her. A whimper in the bushes caught my attention, and I turned towards it, swaying slightly. Everything hurt, and if Theodore was here, he would've had to go and have a little lie down at the sight of my torn palms and the blood seeping through the new rips in my jeans. But nothing appeared to be broken, and neither anything in the garden or the creepy police inspector had bitten me, which seemed like a win.

I picked my way to the edge of the flowerbed and found Effie tangled in the clutches of a rustling vine. Her arms and legs were already buried, and more coils were sneaking across her chest, the leaves damp and shivering in the dregs of light coming from the library. I looked around for a weapon of some sort, but it was hard to even spot if there was a handy stick in the dimness. I took my phone out (the screen had a new crack, but it still came on), and switched the torch on, shining it around hopefully. I didn't fancy sticking my hands in among those vines.

The moment the light touched the creeping tendrils they went limp, the leaves curling up and the coils relaxing, for all the world as if they were playing dead.

"Oh, *yes*." Finally a win. I shone the light straight at Effie, who hissed and squeezed her eyes closed. "Sorry." I kept the torch on her though, getting as close to the plant as I dared. It tried slapping me with a couple of vines, but when I didn't back away they collapsed, retreating into the shadows. Effie wriggled wildly, squirming out of the last few coils, and scrambled out of the flowerbed to join me on the relative safety of the path. She stood up, regarding me solemnly, patted my shoulder, then dropped into a crouch and peered at Lise, snuffling as if to catch her scent.

"Thanks for helping me," I said to Effie. "Um — I have to go and find my cat."

She looked at me sharply, then held her hands out, snapping them open and closed pleadingly.

"You still can't eat him. Although I'd be tempted to let you sometimes."

She hissed at that, then looked back at Lise. Her eyelids had stopped fluttering, and she frowned, half-raising one hand. Effie bared her teeth silently, then turned down the path and started towards the road.

I watched her and said, "Don't you need to go back to the library?"

She paused to look back at me, tipping her head towards the road with her eyebrows raised expectantly.

"Right," I said, and hurried after her before Lise could get any closer to consciousness. Did this mean I had a ghoul now? Or maybe it was the other way around. Either way, Jackie was unlikely to approve.

Jackie. The grimoire. Both of them still sitting there in the car. My brother still staking out the club. Jason still who knew where.

"Sodding hell," I whispered, and broke into a jog. Effie let me catch up, then loped along with me in a half-crouch, her movements effortless. We ran together through the dark, whispering garden and toward the street that would take us into the heart of Darrowdale, dark and damp and festering with magic.

EFFIE KEPT TO THE SHADOWS, ducking into gardens to avoid the pools of the streetlights, patchy though they were. I didn't copy her, not least because I lacked the grace to go flying over walls and fences with such ease. Plus, if the plants in these gardens were as aggressively inclined as those in the hall gardens, I didn't fancy adding any more damage to my already impressive collection of cuts and grazes. And that was assuming I could get out of whatever people-sized foliage traps there were. So I stuck to the pavement, keeping my hood up and my head down. At least Darrowdale was the sort of place where I could pass unnoticed even in this state. In Hollowbeck, I would've had half a dozen people already squabbling over whether to dose me with arnica, witch hazel, or aloe vera.

We were in that crepuscular time, the last vestiges of light draining away, the streets quiet as Darrowdale's daylight residents drew their curtains and settled in around tables, while those with a more nocturnal bent were still getting moving, dosing up on coffee and brushing their beards. It meant I wasn't dodging many people, but I felt awfully exposed too, jogging down the near-empty streets with Effie popping in and out of gardens next to me like my own personal meerkat.

But no one challenged us, or even paid us much attention. A couple hurrying back from town with their heads bent against the rain and their arms entwined crossed the road to avoid us, and a woman with an enormous dog just about got towed through a hedge as she tried to hold it back from chasing Effie, but otherwise our dash from the library went unremarked. Before long (although the stitch in my side informed me it was more than long enough, thank you very much), I was approaching the Witch's Howl with exaggerated casualness, trying not to pant too obviously. Effie walked next to me, shying away from lights and bumping into me occasionally. She was trying to stay upright, but every time a car door slammed or someone shouted, she'd drop back to all fours, arching her back like a cat.

"Ruiner?" I hissed as we approached the car I'd last seen him under. There was no response, and I looked up and down the street uncertainly. We were on the opposite side of the road to the Witch's Howl and a little further down, but I still felt very obvious. A lean, dark-skinned man was leaning against the wall outside the bar, under the shelter of the awning. He had a cigarette in one hand and a beer in the other, like he was just having a smoke break, but I saw him glance across at us. Of course, he could've just been wondering about the tattered woman and the ghoul hissing at cars, but there was something too evaluating in his gaze.

"Ruiner?" I tried again, keeping my face turned away from the bar. Still no answer, no flash of grey fluff, and I dropped to my knees to peer under the parked cars. Sod the guy across the road. I'd tell him I dropped my keys if he asked.

The tarmac under the car was empty of everything except leaf litter. Darrowdale was oddly tidy for a creepy town. Maybe exiled and troublesome magic-workers were quite environmentally minded.

Effie made a questioning sound, and I looked at her. She was crouched next to me, her shoulder almost touching mine, and she looked from me to the ground, eyebrows raised. She had an angular, pretty face, if one didn't mind the excess of teeth and enormous eyes.

"Ruiner," I said to her. "The cat. He's not here."

She blinked at me in a manner that said, *well, obviously*.

"He was here," I explained. "He was watching for someone. I was meant to get the car and come back to meet him."

A stolid stare.

"He's not actually a cat."

She rolled her eyes at that, so evidently ghouls weren't so easily fooled. Which made me wonder if The Dealer was a ghoul too, although I hadn't seen him climbing over any ceilings. Maybe magical creatures were just more perceptive than the average human. It wouldn't be hard. I straightened up, looking across the road, but the man at the door had vanished, whether to report back or simply because he'd finished his cigarette break. I sighed, and took my phone out, poking at it uselessly. Still no signal, and nothing in the call log to show how Jason had called me. The last call still showed as my one to Mum, before we even went to Hollowbeck, and my stomach twisted with guilt. I needed to check on her.

But I needed to find my brother first, and standing here wasn't doing that. The only thing I could think of was that he'd gone looking for me when I hadn't come back, so I shoved the phone back into my pocket and hurried toward town. Effie stayed with me, and I found myself breaking into a jog. Time was running out. I could feel it. Darrowdale was tightening around us, a sea anemone trapping its prey, and I had a horrible feeling that rather than trying to sneak out again, I was wandering around banging on its slippery walls, while the escape hatch got smaller and smaller. I dodged around an elderly woman walking a three-headed goose, giving her a wide berth as I pushed myself to go faster. It was going to be okay. There was still time. Ruiner would be at the car. He had to be.

The car was where I'd left it, although the tree above had apparently decided now was a good time to divest itself of its leaves, and the roof and bonnet were wearing a blanket of dead foliage. I called Ruiner again as we approached, worry making my voice too sharp and too loud, but he didn't appear. My stomach rolled over slickly as I took the car key from my pocket. Maybe Hat Guy had left and he'd followed him, but it was hard to feel convinced of that. Not with that relentless sense of a trap closing in.

My car's remote door lock was finicky at the best of times, so I tended to use the key. I slotted it into the lock, turned it, and stopped, frowning. Then was no clunk, no reassuring grind of old tumblers. I rolled the key back the other way, and the lock clunked shut.

"Oh, bollocks," I whispered, and unlocked it again, hauling the door open. I had locked it. I *had*. I all but dived across the seat, shoving my hand underneath it. "Jackie? Jackie!"

She was gone. The grimoire was gone. Ruiner was gone. I still didn't know where Jason was. And, far too close behind us, Lise would be starting her hunt. I pressed both hands to my forehead and folded into the seat, tears hot behind my eyes and starting to spill down my cheeks.

What did I do? Where did I go? I had no allies, no back-up, *nothing*.

"We're completely shafted," I whispered to the car, and it gave back nothing but silence.

I don't know how long I would've sat there if Effie hadn't tugged my arm. I looked at her, crouched beside the car with the rain plastering her hair to her scalp. Her fore-head was furrowed, and she tugged my arm again, looking down the street then back.

"I know," I said. "But if we leave, I might not be able to get back in. And I don't know where to start looking for Ruiner. I don't even know if he's gone somewhere of his own accord or if someone nabbed him."

She petted my shoulder, a clumsy, uncertain touch.

"Can you find him?" I asked. "Can you track him or something?"

She wrinkled her nose at that, so the answer was apparently no.

"How about the book?" I suggested. "You live in the library. Can you find a book?"

She bared her teeth at that, and I supposed that her living in the library might have been less from desire and more from it simply being how things happened. Some-where she was put, or forced to stay, or had no choice about.

"So what do we do?" I asked, but she wasn't listening. She'd stiffened, her back straightening, staring down the street. If she'd been Ruiner, her ears would've been back. Her teeth were definitely bared. "What?"

She didn't answer, just grabbed my arm, tugging me out of the car. I let her, shoving the door shut behind me.

"Is it Ruiner?" I asked, and she shook her head violently, pulling me towards a concrete path that ran between two of the shops. It smelled as if it was used as much as a loo stop as it was a thoroughfare, but I followed the ghoul. Other than her desire to eat my brother, she was the most trustworthy person I'd encountered here. At least she was honest about wanting to eat him. More people could do with that. It'd save a lot of miscommunication.

"What—" I started, and she hissed, pulling me down to her level and putting a hand over my mouth. Her eyes were opaque pools that reflected the streetlights, and I could feel her trembling. I huddled against the smelly wall of the shop, my own hands starting to shake.

What the hell scared a *ghoul?*

TWENTY-TWO

Breaking, entering, & minotaurs

WE CROUCHED JUST INSIDE THE PASSAGEWAY, STARING AT each other. Effie still had her hand over my mouth, and she smelled of rain and damp books. I pulled away gently, putting my finger to my mouth to show I'd be quiet. She copied me, then shuffled around to peer out at the street. We were only a couple of metres in from the pavement, but the shadows were deep in the skinny snicket, and I figured that if Effie felt we were safe enough here from whatever was coming, she was probably right. Either that, or she knew she could run faster than me and would simply push me into its path and leg it. That was always possible, too.

For a little while nothing happened, and I just listened to my shaky breathing and tried not to think about what was on the wall we were leaning against. Just as I was wondering if Effie was playing some strange game of her own, a car pulled up on the street outside, sliding out of the rainy dark and coming to a halt next to my old Volvo. It was low-slung and looked somehow seamless, its tinted windows melting into its dark, glossy flanks as if one had grown from the other. Its engine was low and wicked-sounding, and it sat rumbling next to my car like a shark nudging up to a geriatric walrus.

At first no one emerged from the car, and it just sat there purring in a self-satisfied manner, but finally the driver's door opened soundlessly. I caught a glimpse of an interior gleaming with leather and low amber light, and Lise got out. She looked as well-groomed and unflustered as ever, but there was a red indent in her forehead the size of a one-pound coin, and the scrapes on her cheek stood out violently against her pale skin. I wondered why she hadn't run here, given the speed of her. Or maybe she needed the car to haul me back to the dungeon.

Lise leaned down to peer into my car, then straightened again, her gaze drifting towards our hiding place. "Hello, little witch," she called, her voice low and soft. "Come out, come out, wherever you are."

I had an absurd urge to jump out, waving like a beauty pageant contestant. It was too like the urge that had made me want to stop and wait for her in the hall gardens, which seemed unfair. Surely she could've just chosen one talent out of super-speed *and* persuasive suggestions.

"You want to be careful with that ghoul," Lise continued, still not moving. "She might be helping you now, but she can't help herself. Ghouls do what ghouls do."

Effie looked at me, baring her teeth in what was probably meant to be a reassuring smile but which missed the mark somewhat.

Lise finally moved, walking to the front of my car. A small grimace crossed her face, barely noticeable, and when I watched closely there was a hitch to her step. It was tiny, but it explained the car. Super-speed was evidently off the cards, at least for the moment. Or she wanted me to think it was. Lise stopped at the front of the old Volvo and bent down by the wheel. There was a tearing sound, then the soft whistle of air leaving the tyre. My poor car slowly listed towards the inspector while I closed my eyes and swore softly.

Lise walked around the bonnet and leaned down next to the other front tyre. She placed her hand on it and casually sank her red nails into the rubber, as if it were no more than a Styrofoam replica. The air whooshed out, and the nose of the car sank.

"I'm not going to hurt you, little witch. Although I *should*, given what you did to me. But come on out and I'll simply deliver you out of town, safe and sound." Her voice dripped warmth, and seemed very mismatched to that pale skin, ghostly in the streetlights. She could've been carved from ice. Effie put a hand on my arm, and I was startled to find I'd been leaning forward. I pressed myself back to the wall, giving the ghoul a grateful look.

Lise walked stiffly down the side of the car, her gait less big cat and more simple human, although I didn't doubt she could still move fast enough if she had to. All she had to be was faster than me, after all, and that wasn't hard.

"Do you think you can hide from me? In my town?" She stopped next to the rear tyre, placing her hand on it and giving it the same vicious treatment before circling the back of the car. "And for what? I won't have troublemakers. Especially not Hollowbeck ones." There was a growl in her voice as she said *Hollowbeck*, and she grabbed the final tyre so tightly it gave an alarmed pop, the back of the car juddering. She really hadn't needed to do that. I only had one spare, like normal people, and I hadn't checked it for so long it was probably flat anyway.

I looked down the little pathway. I couldn't see the end, but the longer we stayed here, the more likely we were to be dragged away by the scruff of our necks. And Lise might *say* she wouldn't hurt me, but the whole crushing tyres thing wasn't making me feel inclined to believe her. We needed to go.

It was dark in the alley, deeply so, and I took one cautious step sideways, thinking I'd keep my back to the wall and shuffle along that way. My foot hit something, and a bottle rolled away with a clatter that seemed to bounce off the walls, multiplying painfully.

"*Bollocks,*" I hissed, and Lise looked towards us, less with surprise than amusement.

"Come out, come out," she called, her voice a singsong. "Come along, little witch."

I turned to run down the path, and never mind what I tripped over in the dark, only to see a huge, indistinct form charging down it towards us, drawn by the sound of the bottle. The faint light from the street lit powerful shoulders and slid off sharp, wicked-looking horns as the sound of pounding feet filled the air. Effie screeched, and I think I made a pretty similar sound. Both of us spun around and bolted for the street.

We came out of the snicket at a dead sprint, Effie using her hands to help her along, me just trying not to trip on anything. Lise stepped out to intercept us, and Effie went straight over her, touched down on the roof of my car with both hands, and flipped herself back towards Lise again. The inspector's attention was on me as she reached out, and Effie's bare feet caught her hard, one to the back of the head and one to the shoulders, sending her sprawling sideways.

I dodged her as she fell and kept running, bolting across the street while a bellow went up behind us. I risked a glance back to see Lise scrambling up, and the beast pounding out of the pathway. Given those horns, I'd been expected a bull, although what the hell a bull was doing lurking in a back alley was anyone's guess.

Instead, emerging into the light as Lise threw herself into her car, was an actual, hulking, black-furred minotaur. Head down, snorting in fury, eyes narrowed, and hands clenched into fists at its sides. It stomped its feet under its … under its spaghetti-strap, floral print maxi dress? I blinked, wondering if I'd hit my head at some point, and Effie grabbed my arm, trying to haul me across the road. I stumbled but stayed where I was, still watching as the minotaur hooked their hands under the side of Lise's car and heaved, lifting two wheels off the ground and struggling to flip it. A slight man wearing round, wire-rimmed glasses ran out of the alley behind the minotaur and yelled, "Dafni! Dafni, sweetheart, please don't!"

She ignored him, dropping the car so hard it bounced wildly, and I glimpsed Lise through the windscreen bracing herself inside. Dafni grabbed the car's frame again, huge shoulders straining, heaving it up.

"*Daf!* That's the inspector! You can't do this!"

She paused, looking at him, snorting so hard I could see the steam rising from her nostrils in the cool air.

"I know people keep … defiling our back wall. But we can rise above it."

She didn't put the car down, but she didn't overturn it, either, and Effie pulled me so hard I almost fell.

"*Cat,*" she hissed at me, and I finally looked away from the minotaur, startled.

"You can talk?"

"Cat!"

"Yes. Yes, cat." I let her pull me away, and we ran across the road. She was still pulling me with her as we passed the front of the Crafty Cauldron. The displays were all gone, tucked inside, and the windows were dark. I stopped suddenly, and Effie lost her grip on me. She spun around, snapping her hands, and I looked at her. "If Edith is behind this, we need to look. Maybe she's even got Ruiner and Jason in there, or something that'll tell us where she's holding them. The grimoire and Jackie, too."

Effie shook her head wildly, hair flying.

"I know this is a really bad idea, but let's see, okay?" I didn't wait for her to answer, just turned and ran to the side of the building, heading down the alley while Lise was still otherwise occupied, and before my nerve could break.

Effie gave a very expressive groan and followed.

THE WINDOWS at the back of the shop were uncurtained, spilling light across the bare flagstones on the back patio, and I stayed at the corner of the building for as long as I dared, watching for shadows inside. I could still hear Dafni stomping around across the street, and her partner pleading with her, but it wouldn't be long before Lise was out, and I had to assume she'd seen where I was going. When I couldn't see anyone inside, I led the way to the low gate and onto the patio, trying to stick to the shadows as we edged up to the nearest window. It was the one over the sink in Hollowbeck, and it was the same here, the kitchen's contents no more nefarious than an off-brand pack of chocolate fingers and a couple of unwashed mugs. As much of the room as I could see was empty, and I sneaked past the door to check the window to the other side, which gave me a partial view of the sitting area. No one by the hearth, and the door to the hall was closed.

I tried pushing up the sash window, but it didn't budge. I went back to the one above the sink, but that was locked as well. I swore, and looked at Effie, who tilted her head slightly, then tried the door handle. It turned easily, and swung open onto the smoke-scented interior with only the tiniest creak.

"Oh. Thanks." I peered inside, but the room was as empty as it had appeared. I crept in, Effie following me with her bare feet silent on the stone flags. I had a moment of dislocation at the almost-but-not-quite sameness of the place. The same big table. The same deep sofas. The same giant cauldron lurking in the hearth. But it was all off by a degree — the colour of the wood, the shade of the cushions, the different herbs dying over the hearth. It was like being in a dream version of the Cosy Cauldron, and I found myself waiting for the walls to blossom flowers, or for eels to swim out of the rug, or tentacles to start flopping out of the cauldron. Although that wasn't so farfetched, really.

But nothing happened, and I hurriedly dug through the piles of recipe books on the table. Unsurprisingly, there was no grimoire, just *How to Use Toxic Herbs for Good Reasons!* and *Sure Remedies for Born Enemies*, which I quite fancied reading. I hurried into the seating area, checking under the sofas and scanning the shelves. Of course it wasn't here. If she did have it, she was hardly going to just leave it lying around. She'd probably be keeping it with her, just as I had. And there was also no handy note on the fridge, saying *Don't forget to take sandwiches to Jason in my private dungeons at 15 Witchcraft Drive*, or something like that. Why couldn't people be more helpful?

I looked at the door to the hall. The office should be down there, just before the shop. It was the most likely place to find something, although I still wasn't sure what I was hoping for. But there had to be *something*. I was running blind, and the place seemed to be empty. It was the best chance I had.

I opened the hall door a crack, peering through the gap. The hall was dark, the shop dimly lit by the streetlights beyond it. I listened. No movement, no voices, nothing but the warm scent of citrus and rosemary, the lingering remnants of a salve or tonic. The Cosy Cauldron never smelled quite so good. Starlight and I had too many near-disasters, so the best we achieved was a whiff of burnt toast by way of ambiance.

I looked around for Effie — then jumped as I found her peering down at me from the wall behind the door. "I'm going to check the office," I whispered to her.

"Cat," she said.

"We'll find him," I said, with more confidence than I felt. I eased into the hall, leaving the door open behind me so I could run for it if I turned out to be wrong about no one being here. I craned my neck as I went past the stairs, peering up, but there were no lights on that I could see.

I made it into the office without anyone jumping out at me and looked around at the crowded shelves. Crowded, but not cluttered. Everything seemed to have its place and was very firmly in it. I could tell at a glance that the grimoire wasn't here. Just file boxes and accounts folders, neatly labelled with months and years, and excess stock stored in carefully labelled tubs. I checked the desk drawers anyway, but even the top, traditionally cluttered one was fitted with an organiser tray, paperclips in one section, rubber bands in another, Post-Its piled next to them. I scowled and moved a paperclip in with the rubber bands, then shut the drawer again. I could try upstairs, but I was wasting my time. Edith was too neat, too careful. Nothing was going to give her away.

I got up from the chair, and as I did so the voices

pounced on me. I almost screamed, clutching my chest with one hand like a scandalised maiden aunt, and my phone started ringing at the same time, as if the voices were too impatient to mess around with teasing me this time. I pawed the phone out of my pocket and tapped answer on the predictably blank screen.

I put the phone to my ear gingerly. "Hello?"

"*Heeere's Jason!*" the voices bellowed, then subsided into giggles.

"Morgan?" Jason said. He sounded breathless.

"Yes! Can you hear me?"

"Finally! I've been trying and trying—"

"Yes, I know. Are you okay?"

"I mean, so far. But why're you taking so *long?* Morgs, I'm really in trouble here." He was whining, and I looked at Effie, clinging to the wall by the door. She rolled her eyes.

"Where are you? You were cut off before."

"The laser tag range. You have to come *now*. On your own."

"Who's with you? Is it Edith? Grace?"

"*Doot-doot*," a voice said cheerfully.

"Jason!"

"*Doot-doot-DOOT-DOOT-D—*" the voice was all but screaming, and I jerked the phone away from my ear, hitting disconnect. A little giggle drifted through the air, and I looked around uneasily. It had to be Edith, didn't it? Who else would know about the grimoire? And it had to be about that, didn't it? And where the hell was Ruiner?

I rubbed my hands over my face and growled, "*Git*."

"Cat?" Effie suggested, and I looked up at her, curled around the light fitting in the ceiling with her hair hanging down towards me.

"I have no bloody idea," I said.

TWENTY-THREE

A bike & a chance

I STOOD THERE IN THE MIDDLE OF THE OFFICE, MY BRAIN stuttering from one impossibility to the next, trying to figure out whether to just serve myself up on a plate at the laser tag place — because if anyone knew how to kill me in just the right way to claim the grimoire, it'd be Edith — or to try and get help, but *how*, and what help? The only person I could think of was The Dealer, and the only thing he wanted was the bloody book too. On the other hand, if it got Ruiner back ... but there I was assuming Edith actually had Ruiner, and for all I knew he'd got bored of waiting and had wandered into the Witch's Howl looking for a catnip fix.

I pressed my hands to my forehead, ignoring the pain from my scoured palms, and wondering how long I had before Lise stormed in to grab me.

I probably would've stayed there, sinking deeper and deeper into indecision, if Effie's head hadn't snapped towards the door. She hissed, and waved at me urgently. Someone was coming, and whether it was Lise ready to strap me to a rocket and fire me out of town, or Edith come to drag me out by the ear, hanging around wasn't going to achieve anything. I hurried to the door and paused, looking up at Effie.

"Which way?"

She skittered out onto the hall ceiling, scampering to the back of the building without hesitating, and I sprinted after her. A moment later we were letting ourselves out into the chilly night, and I hugged my tattered hoody closer to me as we ran across the patio and back into the alleyway. Only once we were out of sight of the kitchen windows did I stop and take the phone out again. I hit dial and said into the silent handset, "Hollowbeck Library."

I waited, but there was nothing, not even a titter. Whatever magic Edith was working to call me, it evidently only worked one way.

"Okay. Okay, think."

Effie crouched in front of me, watching me with a frown, then straightened up and patted my head gently, as if trying to help me kickstart things.

"Thanks. Okay, we need help. We do, right?"

Effie showed me her teeth, which I took to mean she was unconvinced.

"We definitely need a lift. We can't walk to the laser tag. It'll take us half the night." I looked at the phone again. It was pointless. Even if I managed to get hold of Ben, and got him to bring Theodore, it'd take hours for them to get here. Hours in which Lise would have time to hunt me down and do to me what she'd done to my tyres, if Edith didn't get there first. Which left only one option. I needed to make a deal.

"Come on," I said to Effie, checked the street both ways, and headed across it, angling towards the side street that would take us to the Witch's Howl, and the Oubliette above. I had barely reached the middle of the road when she grabbed me, hefting me onto her shoulder in a fireman's lift. I managed a yelp of surprise before we were on the roof of a parked car, then airborne again, leaving a vast dent behind. We slammed into a roof and she grabbed the chimney with one hand, hunkering down in its shelter and sliding me off her shoulder.

"*Huh?*" I managed, which was as close as I could get to demanding to know what the hell was going on, while also trying to dig my fingernails into the moss-encrusted roof.

"Cat," she said, then she was gone again. I gave a strangled scream and tried to become one with the tiles. Below me, someone else yelped, then Effie was back.

"Cat!" she said happily, and thrust Ruiner at me.

"Ruiner!"

"*What the hell—*" He was cut off by a swirl of vast wings, and I flattened myself to the roof, trying to hold onto the treacherous surface and pin Ruiner down at the same time as we were buffeted by the breeze of whatever beast was attacking us. My brother's swearing hit ear-shattering pitch, and Effie leaped over us, hissing in fury. I gave a strangled scream as my fingers slipped on the tiles, and we started to slide. I had a moment of horrifying certainty that we were going to simply keep going, pick up speed and plunge over the edge, and I clawed at the roof with my feet and free hand so hard I felt like I should've been able to bust through to the rafters beneath.

Somehow I managed to get some purchase, my whole body pressed to the roof like a starfish, and we ground to a stop. "*Effie!*" I screamed, not caring if Lise was lurking in the street below. Arrest felt preferable to free-fall.

"Why are we on the *roof?*" Ruiner wailed. He had every claw he owned embedded in my arm, from the feel of things.

"I don't know!" I yelled back

"Why are you both shouting?" a curious voice asked, and I was suddenly aware that the rush of air from the wingbeats had stopped. I lifted my cheek carefully off the tile and squinted at the ridge of the roof. The barista from Bewitching Boos was squatting on it in full soul-eating mode, all big beard and needle-like teeth and huge eyes, with a set of absurdly gauzy wings drifting softly behind him. They looked too delicate to survive the touch of a finger, but it seemed they could create a hell of a breeze.

I stared at him, and went back to my previous, eloquent gambit. "*Huh?*"

"Jim," he said. "Can you call off your ghoul, please?"

I tried lifting my head a little more to see where Effie was, then gave another little shriek as I slid a bit further down the roof.

"*Stop moving!*" Ruiner yowled.

"Help me," I begged Jim.

He cocked his head, forehead furrowing gently. "You won't fall."

"It bloody well feels like I will." All the breath was being squeezed from me by the effort of holding on.

"You're a witch. Just float down." He got up and strolled casually to the edge of the roof, his booted feet surefooted on the tiles. I saw Effie then, clinging to his back and trying various angles to get her teeth into his neck, but his wings were in the way.

"I'm not that good of a witch! Please help me!" My fingers and toes were cramping with how hard I was jamming them into the roof, every muscle shaking.

He turned to look at me, frowning slightly, and Effie gave up on biting. She let go and scampered towards me, shouting, "Git!" over her shoulder at Jim.

He raised his eyebrows, looking at me.

"I don't know where she learned that."

"Cat," Effie said, picking up Ruiner in one hand, then grabbing the back of my coat in the other and dragging me up to the ridge of the roof. I clutched it gratefully, scrabbling up until I could hook both elbows over it and feel a bit more secure.

I peered over my shoulder at Jim, who was watching with a vaguely bemused air. "What're you doing up here? I didn't eat anything!"

"That's quite hurtful," he said. "Fae can't help being Fae."

"You could try not setting traps for people."

He shrugged. "It's just my nature. And in answer to your question, I thought she was going to eat the cat."

I looked at Effie, squatting on the roof with Ruiner bundled in her arms. "Cat," she said, baring her teeth at Jim. He bared his back.

"Why were you worried about the cat?"

"Well, I don't like seeing animals hurt. Plus he's a little unusual. And really sweary."

"Oh, excuse *me*," Ruiner said. "But being grabbed off the street by a bloody Fae requires more than *meow*."

"I only *grabbed* you because I saw you wandering around on your own. Darrowdale's not exactly safe for that sort of thing when you're that size." Jim looked at me. "I was going to keep hold of him until you turned up, but then Effie went and snatched him."

I looked at Effie, who licked Ruiner's head. He wrinkled his snout, ears back. "I'd quite like to get down now."

I wriggled myself further up the roof, until I could grab the chimney and sit next to it. Jim ambled up the slope and sat down next to me, regarding me with interest.

"Are you sure you can't float?" he asked me.

"Very sure." I examined him warily. His wings were

delicate confections, glittering with pale rainbow colours, and softly translucent between fragile-looking, bony supports. They were big, even concertinaed together, but they still looked like they shouldn't've been able to support a toddler, let alone a large, well-muscled barista.

He smoothed his beard, petting the little silver lizards nestled in it, who were goggling at me with bright, round eyes. "I thought you must be a really powerful witch, having two familiars. Plus Edith got all upset when she saw you, like she felt you were a real threat." He watched me, waiting for an answer, and I was suddenly aware of how precarious my perch was. I wondered if Effie would be quick enough to save me if Jim decided to pitch me off the roof to appease the town witch.

"Where is Edith?" I asked.

"At home, probably. She tires easily now her magic's been drained."

I stared at him. "Now it's what?"

"Now it's gone. When she got chucked out of Hollow-beck, she was stripped of her magic. It's part of the punishment when someone's exiled. Pretty harsh, if you ask me."

This was new. "Does that mean Edith's not a witch anymore?"

Jim shrugged. "I'm not an expert on human magic, but I think so. Not a witch with power, anyway. She can build it up again, but it'll take time."

I was torn between feeling vaguely guilty, horrified at the thought of anyone being *drained* (and wondering how something like that happened, and if it was anything to do with Theodore's vampirism), but also a little relieved. At least I wasn't dealing with a super-strong witch. Although, to be fair, even a not-very-strong witch was going to be a challenge for me.

Then something occurred to me. "But isn't she the town witch? I saw her at the Crafty Cauldron."

Jim snorted. "Sure, she works there. But Luna's the town witch."

"Who?"

He waved vaguely. "She'll be around. Spends a lot of time forest bathing, and not much in the shop. She had Edith making some salves and basic charms, easy things that don't need much magic."

Now it made even more sense that Edith was after the book. After all, if she had no magic, it'd be a great way to get it back. But if she no longer had power, it meant she couldn't do that horrifying thing she'd done in Hollowbeck, where she'd sucked all the air out of the room and made it feel like we were burning alive. She couldn't do *anything*, and I was pretty sure I could take a woman who looked like she was in her sixties. With a bit of luck and the element of surprise, anyway. Or, preferably, I could sic Effie on her, if the ghoul was still feeling helpful. Suddenly this wasn't an impossible rescue mission. This could *work*. I had to get to the laser tag.

"Thanks for looking after Ruiner," I said.

"I didn't need *looking after*," Ruiner snapped. "Dragonfly boy here just up and *grabbed* me like I'm some alley cat."

"I could tell you weren't that," Jim said. "But I just thought you were a familiar until you started telling me what I'd apparently done to my mother."

I winced. "Sorry. Being a cat hasn't improved his disposition."

Ruiner huffed, putting both front paws against Effie's chest and straining away from her. She pouted. "Can we get off this sodding roof yet?"

I looked at Jim. "Are you letting us go?"

He shrugged. "Effie brought you up here, not me." He looked from me to Ruiner. "I heard you brought down Masters of Mayhem. The carnival."

"That was sort of an accident," I said.

"Yeah, that makes sense. You're not quite what I expected."

Before I had time to feel properly insulted, he got up and wandered off the edge of the roof, his wings swirling into a muted rainbow of movement as he drifted gracefully to the ground.

I watched him go, then looked at Effie. "I can't float. You know that, right?"

"Cat," she said helpfully, then grabbed the back of my hoody in one hand, shoving Ruiner at me. I just had time to catch him before she dragged me over the edge of the roof and straight down the wall, the ground coming up alarmingly fast, but nowhere near as fast as it could have. A moment later I was standing somewhat unsteadily on the pavement just down from where my poor, wounded car was parked. Dafni the minotaur had vanished, as had Lise's car, although there was some shattered safety glass on the ground. Jim was waiting for us, looking fully human again, his hands tucked into the front pockets of his jeans.

"What're you up to now, then?" he asked.

"Um..." I had Ruiner, and Edith had no power. We didn't need The Dealer anymore. "We need to find Edith."

"Sod that," Ruiner said, clambering to my shoulder. "Let's get the car and get out of town before Lise catches up to you."

"Can't," I said flatly.

"Look, forget bloody Jason—"

"No, *can't*. I've got four flat tyres. And Edith has ... my bag."

"Your *bag?*" Ruiner demanded.

"And everything in it."

"Yes, genius, I got that." He sighed deeply, his whiskers tickling my ear.

"I didn't get it," Jim said amiably. "But Edith lives in a guest house over that way." He waved vaguely in the direction of where Petunia's WitchInn' would've been in Hollowbeck. "If the shop's shut, she might be there."

"We need transport," I said.

He frowned. "It's not that far. Are you hurt? You do look a little ... tatty." He looked me up and down curiously, and Ruiner leaned over on my shoulder to take in my battered clothing and assorted injuries for the first time.

"Bloody hell," he said. "Did Lise do this?"

"No. Small altercation with a garden. But I really do need transport." I looked at Jim. "I don't suppose you have a car we could borrow?"

He snorted. "Saved your cat and now you want to borrow my car? *And* you wouldn't eat my shortbread?"

"I'm sure it was lovely," I said. "I just wanted to keep hold of my soul."

He rolled his eyes. "Your *soul*. I'm not The Dealer. It'd just have been a few hundred years of dancing. And I'm a good dancer." He pirouetted, demonstrating.

"Sorry. I have plans."

He laughed at that, then shrugged. "Look, it's just habit. No hard feelings, right?"

"Not if you let me borrow your car."

"Well, I would, but I don't have one. You can borrow that, though." He pointed at Bewitching Boos, and I spotted a town bike leaning against the wall, shiny black and chrome with a big tan seat, a parcel rack, and a basket on the front. "Best get moving before Lise comes back around. She doesn't lose people. Not for long, anyway."

I garbled my thanks, already jogging for the bike with Effie scuttling after me and Ruiner wobbling on my shoulder.

Of course it had to be a bloody bike, rather than something that could get us there quick enough to surprise Edith. But it was a chance. And sometimes all you need is a bike and a chance.

TWENTY-FOUR

Midnight riders

JIM'S BIKE WAS RATHER NICER THAN STARLIGHT'S. IT HAD gears that worked, for a start, and the chain wasn't threatening to come off every time we went over a bump. It also had a little headlight on the front, but I didn't use it. I felt we were attracting enough attention as it was without carting our own personal beacon around with us. The seat was too high for me to be able to reach the ground from sitting, but I could manage the pedals, and I didn't want to take the time to change it. I just dumped Ruiner in the basket and pushed off, standing on the pedals to get us powering down the street. My brother perched in the basket without complaint, ears back and snout wrinkled against the ever-present drizzle and the wind of our passage, and Effie ran alongside us, taking to walls and rooftops whenever the fancy took her. It was like being accompanied by some sort of Labrador/spider hybrid.

Getting out of town was nerve-wracking. Lise's shark-like car hadn't reappeared, and I still didn't know what — or rather who — Effie had hauled me out of the shop to avoid. Edith could be watching me from behind the darkened display windows, waiting to run out and grab me. Although at least probably not to zap me with a spell, which was a relief.

But Jason had said the laser tag place, so that's where we were going. There was no point poking around here. It'd be too much of a coincidence for Edith to snatch the book and someone else entirely to have snatched my ex-husband, so I was working on the assumption finding one would lead to the other. We were getting out of town.

Straight down the main road seemed like a good way to get picked up by Lise, and while there was only one route in and out of town, I could at least stay off it for as long as possible. I swung the bike into a side street, planning to do a few blocks in a somewhat more circumspect manner. But a block isn't really a block unless the town's been laid out by someone with an eye for advance planning, which means plenty of the regular, non-magical small villages and towns in Cumbria weren't great at them. When somewhere's sprouted with the same organic enthusiasm as a mushroom colony, a block can mean anything — and in a magical town like Darrowdale, that goes double.

I found myself pedalling frantically down an avenue of ghostly, groaning trees, trunks pulsing with luminescence while things laughed and tittered somewhere out of sight. There were no houses, no shops, just the palely glowing trees, seeming to move as I passed, so that I was scared to look back in case the road had been swallowed. Effie drew close to the bike, staying well away from the verges, and we shot through the gauntlet of trees as fast as my legs could manage.

A street loomed to our left, one that should, in theory, run parallel to the main road, and I turned into it so hard I almost fell, Ruiner yelping as he nearly tumbled out of the basket.

"Watch it!" he hissed.

"You want to do it?" I panted, and then we were wobbling into an area so different it was as if we'd just gone through a set change at a theatre.

Packed terraced houses lined both sides of the street, swallowing the pavement, their walls a patchwork of colours and warped dimensions. Terraced houses are characterized by their sameness, the fact that they're just one long building divided into different houses, but this was more as if someone had picked up a bunch of entirely random places and simply squeezed them together, with zero regard for if anything lined up. Some were one storey, others four or five, gabled and flat-roofed, with balconies and turrets and gargoyles, all of them leaning over the street with an alarming precariousness.

Lights burned in some of the windows, and music tumbled from others, and somewhere a man was repeatedly shouting, "Ho ho, lads!" with frantic cheerfulness as the scent of roasting meat drifted into the street, fragrant and repulsive all at once. It was dawning on me that the detour had not been one of my better ideas.

I took the next left I came across, less because I thought we'd gone far enough and more because I had the sneaking suspicion that, if I didn't get back to the main road soon, I could end up cycling the back streets of Darrowdale for all eternity, taking turn after turn through stranger and stranger neighbourhoods and never finding my way out.

I was a little more careful on the corner this time, slowing right down, although my back was itching with the sense of being observed. But nothing chased us or sent tentacles rushing out in pursuit, and the scenery changed as quickly as it had on the last corner, delivering us into an overwhelming scent of caramel and baking apples.

The road was lined with cute, compact log cabins with red curtains, and squat little white-washed bungalows sporting thatched roofs, and two-storey houses with chalky pink walls cross-hatched with heavy Tudor beams. They were all set back behind low wooden fences, the gardens a frenzy of pretty birdhouses and overflowing flowerbeds and welcome signs. Somehow they were even creepier than the terraces and ghost trees had been.

I kept to the centre of the street even as the toffee apple smell intensified and Ruiner put his front paws on the edge of the basket, standing up with his nose twitching. "Can you smell fish?"

"Cat," Effie said sternly, keeping pace with me easily, her eyes on my brother.

"I don't think it's real," I panted. The smell shifted, taking on the cinnamon-y, toasted oat scent of apple crumble, making me think of warm custard and cream held up as a shield against dreary days. I pedalled faster.

The main road appeared so suddenly it took me by surprise, and I jammed the brakes on, stumbling off the pedals. Ruiner almost fell out of the basket and gave me a dirty look as we halted at the T-junction, barely avoiding running down a very old man sitting in a small metal cart, being towed along by a stoic-looking pig. He looked me up and down as they trundled past, and said, "Bah."

The pig didn't say anything, but Effie spoke up from the lamp post she was clinging to. "Git."

The old man turned in his cart to glare at her as the pig plodded on. "*Bah*."

"*Git*."

"Good to see you helping expand her vocabulary," Ruiner said to me.

I ignored them all and pushed off again, pointing the bike out of town. The back streets experiment had at least gained us some ground towards the edge of town, where the houses were left behind and that one straight road ran through the cornfields to the cliff of buildings that held the valley. We didn't have many more options for hiding. I checked over my shoulder for Lise's car, but the streets were empty of it and every other, so I stood up to pedal harder, my heart going too fast for the physical effort to justify. I felt as if someone had pinned a target to me.

None of us talked again until the last of the buildings fell away behind us, and I sat down on the seat, changing down a gear to give my legs a bit of a break. "Bloody Jason," I complained. "This whole mess is all his fault."

"Told you to ignore the message," Ruiner said. "You have to stop trying to save everyone."

"Oh? And where would you be then?"

"I'm your brother. That's different."

"It really isn't. Anyway, what happened to you? Where did Hat Guy go?"

"I don't know. I didn't see him come out, but when you hadn't come back, I went to check on you. I saw the car was still there, so I went for a nosey into the coffee shop in case you'd sold your soul for an Americano. Next thing I know our mate Jim had bundled me up in a sweater and was asking me if I liked cream."

"You didn't have any, any did you?"

"Obviously not. I bit him, he squirted me with a spray bottle, and the next thing we were in a shouting match. He shut me in a bloody *box*, and only took me out just before Ghoulie here grabbed me off him." Effie glanced at him and made a little purring sound. Ruiner huffed. "To you too. Anyway, he was off to find you and give me back, so I suppose he was alright. Other than the box."

"He does seem pretty decent for someone who wants to steal everyone away for a hundred-year dance."

"Everyone's got their thing. Anyway — how the hell did you lose the book?"

I sighed. "I left it in the car when Lise grabbed me."

"You left it in the *car?*"

"It seemed safer. Remember the carnival and Aubrey getting hold of it?"

Ruiner didn't answer, and we rode on in silence. Fields spread out to either side of us, pocked with the round, glossy humps of wrapped hay bales, only just visible in the dark. I could see a wall of deeper shadow looming up ahead, the corn waiting to swallow us up, and I shivered, aiming the bike straight down the centre line. It made me feel marginally safer.

"I spoke to Grace," I said.

"*Grace? Really?*"

"Only she's not Grace. She's Faith, and she's the mayor."

Ruiner wrinkled his snout. "What?"

"They're identical twins."

"Absolute bollocks." He turned in the basket to look at me. "She and Edith are in it together. Got to be."

"It seems the most likely," I agreed. "But what can I do? I tried to call Ben from the library, and I thought someone answered, but I couldn't hear anything. And now on top of everything I've lost Jackie and the book."

"We have," he said absently, and I had the sudden urge to scritch his head, but I held back. He was still my brother, not actually a cat. "How did you get away from Lise?"

"Grace — Faith — told Lise to escort me out of town, and that I'd be banned from coming back. Only I sneaked out the bathroom window and now I think Lise would quite like to tear me into small pieces."

"Ah. So you've gone from being offered a very civilised retreat to starting a Hollowbeck/Darrowdale war in the space of one afternoon? I knew you were my sister."

"I haven't started a war," I protested. "And it's been two days."

"If Tango-tinted Theodore discovers someone wants to tear your head off, it will be war."

"Well, it's your fault too."

"How?" he demanded. "I was being held by the Fae Coffee King!"

"You're the reason Jason ended up here in the first place."

"Absolutely not. He did not learn about Darrowdale from me."

"Oh? Who from, then?"

"I don't know," he said. "And that's something we should both be worried about, actually."

I was still digesting that when Effie gave a hiss of warning, so close to me that I flinched. The bike wobbled wildly and Ruiner gave a squawk of alarm.

"What is it?" he demanded.

I checked over my shoulder, but there were no head-lights sliding down the road towards us. "Effie?" I asked.

She looked ahead rather than back, to where the road dived between the leaning, rattling husks of the corn. We were close enough to hear the rain sighing as it pattered down into the brown, slowly flaking stalks, and the road was nothing but a black river running between the cliffs of dead plant life. I stopped pedalling, sliding off the seat and putting both feet down as we coasted to a stop. None of us spoke, and the corn seemed to pull a little closer. The passage hadn't been this narrow when we'd driven in that morning, had it?

Effie's teeth were bared, and she spun to look back at town, then turned again to the corn, then again, moving ceaselessly, trying to see everywhere at once. Ruiner had a strikingly similar expression, and he'd hunkered down so low in the basket he was just a wide-eyed shadow. I licked my lips, my mouth suddenly dry.

"*Ring-ring!*" someone shouted. "*Ring-ring!*"

I swear the road behind us had been empty all the way to town. I was *sure* of it, but maybe there were side trails I hadn't seen in the dark, or secret, unsigned paths known only to kids, like some things are. Because suddenly they were just *there,* the pack on their bikes charging down the road towards us like a stampede, girls in rolled up jeans and boys in zipped-up tracksuit jackets, hair flying in the wind of their passage, legs pumping and arms braced on the handlebars. I glimpsed a very small boy on a flower-decaled BMX pedalling wildly to keep up, while the oldest girl popped a wheelie as she swept past me, teeth flashing with laughter.

"*Ring-ring!*" they chorused, and Effie just about tried to join me on the bike as the pack washed around us like a storm surge. "*Ring-ring!*"

"You've got one new voicemail," a skinny girl with beaded braids intoned, coasting past me with a chuckle. She flung a sheet of paper into the basket on top of Ruiner, who promptly attacked it. The pack reformed beyond us, arrowing toward the corn.

"Hey!" I yelled. "Hey, who gave you that?"

I got nothing back but a laughing "*Doot-doot-doot*" from the girl, and the little boy extended a hand behind him, suspiciously like he was giving me the finger, although it was hard to tell in the dark. Then they were gone, lost in the shadows of the corn, or back to their secret paths, vanished as quickly as they'd appeared. I grabbed the note off Ruiner, who'd already put teeth marks in it. I pulled my phone out and leaned down next to him so he could see, Effie huddling close to my shoulder.

The light of the torch from my phone revealed a line drawing of a phone at the top of the page, and the text at the bottom, *Someone called for you!*, just the same as the paper in Hollowbeck. The writing was different, though, in neat block capitals.

WE'RE COMING FOR YOU.

I turned the paper over, but there was nothing else. No name, no return number. No more details and no explanation.

"Well, that's just great," Ruiner said. "Sod the muppet. Leave the car. Just keep pedalling and let's get the hell out of here."

"I can't just leave Jackie. Or the grimoire, for that matter."

"Edith can't use it unless you give it up. And she can't force you to do that unless she gets hold of you, which is all the more reason to get out of here. And now we've got this?" He pointed his snout at the note. "Is it Lise? Edith? A bloody plant you upset?"

"It doesn't change anything. I can't just abandon Jackie. Even if that was an option, what if they kill her and that breaks my bond with the book? Then they've got all its power and all of Hollowbeck's deals." I looked at him levelly. "Including yours."

He huffed. "So what're we going to do? Just ignore the note and go up against a seriously experienced witch with no one but Jaws there?"

Effie bared her teeth at Ruiner.

"A witch with no powers anymore."

"A *desperate* witch, who's probably got herself some help. We saw Grace go to the shop. I bet the whole thing of telling Lise to escort you out was just a ploy. She knew you'd escape, and this way she can legitimately kill you off as having broken Darrowdale's laws."

"It has laws?"

"It does. And Lise keeps them. She probably would've just escorted you out before, but now you're an escaped prisoner who's refusing to leave her valley."

"And I did kind of make a minotaur trash her car."

Ruiner stared at me. "I think this role reversal's going a bit far."

"You're probably right." I looked back towards town. The road was still clear. "But we've come this far. I'm not losing Jackie."

"And the Muppet?"

"Eh. If we get him out, maybe he'll give me my books back."

"That's make everything *totally* worth it," Ruiner said, sinking back into the basket. "Especially given the mysterious note-writer."

He was right, of course. But that didn't change anything.

TWENTY-FIVE

Reunited & it feels no good

AS CREEPY AS THE STANDS OF CORN WERE, WE STILL ended up diving off the road into their cover twice when cars appeared on the road. One came out of town and roared past us with all the windows down and a confusing amount of people jammed inside, all bellowing that they were the real Slim Shady. The second car slid out of the avenue of corn ahead, bearing down on us from the borders of Darrowdale, headlights hungry eyes in the night. It was all but silent as it passed, cruising slow and smooth on the damp tarmac. I pressed myself deeper into the ditch that bordered the road, ignoring the ceaseless rustling of the corn, barely daring to watch the car pass. The tinted windows hid anyone inside, but there was no mistaking that car, especially not with a couple of smashed taillights and a missing side window.

But it didn't slow, and once the red embers of its lights had vanished, I dragged Jim's bike (distinctly muddied — I was going to have to find somewhere to give it a wash before I returned it) onto the road and swung back on.

We'd passed a couple of signs for the laser tag already, one of them showing a man being cut in two by a red beam. He was laughing delightedly, as was the guy shooting him, and I really hoped it was artistic license. No telling in this place, though.

I pedalled harder in the wake of Lise's car, painfully aware of how long it had already taken us to get this far. She was going to find me at some point, and I was surprised she hadn't already. Maybe Darrowdale's surveillance didn't work so well at night.

Finally another sign loomed out of the corn ahead, an arrow pointing down a gravel track that dived away from the road. *LEGENDARY LASER!* it announced. *TURN HERE FOR YOUR BEST GAME EVER!* The lights on the billboard were off, and a chain was pulled across the track, blocking it to cars. I got off the bike and dragged it under the chain while Ruiner clung to the basket and complained.

"You could get out," I said to him.

"Are you kidding? Something'll eat me."

"Cat," Effie said, making grabby hands.

"Like her," Ruiner said.

"She's not going to eat you. She's been very helpful." At least the second half of that was true.

"Can you maybe make friends with powerful witches who can break curses and other thinking creatures, rather than librarians and cat-hungry ghouls?"

"At least I make friends." I got back on the bike, looking at Effie. "Ignore him."

She looked from Ruiner to me and said, "Git?"

I burst out laughing, trying to smother it with one hand, and Ruiner put his ears back. "Can we just get the bloody book and get out of this place?"

"That is the plan," I said, once I had slightly better control of myself.

We followed the curve of the drive though the chattering wilderness of the corn, leaving the road behind. There were no lights and no more signs, only the sweep of star-scattered sky above us and the leaning, dusty plants to either side. I wondered about trying to sneak up on the place, but we were hardly equipped for a tactical assault, and I also had an idea that even if nothing in the corn tried to eat us, we'd likely end up so lost we'd never get out. So I just kept going, the bike's lack of suspension jarring my bones, until we rounded a corner and the laser tag building was revealed in front of us, crouching long and low on the other side of a rough car park.

It was a flimsy, insubstantial-looking place, with a slanting corrugated iron roof and walls that looked like some sort of prefab kit. It was raised off the ground and had a deck running along the front, two cars snuggled up to it. Another billboard sprouted from the roof, depicting a pack of three fatigue-clad figures chasing two others, while another lay on the ground, separated from his legs. All six were laughing, and the text read, *LEGENDARY!! PICK YOUR TEAM! DESTROY YOUR ENEMIES! (OR YOUR BOSS!)* Yellow spotlights lit it up, and fat orange bulbs strung from unevenly hung wires illuminated the front of the building. A man leaned against the wall, smoking a cigarette and staring vaguely off into the corn.

I'd stopped as soon as the place came into view, the darkness giving us some cover.

"What's the plan?" Ruiner asked, his voice low.

I stared at the building, not answering.

"Morgan? Do you have one?"

"I hoped something would come up," I admitted. "Isn't this more your sort of thing, anyway? Dodgy dealings and so on?"

"Maybe. But plans are more yours."

We looked at each other in the dark, then I said, "I just walk in and do the *I claim the grimoire* thing, like I did in the carnival?"

At the same moment he said, "Ghoulie and I sneak in the back and try to bust Jason out while you distract Edith?"

We considered each other's suggestions, then said together, "Both."

I held out a fist and he bopped it with a paw. "They're both terrible plans," he pointed out.

"Agreed," I said.

Ruiner jumped out of the basket and looked up at Effie. "No eating me."

She chattered her teeth at him in a way that almost promised she was going to eat something, then winked. They vanished into the corn and I took a deep breath, then pushed off, pedalling across the car park towards the building. The man straightened up and watched me come, not speaking until I got off the bike and put the kickstand down, then stood in front of the deck looking up at him.

"Hi," I said. "I think you're expecting me."

"Find your cat?" he asked, and I squinted at him.

"You're from the Witch's Howl," I said. "You were outside."

"I was." He flicked the stub of his cigarette into a bin and waved me up a set of creaking steps to the wooden deck.

"Why didn't you just grab me then?" I demanded as I joined him.

"From outside the club, when you'd been all chummy with The Dealer? I don't have a death wish." He sounded vaguely impressed, and as he reached for the door I saw a mark on his right hand. It was the spade off a playing card, torn down the middle, and formed from curling, ridged scar tissue. I knew that mark. I'd seen it on the dead man in Jason's kitchen, although I hadn't realised it at the time.

I pointed at it. "Is that an anti-Oubliette mark?"

He glanced at it. "It is. More reasons not to draw too much attention from The Dealer."

"Why're you hanging out on his doorstep, then?" Or around Edith, for that matter. Maybe she'd promised to remove the mark or something.

"Anyone can go to the Witch's Howl." He opened the door onto a room furnished with a couple of stained sofas, a listing coffee table, a stack of cheap metal stools, and three softly glowing vending machines. "I'm Stu, by the way."

"Hi Stu," I said, and walked past him into the room, trying to keep my breathing even. I hadn't seen Edith since she tried to kill me. I didn't even know how to prepare for a reunion like this. *Was* there a way to prepare to meet your almost-murderer? Stu shut the door behind me, staying outside, and I looked around warily.

A reception desk sat off to my right, just a high counter built out from the wall and equipped with a computer monitor. There was a door next to it that said *Private*, and souvenir caps and T-shirts, all declaring the wearer had survived Legendary Lasers, hung above the counter. One of the vending machines dispensed energy drinks, another miniatures of vodka and whisky, which seemed unwise, and a third contained chocolate bars and first aid supplies. Posters of people looking tough in fatigues papered the walls, and a very small sign said, *PLAYERS MUST TAKE ALL LOST ITEMS WITH THEM WHEN LEAVING*, which seemed confusing, until I read the even smaller print underneath. *Abandoned teeth, limbs, & organs cannot be reclaimed later*.

There was only one person inside, lying on one of the sofas with their feet up on its arm.

It wasn't Edith.

They had a rumpled shock of red hair, and light glinted on their glasses as they rose to their feet.

"*Connall?*"

"There you are," he said, his voice warm. "I was a bit worried when Lise spirited you off. This was going to be much more difficult if you were banned."

"But..." I pointed at him, as if he might not have realised what was happening. "You're the librarian!"

"Sure. But it's not the best income in the world, you know? Lots of time for research into other options, though."

He rubbed a hand through his hair, smiling at me, and my gaze fixed on the inkwell tattoo decorating his right hand. "Other options. Like games? You were banned from the Oubliette?"

"Excellent deduction." He was still wearing an encouraging sort of smile, as if I was a slow reader who'd suddenly started making progress.

My progress stalled out, though. "I don't get it. Why d'you want the grimoire? How's that going to help? That's what this is about, isn't it?"

He rocked his hand from side to side. "Yes and no. It's mostly about you."

"Me?"

"Edith is pretty upset at you."

I *had* been right. "I knew she had to be behind this. I knew it!"

"Oh, not at all," he said. "I mean, I'm sure she'd love to get hold of the grimoire, but she's not really in a position to. She's got a black hole where her magic used to be, and it's going to take a while to fill it. But she was very happy to air her grievances to me one night over a bottle of vodka, so I heard all about the plain old human who took her down, and ended up the new owner of a ridiculously powerful book."

"So you *do* want it."

He *hmm*ed. "Like I said, I'm more interested in you. I got *very* interested, in fact, when I discovered you'd managed to destroy an entire *carnival,* with no training. Amazing!"

"I don't know where you're going with this." I was sweating, but the more he was talking, the more time Ruiner and Effie had to find Jason and get out.

He waved at the sofas. "Do you want to sit down? Something from the vending machines?"

"I'm fine," I said.

"Suit yourself." He leaned against the sofa, crossing his arms. He didn't look any different than he had in the library, but he *felt* different. Something about the way he stood or moved, something predatory and watchful.

"You didn't accidentally get trapped under the books, did you?"

"I did not. I mean, it has happened, but not since my early days here."

"You were trying to get the grimoire off me, but Effie kept messing it up."

"I was trying to forge a *connection* with you," he said, somehow making the word feel a little greasy. "And yes, she did keep messing it up. Took a liking to your bloody cat, which is not a cat, according to Edith."

I took a breath. "So where's the grimoire now, then? I assume you took it from the car when Lise grabbed me."

"I did," he agreed. "And it's safe and sound, along with your familiar. You can have them both back."

"If?"

"If you agree to work with me."

"Doing what?" I asked, bewildered.

"Darrowdale and Hollowbeck are *stagnant*. The same people running the show for ages. With that grimoire, we could take over both."

I stared at him for a long moment, then burst out laughing. He just watched me, head on one side, until I got myself under control. "You want to overthrow the government of two little towns? High aspirations there."

"Higher than you realise," he said. "They're the two oldest magical towns in the north. There's a lot of power in them."

My smile faded. "I'm not doing that. Zero interest, thanks. Give me back Jackie and the grimoire."

"I like your priorities. What about your dear old Jason?"

"Well, him too, I suppose." I folded my own arms. "I can't believe you kidnapped him. He knows *nothing* about this world."

"Oh, I didn't."

"What?"

"I didn't kidnap him." Connall wandered over to a door at the back of the room. A roughly stencilled sign declared *This way to begin the games!* He opened it, stuck his head through, and called, "Come on out, Jason."

I rubbed my forehead. "You told him it was a good way to earn some money?"

"No, not that either."

Jason emerged from the door, leaving it open onto the glimpse of a hallway. He gave me a sheepish smile, running one hand through his hair. "Hi Morgs," he said. "I knew you'd come."

"I shouldn't have," I snapped. "Do you have *any idea* what you're caught up in here?"

He crossed his arms, lifting his chin. "Look, I get to make my own decisions, right. Connall's been helping me, and—"

"And he had you pretend you were *kidnapped?*"

Jason paused, his chin still lifted but his gaze sliding away. "I mean, I can see how that looks bad—"

"How much?" I demanded.

"What?"

"How much money do you owe him, Jason?"

"I don't—"

"Enough that his car wasn't going to cover it," Connall said. "And not me specifically. Let's say I took on his debts for the simple price of a phone call or two."

"Did my brother get you into this initially?" I asked Jason, ignoring Connall.

"No," Jason said, and he actually looked annoyed. "I know he was playing really good games, but he wouldn't let me join him. He kept saying—"

I turned away from him, looking at Connall. "Let him go now. Get him out of here before I brain him myself."

"Morgs—" Jason started.

"If you call me Morgs again, I will smother you with a sofa cushion."

Jason looked so startled I almost laughed. Connall did. "He can go," he said. "Once you've agreed to help me."

"I'm not helping you. I like Hollowbeck just as it is."

Connall put his hands in his pockets. "I do have the book. And the rat."

"You can't use it without me. I claimed it."

"I can break that claim."

"Are you sure? Because someone else tried to do that and I destroyed their whole carnival. I thought you'd done your *research*." I spat the word with a whole lot more conviction than I felt.

"Oh, I've done my research. You've still not quite got the hang of the whole witchy thing, have you?"

"Didn't stop me before."

"You weren't dealing with me."

We watched each other, and I could feel his wariness in an echo of my own. I *had* brought down the carnival. But he was right, too. It had been a desperate, last-ditch effort, and right now I had no book, no Jackie, and no Ruiner. I wondered where all three were. And Effie. I seemed to be losing more people rather than less as the night went on.

"Did you just call her a *witch?*" Jason asked.

"Shut up, Jason," we both said, and Connall grinned.

"We'd work well together. I'd definitely prefer it than the alternative. Your power and mine would make for a rather nice alliance."

"You seriously think you can take down The Dealer? That's what you're talking about, isn't it? He's the one really in charge of Darrowdale."

He shrugged. "He's old-fashioned. No taste for change. Darrowdale's so stuck on being this poor copy of Hollowbeck, when it can be so much more. It just needs to up its game a bit." He pointed at me. "And you, you see, are still welcome in Hollowbeck. You can effect change from the inside. I'll help you develop your skills, really get to grips with the book. Help your brother, too."

I hesitated. "You know how to do that?"

"I know a lot of things."

"That's *unbearably* cheesy."

He laughed. "True. But it's accurate. Things like … how to make phone calls when no one's phones work."

I stared at him. "I thought I was being *haunted*."

"*Hmm.* You were, sort of."

"Those were ghosts?"

He seemed to consider it, but his eyes were dancing, a kid who can't wait to show off. "Ghosts don't need phone lines. Just a way to find someone. There's all sorts of things you can do with the dead."

I made a face, then something occurred to me. "Like dead bodies that vanish?"

"See, I knew you'd be interested. It's cool, right? Work with me, and we can do *all* the fun stuff. What're you going to do otherwise? Hang around in Hollowbeck making love spells and arthritis creams?"

"Sounds pretty pleasant, really. And are you even a witch?" I squinted at him. "You don't look like one."

"Why are you talking about being a witch?" Jason asked. He sounded far too troubled by this for someone who'd been faking a kidnapping. "You're a *bookkeeper*, Morgs — Morgan."

Connall started to say something, but movement at the hall door caught our attention. We all turned towards it, and Effie came barrelling through the doorway, scampering along the ceiling and hissing mightily. A pot-bellied man was in hot pursuit of her, bleeding liberally from what looked very much like Effie-sized bites on his arms, and a younger man pounded behind him with Ruiner clutched by the scruff of the neck in one hand. Effie threw herself towards Connall, hands outstretched and hooked into claws, lips pulled back from her teeth in a terrible rictus.

Connall pivoted away from her, snatching something off the sofa. He lashed out as Effie twisted mid-air, catching his arm and tearing a snarl from him. He landed his own blow, though, and a fine silver chain whipped around the ghoul, trussing her up so firmly that she rolled across the floor until she fetched up against the wall, hissing and struggling, but unable to break free.

"Sorry they got past us," the pot-bellied man said, cradling his injured arm in a rather pointed manner.

"*Yours* did," the young man said, brandishing Ruiner.

Connall looked back at me. "Oh look," he said. "I think I may just have scored a little leverage."

"Dammit," I said with a sigh.

TWENTY-SIX

Good bodies

"YOU'VE ALREADY GOT LEVERAGE," JASON POINTED OUT. "You've got me."

I looked at him. "You do remember we're divorced, right?"

"You're *here*."

"And regretting every moment."

"I think you may be rather less effective leverage than her brother and her new favourite pet," Connall said, glancing at Effie. She was twisting frantically, and I could see the chains cutting into her skin, so fine they were like fishing line.

"Let her go," I said to Connall, and Ruiner gave an outraged growl. "Him too."

"I will, if you work with me."

We looked at each other, ignoring Jason saying, "And me?"

"What if I won't?" I asked.

"Well, I could make a bunch of threats, but I'm sure you can work it out," Connall said, gesturing at Ruiner. "I just keep going until I finally have to kill you and figure out how to claim the grimoire. Not sure how to do it yet, but I'll manage."

Well, at least he wasn't hanging around being dramatic. Always nice to have someone be efficient about such things. "Maybe we could play for it?" I suggested. "Since you seem to be into that."

He grinned at me. "Are you a secret card shark?"

"No, she's awful," Jason said. "She can never even remember the rules to Hearts."

"I didn't say cards," I protested. "We could play Trivial Pursuit or something."

"She is good at that."

Connall laughed. "Well, as tempting as it is, I'm going to have to say no. Doesn't gain me anything, does it?"

I sighed. "Worth a try."

"Sure. And if I was The Dealer, it probably would've worked. He can't resist any game. It's his nature."

"But not yours." He might be efficient, but he did like his own voice. Potbelly and Skinny both looked bored, and I had an idea it wouldn't be hard to keep Connall talking. And I really needed to, because I was facing the window, while Connall's back was to it, and Potbelly and Skinny were too intent on stopping their bleeding to pay attention. There was a silhouette beyond the curtains, and the build wasn't right for Stu. Of course, it could be another of Connall's team, but I was going to hope it wasn't, even if I had no idea who might be coming to our aid.

"Not mine," he agreed. "That's why I'll be better for this place than The Dealer. Move him on, and get the rest cleaned up too. Trifecta of try-hards, Lise and Faith and Luna. Trying to turn the town into something it isn't."

"How d'you mean?" I tried to look at him and the window at the same time. The silhouette had just sprinted past, followed by another, larger silhouette that looked like it'd be Stu.

"I mean Darrowdale needs to stop trying to be something it's not. There's room for plenty of types of magic in this world, so why not embrace what we're good at?"

"Which is?" Neither silhouette had come back, and there was a thud from outside that sounded like someone slipping on the stairs. Connall looked at the door, frowning, and I said quickly, "I mean, Darrowdale seems good at lots of things. Um, metal bands and ... teeth, and coffee drinking competitions and all that."

"Yes," he said doubtfully, still looking at the door. It was silent outside, and after a moment he looked back at me. "I mean Darrowdale could be a haven for the sort of magic no one dares do elsewhere, but they're holding us back. It's ridiculous. We could be a *powerhouse*."

"Oh?"

"Like they think we need to adhere to Hollowbeck's narrow little moral code." He cocked his head. "You haven't decided what sort of witch you are yet, have you?"

"I didn't know I got to decide. I thought it just kind of happened."

"For some people." He looked at the door again, taking a step towards it.

I grabbed his arm, catching the scent of him as he glanced at me in surprise. He smelled of soap and honey. "You mean I get to choose? Would you help me?"

For a moment I thought I'd pushed it too far, my eyes wide as I looked up at him, but he turned towards me, all but puffing his chest out. "You've got all the natural power, Morgan. You can choose how you direct it."

"Oh, *wow*," I said, and Ruiner made a strangled sound.

"You're being limited where you are. Theodore and Isabella keep such a tight leash on things — on *you*.

They've made sure there's no one in town you can learn from. They don't want any threat to their tidy little arrangement."

"What arrangement?" Neither silhouette had come back, and I was going to have to do something soon. I couldn't keep up the awed little woman act for much longer, and Ruiner was going to choke if he had to hold back his laughter any more. Even Jason looked like he was catching onto the fact that I was up to something.

"Everyone in debt to the town witch, and the town witch controlled by them." Connall smiled almost indulgently. "They could've stopped Edith before she killed Norma. You think they didn't know what Edith was like? They just let it happen, then defanged her and sent her away."

That got my attention. "No," I started, but he cut me off.

"So they've been helping you achieve your full potential, have they?"

We looked at each other, his smile still dancing on the edges of his lips. I found my voice finally. "I want to see the grimoire."

"What, you don't trust me?" He grinned, then added before I could answer, "Good. I wouldn't either." He headed for the office door, still talking. "I'm not lying about helping you, though. Unlike others I could mention."

"Oh? You have a list?" I wasn't sure what I was playing for now, but I had the sense that something was about to happen, a tightness in my chest, my breath faster than it had been, a sucker punch of adrenaline setting sparks on the edges of my vision. And I knew part of it was simple rage at this utterly, utterly ridiculous situation, brought here by a lingering sense of obligation to an ex who was a willing accomplice in the set-up, the grimoire snatched away again by some man I'd barely met but who thought he knew me, telling me my friends were controlling me when he was trying to do the same thing. I knew that's where the fury was coming from, knew I didn't have time for it, but at the same time I welcomed it. *Something was about to happen*, and if that something was me, well, at least it'd stop this horrible impasse.

"Oh, I have a list," Connall said. "You'll love it." He opened the office door as he spoke, looking back at me, so he never saw the blur of grey fur launch itself out of the office straight at his face.

"*Jackie!*" I shouted.

Connall shrieked, more in fright than pain, and staggered back, slapping Jackie away. He only caught her a glancing blow as she leaped clear, but it was enough to send her somersaulting across the room.

I threw myself forward, arms outstretched as I stumbled into a fall like a rugby player diving for a ball, and Connall swung back toward the office door, his smile replaced with hard-edged fury. I caught Jackie with one hand, and I reached toward the office with the other, those sparks of rage flashing at the edge of my vision. How dare he! How *dare* he hurt her! How *dare* he touch my grimoire!

"That is *mine*," I roared. And it was a roar. I could feel it echoing in my bones, the power vibrating between Jackie and myself, and the satchel flew out of the office in answer. Connall grabbed for it, snagging the trailing strap of the bag and sending it off course. It tumbled to the floor, rolling end over end, and both the librarian and I threw ourselves towards it.

"*Get it!*" Connall bellowed, and Potbelly jumped forward, rushing for the grimoire.

Ruiner, who'd been hanging helplessly from Skinny's

hands, executed a tight, furious flip and wound up with his teeth and claws buried in the young man's hands, who squawked in pain. Potbelly kept going, closer than both Connall and I to the book, but Jason almost casually stuck one foot out, a bewildered look on his face, and Potbelly tripped, going down hard. All three of us scrambled across the floor, desperate to reach the grimoire. Ruiner shot past us, coming to a skidding stop atop the book and yowling like a cat possessed. Connall reached him first, making a grab for the bag, and Ruiner went straight for his face. I grabbed Potbelly's shirt, jerking him backwards, and then I was past him and had the strap of the satchel, reeling it in towards me.

"Go!" I yelled. "Ruiner, *go!*"

He didn't hesitate, racing for the main door. Jason was still standing in the middle of the room, looking confused, and as I scrambled to my feet, I yelled at him, "Open the damn *door!*"

He lurched forward, and Jackie, who'd scrambled to my shoulder and was clinging to me desperately, hissed in warning. I tried to duck but I wasn't quick enough, and Connall snatched a handful of my hoody, hauling me around to face him as he grabbed the bag. I fought back, but he was bigger and stronger than me. My fingers slipped on the cloth of the satchel, and he grunted in triumph, pulling harder. I tried to recapture that commanding rage, the one that had called the book so violently to me, but all was white panic, and I'd never even been in a fight before, if I didn't count the tussle with Edith, oh and the ones at the carnival, but other than that I hadn't, and I didn't—

"*Morgan!* Use your *head!*" Ruiner's yowl cut straight through my babbling thoughts, silencing them, and I reared back, then slammed my head forwards, not even thinking about it. There was a hideous crunch as my forehead crashed into Connall's nose, and he yelled in wordless pain.

"Not quite what I meant," my brother said, sounding impressed.

I staggered, spots swimming in my vision, but I had the grimoire back. I swung towards the door, then spotted Effie though my streaming eyes, still trussed by the wall. "Effie!" I managed. "Someone get Effie!" I looked around wildly, but there wasn't anyone to get her. Potbelly was up off the floor advancing on me, and Skinny had tackled Jason before he could reach the door, both of them crashing onto one of the sofas, bouncing off it to the floor.

"Give it—" Connall was coming for me again, blood dribbling undramatically over his top lip. Potbelly flanked me on the other side, like a pair of farmers trying to corner a particularly recalcitrant sheep. I backed up, clutching the bag to my chest. Connall made a grab for me and I jumped backwards. I was going in the wrong direction, away from Effie and away from the door, but I couldn't get past both of them. I kept backing up until I bumped into the wall and stopped, trapped. Ruiner was by Effie, and Jason was still tussling with Skinny, and none of us could help the other.

I brandished the satchel warningly. "Don't make me use it." Potbelly looked a bit worried, but Connall snorted, spraying blood off his lip. "*Ew*."

"You can't use it," he said, his voice nasal and distorted. "That was pure luck." He reached for the bag.

"You sure?" I asked him, and he hesitated. As he did, three things happened in rapid succession. The room had been silent but for Jason and Skinny grunting and swearing, and a fine, tinkling sound rang out, high and sharp. Connall spun away from me, eyes widening as Effie exploded off the floor, bounding towards us and leaving

Ruiner still holding one end of the chain in his mouth. I shifted my grip on the satchel, readying myself to swing it, and the door to the deck was ripped open, revealing a man in a rather respectable waxed jacket, his jeans torn at the knees, and a length of wood raised over one shoulder in a very non-respectable manner.

"Morgan?" he shouted, staring in at us. "*Morgan!*"

"*Ben?*"

"*Leg it!*" Ruiner yelled.

Effie, who'd paused in her charge as the door opened, launched herself forwards again. I swung the bag as hard as I could at Potbelly, who was still looking at the door. The book connected hard, and he pitched over barely getting his hands out before he hit the ground. Effie slammed into Connall, teeth snapping as she clawed for his face, and he jammed one arm against her throat, holding her off like someone might a dog.

"Morgan, *move!*" Ruiner shouted. He was at the door, Ben stepping over him and peering into the bedlam, shifting his grip on the plank as if wanting to hit someone, but not sure where to start. He'd caught a split lip from somewhere, and he pointed at Jason and Skinny.

"Which one's with you?"

"Neither," Ruiner said, and I smacked Connall on the back of the head with the grimoire. He gave a startled grunt, knees buckling, and I grabbed Effie as she lunged at his face, teeth bared.

"We're going," I told her, pulling her with me as I ran for the door. "Jason!"

"Jason? Really?" Ben said.

"My feelings exactly," Ruiner said, but Ben stepped forward and swung the plank at the back of Skinny's legs. He went down with a yelp, and Jason wriggled free, bolting for the door. Effie and I were just behind him, Ben waiting for us, his eyes on the men on the floor.

Ruiner flew across the threshold, breaking into a run as Effie, Ben, and I burst out of the building behind him. Jason was already running down the steps that led from the deck to the car park, but even as I gasped a deep breath of fresh air, hugging the grimoire close, he skidded to a stop. It was dark beyond the reach of the lights on the deck, and I squinted to try and see what had made him stop. Was Stu still out there? More of Connall's cut-rate henchmen?

Jason pounded back up the steps. "Back inside. Get back inside!"

Effie leaped to the railing, balancing there as she peered into the dark, and I ran to join her, shading my eyes. She gave a sudden hiss and grabbed my shoulder, still staring into the night. I followed her gaze, and as the shadows took form I might've hissed a little myself. Because emerging from the corn and marching purposefully toward the building was, if not an army, at least a good rugby team's worth of people. They were entirely silent, other than the crunch of gravel as they reached the car park, and as I watched, one's arm fell off. He stopped, picked it up, and kept going.

"What," I started, and Ruiner jumped onto the railing next to Effie.

"Did that—?" Ben said beside me, and I turned to look at Jason, who was back at the door, waving at us wildly.

"Get back *inside!*" he yelled. "Hurry *up!*"

The rugby team approached across the car park, their eyes fixed on us. They didn't talk, didn't glance around, and as the light hit them it revealed tattered clothing and bare feet, milky eyes and skin with a strange grey cast. Effie snarled, jumping lightly to the ground and tugging my arm.

"*Huh,*" Ben said, in the tones of someone trying very hard not to panic.

"Zombies," Ruiner said. "Those are sodding *zombies.*"

That broke the strange paralysis that had gripped us all. I shoved myself away from the railing, Ben grabbing my arm to pull me with him, as if I wasn't already breaking into a sprint. Jason had shot inside, Effie and Ruiner a stride ahead of us as we dived into the relative safety of the room. Ben slammed the door and turned the lock, putting his back to it, and I said, "Zombies? *Zombies* exist?"

"You saw them," Ruiner said. His tail was puffed out as far as it could be, given the damp, and Effie looked just as horrified.

"Out the back." I was already running for the door to the hall, swerving around Skinny, who was sitting on the sofa massaging the backs of his legs. The door was still ajar, and the white light of the hall shone on the bald head of a large man lumbering toward me. His skin had the same sickly grey — or *dead* grey — cast as the people outside, his eyes murky and opaque and yes, very zombie-like. I slammed the door and looked around the room wildly. "Vending machine," I said. "Quickly!"

Ben, Jason, Effie and I ran to unplug the machines, putting one in front of the door to the hall and another at the front door, while Potbelly and Skinny looked on as if unsure if they should be helping or not. Connall was sitting on the floor with his knees up, one forearm resting on them while he used his other hand to investigate the back of his head where I'd hit him with the grimoire. He looked entirely unconcerned by the fact that we were being laid siege to by the walking dead.

"Why are there *zombies?*" I yelled at him, as I unplugged the third machine and looked between both doors uncertainly, not sure where to put it. We had the sofas too, of course, and I was suddenly frozen by the logistics of building effective zombie barriers.

"Very useful to add a bit of realism to the laser tag," Connall said, checking his fingers for blood. "Everyone likes shooting them up."

"You have *live* — well, dead — zombies at your laser tag?" Ben asked. "What sort of place *is* this?"

"It's not his," Ruiner said. "He's the librarian."

Ben grimaced. "Sorry. On behalf of librarians in general, I mean. We're not all like that." Given the plank of wood and his torn-up clothes, he wasn't that convincing.

"The zombies *are* mine, though," Connall said. "I provide them to the laser tag for a fee. That way they can use real laser guns, which is quite the draw. Well, magically tweaked laser guns, so they actually work. And no point good bodies going to waste."

The good bodies in question were piling up at the door, making the wood creak under the pressure. "They're yours?" I demanded. "How?"

"Oh, you didn't ask me what sort of witch I am, did you?" He grinned at me, the blood making his expression terrible. "I'm a necromancer. How else d'you think you had a vanishing body?"

"No," Jason said, covering his head with both hands and sinking onto the sofa next to Skinny. "No, this is *not* what was meant to happen."

Ruiner and I looked at each other. "Best get the hang of that bloody book," he said. "You know, other than hitting people with it."

Easy for him to say.

TWENTY-SEVEN

What a witch

THE OUTER DOOR GROANED UNDER THE WEIGHT OF THE bodies, and the lock abruptly splintered. The vending machine held, but it was wobbling, and Ben put his shoulder to it, which seemed more optimistic than effective.

"Can you *help?*" I shouted at Potbelly and Skinny.

"They won't eat us," Potbelly said cheerfully. He'd helped himself to a can of energy drink at some point. The can was black and neon yellow, and said *Carnage,* which seemed appropriate.

"Sure about that, are you?" Ben demanded.

Both henchmen looked at Connall, but he ignored them, getting up and straightening his jumper. Effie hissed, backing away until she could hide behind my legs. It was a nice vote of confidence.

"I did not have being eaten by the undead on my Darrowdale bingo card," Ruiner said, looking at the hall door, which sounded like it was going to go the way of the front one at any moment. "Is there another way out?"

Connall looked up. "Sorry, are you asking me? You may have misunderstood my role here."

"Call them off," I said, hurrying to the hall door and bracing myself against the vending machine. It sounded like the dead were trying to claw their way through.

"Well, I would, but I want the grimoire," he said. "And you, obviously."

"Excuse me?" Ben said.

"Not like that," I shouted, and immediately realized it was hardly the most important thing right now, partly because Jackie clawed my ear. "And no to both, anyway."

Connall nodded as if that didn't surprise him, and said, "The thing is, the dead are very much *my* dead. I'll simply let them eat everyone else while you watch. I wonder if it'll be your brother or your boyfriend that's your breaking point?"

"Ex," Jason said.

"Not you. I mean, either of you. I mean, I don't have a —" I shook my head while Connall laughed softly. "Let them go."

"It's up to you, little witch."

I really wished everyone would stop calling me *little*. It was one thing when it was Lise, given that she was tall and terrifying and an entirely supernatural creature. Some bloody librarian who messed with the dead had no right.

My attention had lapsed, and as I tried to decide how to respond, the dead shoved the door behind me so hard the vending machine toppled over. I barely jumped out of its way, stumbling forward and crashing into the nearest sofa. Ben gave a yelp as he was thrown away from his own door by the force of the attack from that side, and I shouted at Connall, "*Stop!*"

"Say the word," he said cheerfully.

The dead poured in, Ben fending them off with his plank, Effie hissing in fury, Ruiner shouting at me to do something. I backed away as two slack-faced women tried to squeeze through the hall door at the same time, gaze fixed on me. I was out of options. We were trapped.

Which was when my utter waste of space of an ex-husband surged to his feet, snatched up the stack of metal stools, and sprinted straight at the big, curtained windows. He didn't slow, didn't stop, simply launched himself forward with the stools held like a battering ram. If it had been double-glazed glass, or even a smaller window, he'd probably have taken himself out, but the place was both cheaply built and old. The glass blew out in an explosion of shattered fragments, and Jason crashed into the wall beneath it.

"*Move!*" Ruiner yelled, and we surged towards the broken window.

Connall lunged for me, closer than the dead, and Ben swung the plank at him before he could reach me. Connall twisted away, but the wood still caught him a glancing blow on the shoulder, sending him staggering.

Jason cleared the last of the glass with a sweep of the stools, then dropped them in front of the window and used them as step to vault out. I bolted after him, Ben right behind me, scrambling out onto the deck beyond as Ruiner flew effortlessly past us. Effie lingered, snarling at Connall and his men, although they seemed content to sit on the sofas and let the dead do the work.

"Effie!" I shouted, and she bounded through the window to join us, not bothering with the stool. Then we were out, all of us, in the cold rain and the dead-filled night, the zombies at the door turning towards us.

We didn't bother trying to get to the steps off the deck,

or wasting time discussing it, simply scrambled over the railing and dropped to the gravel below. I almost landed on top of Stu's unconscious form, sprawled in the shadows, and I threw myself sideways, twisting my ankle enough to hurt. I yelped, and Effie grabbed my arm to help me up.

"Morgan," Connall called, leaning out the window. "Come *on*. It'll be fun! I'll teach you necromancy!"

"That is not fun. That's sick!" I yelled back. We were already moving again, running into the car park, aiming for the drive. Or trying to run. My ankle was protesting mightily.

"You're thinking of necrophilia," Connall shouted, as the deck's railings cracked behind us with the weight of the dead crashing through them.

"I really want to say *not all librarians*," Ben said, slowing for me to catch up. "But you've not forgiven me for the tea yet, have you?"

"Ben, if your car is here, I will forgive you for everything, forever, in eternity," I replied.

"It's on the road."

"Oh, bloody *hell*." We were almost to the drive, and I tried to go faster, but my ankle was really smarting now, stabs of pain shooting up to my knee. The dead weren't super-speedy, just lumbering doggedly after us, and when I glanced back, they were still far enough behind that we might escape them. Connall, Potbelly, and Skinny were running down the steps, though, and they were faster.

Jason was ahead of us, running hard, his head down and his eyes on the ground. That was why we saw them before he did.

"*Jason!*" I screamed, as half a dozen dead ploughed out of the corn from his left, some of them still dressed in fatigues with laser guns hanging from their necks, arms outstretched in good, classic zombie fashion.

Jason screeched and swerved, but more were emerging from the field to the right of the drive. He stumbled, sliding in the loose gravel, and went down under a mass of unbreathing bodies. I tried to push my protesting ankle into a sprint, but Ben had already reached the pile-up, laying into the dead with his piece of wood.

Some of them turned towards him, and he backed up as they advanced down the drive.

"Into the corn!" Ruiner shouted, already veering that way.

"We can't leave Jason!" I stumbled to a stop, caught between the approaching necromancer at our back, and his splinter pack ahead.

"We can't *save* him!"

Effie snarled, one hand still clutching the back of my hoody as she supported me. Ruiner tried to leap the ditch into the field, and an arm snapped out of it, snatching him out of the air. He yowled, and I patted Effie's shoulder.

"Go. Grab him."

She abandoned me, bolting after my brother, and I turned to face Connall's approach, unsteady on my bad ankle. The corn rustled violently as more dead approached, and Ben hurried to join me.

"What do we do?" He was panting, his arms shaking slightly, from exertion or adrenaline or both. The dark skin of his cheeks was marred with dust from the drive, and his jacket was torn along the seams.

"Thank you," I said, and he gave me a sideways look.

"It was a terrible rescue effort."

"Thank you anyway."

He smiled, then shoved something into my satchel. I glanced down, seeing the handle of what looked very much like a gun sticking out of the bag. I adjusted the top to hide it, wondering what the hell I was meant to do with that. I'd've preferred the plank of wood, to be honest, but he gave no sign of relinquishing that.

Effie screeched triumphantly, and an arm flew onto the drive, the hand still gripping Ruiner. It hit the ground and the fingers flew open. My brother bounced free, rolled twice, and came to all fours just as Skinny reached him. The young man tried to leap over Ruiner, Ruiner tried to run, and they both went down into the gravel with a chorus of inventive swearing.

"Effie?" I peered into the shadows of the corn, but I couldn't see anything except a tangle of shadows, the plants snapping and swaying, the ghoul snarling and occasionally shrieking, "*Git!*"

Ben gave a sudden yell, and I jerked around, crying out as my ankle gave way. I stumbled to one knee, watching as two of the grey-skinned dead seized him, a third wresting the plank away. He fought back, but they were implacable, ignoring every fist and kick.

I pushed myself back up to my feet, turning to Connall. He slowed to a walk, then stopped a few metres from me. Potbelly stood a little behind him, eyeing the dead nervously, and Skinny was trying to grab Ruiner, which wasn't going well. My brother had gone into a full, feral rage of the sort I vaguely remembered from when we'd been kids. He hadn't had so many sharp bits then, though.

"Call them off," I said to Connall. This far out on the drive, the light from the building was dim, shadows woven deep with the night and the corn, but I could see him smile, a tighter effort than previously.

"You know the deal."

I put my hand on the satchel, and Jackie clawed my ear. She wasn't hissing, though. She knew an impossible situation as well as I did.

"Fine," I said. "I'll work with you." The grimoire was

hot through the cloth, as if in sudden anticipation. Probably it rather fancied the idea of someone who'd use it rather than trying to make it give up deals and behave itself. "Now let them go."

Connall took a step forward, one hand out. "Give me the book first. Forgive me for not being entirely trusting, but I'd prefer to keep hold of it."

I fished in the satchel, trying not to fling the gun out and laser my own face off. But it was the grimoire that almost singed my knuckles as I seized the book in my left hand and pulled it out, holding it aloft rather than towards Connall. "This?"

He frowned. "What're you doing?"

I pulled the laser gun from the bag with my other hand, hoping it worked the same as a water pistol, since I'd never used so much as a paintball gun. If there was a safety catch or some other trick, I was screwed.

"Morgan," Connall said, his voice flat. "I don't know what you think you're doing—"

I squeezed the trigger and it belched red light, illuminating the corn in neon shades and shearing a corner off the book. "*Ooh*. It's like Star Wars!"

"*Morgan!*" Connall held both hands out to me, in supplication or placation. "You can't do that!"

"Can," I said, and fired again, this time merely nipping the edge. A faint smell of burning paper drifted in the rain.

Ruiner had disentangled himself from Skinny and now stood between me and Connall. "Now *that's* a witch," he said, and I shot him a grin, lowering my arms. The book was heavy, and I was worried I might shoot my fingers off.

"That's a dead witch if she keeps it up," Connall said. "Do you have *any idea* how precious that book is?"

I looked around. "I don't see you doing anything about it."

"*Give it to me.*"

I aimed the laser at the book and fired again. A huge chunk tore out of the corner, and the beam carried on going, disintegrating the knee of one of the dead holding Ben. It keeled over sideways, and he yelped.

"Oops. Sorry."

"*Stop it!*" Connall's voice spiked with panic.

"Call off your horde, then."

This time he didn't argue, just clicked his fingers irritably. I didn't look away from him, the dead moving on the edge of my vision, corn rustling and shifting.

"Ruiner?" I said.

"They've let Jason and Ben go. I can't see your ghoul." A screech rose from the corn, and he added, "You might have to tell her to let *them* go."

"It's done," Connall said, taking a step forward. "Give me the book."

I raised the gun threateningly. "No. We're just going to leave, otherwise I'll burn the whole damn thing up."

"That wasn't the deal."

"It wasn't *your* deal."

I caught the movement in the corner of my vision just as Ruiner yelled, "Duck!"

I jerked away from the attack, Potbelly lunging forward and slinging the fine chains that had entangled Effie at me. They whispered and snapped as they arced through the air, hungry and *other*, and my ankle gave way as I tried to avoid them. I went down hard, crying out as the chains snapped tight around my legs, and my finger jammed down on the trigger of the laser gun involuntarily. I had one horrified moment when I imagined slicing my brother in half with it, but the gun gave a petulant whine and nothing happened.

Connall threw himself forward instantly, running at me

with his face twisted in a snarl, and the dead surged into action, their movements an echo of his own as they resumed the attack. Ben and Jason went down under separate mobs without even a chance to fight back, and Potbelly aimed a kick at my gun hand. I threw the weapon at him, and he ducked. The gun went sailing into the darkness and landed somewhere in the corn, sending a startled blast of red light into the sky and making me wish I hadn't given up on it quite so quickly.

"That's got you," Connall said, and grabbed for the book. With my legs enmeshed, I couldn't do much except cling on grimly, trying my best not to let him steal it.

But I couldn't keep my grip. With a final grunt of effort, he ripped the book away with a hiss of triumph.

"Now," he said. "You've been a complete pain, but I'll have to keep you alive for a bit until I can figure out how to claim this." He hugged the book more tightly. "The rest can go, though."

"Connall," Skinny said.

"Yeah, just grab them."

"No, *Connall!*"

I rolled onto my belly and lifted my head, suddenly aware that the air was choking with smoke, and, despite the rain, I could hear the crackle of fire. Ruiner came bolting out of the corn with a burning leaf in his teeth, yowling frantically, and Effie charged after him, stalks of burning corn in each hand. They barreled onto the drive, coming straight for us, a battalion of the dead in hot pursuit. Literally hot.

The laser had set fire to the crops, and Effie and Ruiner had evidently been leading the dead through the flaming plants. Their hair and clothes were ablaze, turning them into lumbering bonfire guys at a really unpleasant Guy Fawkes night.

Skinny backed up rapidly, then took off towards the road without bothering to speak. Potbelly hesitated, then ran after him, shoving past the wall of dead blocking the drive.

"They're *dead!*" Connall shouted at Effie and Ruiner as they scampered through the crowd, spreading fire wherever they could. "What d'you think that's going to do?"

"Distract you," I said, and as he turned back to me, I came from prone to my feet in the best burpee I've ever done, ignoring the scream of pain in my ankle as I landed. He opened his mouth, probably to call me a little witch again, and I slipped the grimoire — the *actual* grimoire — out of the satchel, Jackie racing down my arms to place both paws on it as I thrust it out towards him like a preacher ordering the devil out. "It's mine," I said. *"I claim it!"*

My voice rose on the last words, louder than I'd intended, louder that seemed reasonable, and the fury all but swallowed me. That this person, this *man,* would presume to take what was mine? My brother, my rat, my *book*? Everything was white-hot incandescence, and the fire in the corn roared, reaching furiously for the sky. I'd raze him to the ground. Raze this *town.*

Then Jackie bit me, which was fair enough, and Ruiner skidded to a stop at my feet and yowled, "Just *him,* you muppet!"

"How?" I yelled, as the world lost its furious edges, and it was suddenly just me waving a book at a bloody *necromancer*, and the book only worked when I was angry, but when I was angry the book tried to eat the world, and how was I meant to find the middle road, but I needed to find it *right now*, and I couldn't banish Connall like I'd banished the carnival, and he was coming towards me, the dead closing in, and—

And for some reason I thought of how everyone wanted the book to give *them* power, Connall, and Edith, and maybe The Dealer too, but it had to get its power from somewhere in the first place, and it was a hungry thing. Such a hungry thing, always trying to hold onto those deals and gobble them up.

I opened the grimoire, holding it out towards Connall as the dead grabbed my shoulders, trapping me in place as if he thought I might rush him, bound legs or not. "Go on, then," I said. "This is the real one. All you have to do is promise to give it all the power it wants."

He looked at the book he was holding, then at me, and I could see him searching for the lie, but there was none. It really was all the book wanted. "I promise," he said, dropping his book on the ground and grabbing the grimoire with both hands. I didn't let go.

Go on, I thought. *Take the deal.*

The air rushed out of the night. Connall's face, set in triumphant lines, changed, his eyes widening and his mouth dropping open. He screamed, trying to pull away, but he'd promised. He'd taken the deal. He twisted and fought as the fire raged around us, and the book fed, and fed, and fed, my hands burning with its ravenous energy. Wind whipped across the field, growling in my ears, and he fell to his knees, his hands still trapped. There was a nasty twist of satisfaction in my belly as he looked up at me.

"You *witch*," he hissed.

"You better bloody believe it."

He sagged, eyes drifting closed, and the book released him. The necromancer went down like a sack of power-hungry, anti-ghoul potatoes, and I gasped, almost dropping the grimoire on top of him. My hands were tingling like I had the worst case of pins and needles in history.

"*Yes, team!*" Ruiner yelled, and the dead ground to a halt as the necromancer's hold on them vanished. Silence rose, broken only by the patter of the drizzle as the corn burned and the dead smoldered, and I looked at Connall's prone form and wondered what I was meant to do with him now. I hadn't thought that far ahead.

TWENTY-EIGHT

Strange, messy, & formidable

BEN GINGERLY MOVED THE DEAD ASIDE UNTIL HE COULD pull me out of their midst, slinging one of my arms over his shoulders. Effie hissed at him, then picked up Ruiner.

"No!" he yelped, but she just stroked him with long, clawed fingers, crooning softly. Jason had crawled out of a pile of zombies and sat down on the drive, watching the burning fields. The rain was stopping the fire spreading too fast, but I supposed I should be doing something witchy to stop it entirely. I couldn't think of what, though, and my head was pounding with what I assumed was some sort of magical hangover.

We started down the drive towards the road, leaving Connall where he lay, and we'd barely made it fifty metres before a set of narrow white headlights pulled into the lane ahead. They rolled forwards, and even over the sound of the fire I heard the clatter of the chain collapsing.

"Oh, sodding hell," Ruiner said.

"What?" Jason asked. "Who is it?" He looked around, panicked, as if hoping for another way out.

"The cops," I said, although *cop* was more appropriate.

We stood there waiting as Lise's car crunched to a stop, headlights washing the battlefield around us. The dead were still frozen in place, Connall spreadeagled on the ground among them, and the burning fields fought with the car's lights to give the nastiest colour to everything.

Lise got out, her movement languid, and stood with one hand on the roof of the car, surveying the scene. "Well," she said, her gaze settling on me. "This is a pretty spectacular effort."

"Self-defence?" I offered.

"Oh? And escaping police custody?"

"*What?*" Jason asked, and I ignored him.

"I was worried about the ducking stool," I said.

"You didn't need to be before," Lise said. "Now I think we might have to rethink the simple banishing. Wholesale destruction, this."

"He set *zombies* on us," I said. "Also, he's been abusing the library ghoul. Strapping her up with chains and things." Effie had been too scared of Connall for that to be a first.

Effie nodded firmly. She was still holding Ruiner, who looked surprisingly comfortable. They seemed to have bonded over their cornfield battle with the dead, and she pointed back at Connall. "Git."

Lise frowned. "Well, that's unacceptable behaviour, obviously, but we don't deal with it by trying to burn him alive."

"That was an accident."

She shrugged. "Well, you'll all have to come with me." She beckoned to us, with the sort of authority that meant we all took a step forward before our brains had time to engage. Even when mine did, I couldn't seem to figure out a way to argue. We *had* just set fire to the whole place.

What stopped us was a new voice, smooth and warm, that cut through the crackle of the fire effortlessly.

"I hope you're not harassing my guests, Inspector."

It was coming from the direction of the laser tag building, and as we watched the jumble of dead parted like sand blowing across paper. The Dealer strolled between them with his hands in his pockets. He wasn't wearing his jacket, and his shirt was open at the collar, sleeves rolled up. His skin shone in the ruddy light as if on fire from the inside, and he looked around with a mild sort of interest, as if he'd stumbled on a somewhat substandard street theatre troupe and was too polite to walk away.

"She was instructed to leave," Lise said. "I was going to escort her. Instead she escaped and did … this." She waved to indicate the general carnage.

"The dead aren't mine," I said. "They were his." I pointed at Connall.

"Obviously," Lise said. "But the rest was you."

"He was trying to steal my book," I offered, hugging the grimoire closer.

"And my business," The Dealer said, nudging Connall with the toe of one well-polished boot. He glanced at me, then at Ruiner.

"Took your time, didn't you?" Ruiner asked.

"I needed to confirm a few things. One should never simply take the word of a cat."

I looked from one of them to the other. "When did you go to The Dealer, Ruiner?"

"Doesn't matter."

"Did you do another deal?"

"*Doesn't matter*."

"You said we shouldn't go to him."

Ruiner hissed at me. "Leave it, will you?"

I scowled but left it. It wasn't the most important thing, I supposed. Not right now, anyway.

Lise crossed her arms. "The little witch ran from me."

"So would I," The Dealer said. "You can be quite intimidating."

"She hit me!" Lise pointed to her forehead with one well-manicured finger.

"You *were* chasing me," I protested. "I thought you were going to tear my head off or something."

"Really? I'm *police*."

"Well, I don't know. Our police is a vampire. I don't know what he does, either."

Lise shook her head and looked at The Dealer. "So, what — you're excusing her?"

"I am. She has my welcome, as do her friends." He looked at Ben, then Jason. "Except for him."

"Oh, come *on*—" Jason started.

"It's that or I'll tear your soul into itty bitty pieces and have it as an appetiser. With dipping sauce," The Dealer said. "You conspired with the necromancer, thinking to challenge me. Being banned from Darrowdale is a truly generous gesture on my part. If I get even a whiff of you again, well. Appetisers."

Jason, for once, didn't argue. He just nodded violently.

"Faith won't be happy," Lise said. "She wanted the witch excluded."

"Faith may be mayor, but this is not her town, is it?"

Lise threw her hands up, an oddly human gesture for someone who looked so otherworldly, her skin milky as sea glass in the warm light. "This is just brilliant. Let one bloody Hollowbeck-er in and half the valley burns up."

"A slight exaggeration." The Dealer turned to me, and Ben's arm tightened where he was supporting me. The Dealer indicated my ankle. "May I?"

"What?"

"Fix it."

I scowled. "How much is that going to cost me?"

"Nothing. You have uncovered corruption in Darrowdale, in my realm. You are my guest, and nothing will cost you anything here, now or any other time." He smiled, wolfish in the red light. "And if anyone tries to charge you, you can tell them to see me."

"So all debts are forgiven?" Ruiner asked. "Since I was key in all this, you know."

The Dealer looked at my brother. "Your previous debts are cleared."

"Sweet," Ruiner said.

"But our business is not concluded."

"Ugh."

"May I?" The Dealer repeated, and this time I let him place his hands on my ankle, almost unbearably hot. The skin and tendons shifted under his touch, mending and knitting, painful but not unbearable. A moment later he stood up, and I let go of Ben, testing my weight while he kept one hand in the small of my back, cooler than The Dealer's but more comforting. My ankle seemed fine. If anything, it felt better than the rest of me.

"Thanks," I said.

The Dealer stepped over to Connall and picked the scorched book up from the ground, stroking one finger down its cover gently. *"Miss Edna's Guide to Proper Comportment for Young Witches,"* he read. *"Including how to eviscerate your enemies with style."*

"I was looking forward to reading that bit," I said.

"I'm not sure you need the help." He handed the book back to me, and I tucked it into the satchel with the grimoire, singed edges and all.

"Alright," Lise said. "Out of my town, the lot of you. I'll deal with Connall."

"I rather think I'll do that," The Dealer said, looking down at the necromancer. "Maybe Morgan can give me some tips." He winked at me, and I shivered.

"My car's still in town. And I need to give Jim his bike back."

"We'll deal with that," Lise said. "I don't *owe* you a car repair, but I'll do it. Anything to not have to look at any of you again."

"Harsh," Ruiner said. "I mean, she's no picture, but I'm adorable."

"It's the toes," The Dealer said. "He has fluffy toes."

BEN'S CAR was on the other side of the chain, which was, inexplicably, back in place despite the fact Lise had driven right through it. But considering we'd just been battling literal zombies, I didn't even question it. Effie walked with us to the car, still cradling Ruiner, then put him on the back seat and looked at me.

"You can come," I said. "I'm sure Isabella will be happy to have you in Hollowbeck." I wasn't actually sure, but I was sure I'd have my first ever argument with a ghost over it if I had to.

She thought about it, then said, "Books."

"You want to go back to the library?"

She shrugged, an uncertain little motion, and I nodded. It was familiar. Without Connall and his chains around, perhaps it was even safe.

"Okay. Thank you, Effie. So much."

She grinned, showing all those alarming teeth, and threw her arms around me, hugging me tight and snuffling my hair as if to catch the scent of me, although I was pretty sure I stank of smoke and sweat. Then she waved at Ruiner, gave him a grave, "Cat," and loped off into the darkness, heading in the direction of town.

Jackie put her head out of the satchel and eyed me. "I know," I said. "But she didn't try to eat you once."

"She did me," Ruiner said.

"That's understandable, though."

Ben had started the car, and now he looked out at us. "Are you coming? We need to get Theodore back to Hollowbeck before it gets light."

"*Theodore's* here?" I asked, as we clambered in.

"Well, not here, evidently. He couldn't get over the border. Every time we tried, the walls slammed shut on us, so I had to come on my own." He frowned. "He gave me that bit of wood and said *do what is needed, Ben*. What does that even *mean?*"

"It looked like you knew what you were doing," I said, and meant it.

He rubbed a hand over his head, not looking at me. "Oh. Thanks."

"How'd you find us?" Ruiner asked. "You got tracking on my sister, or something?"

"*No.*" Ben pulled onto the road, headlights flooding the corn. "We got a delivery notification on our message from the road here, so I was just checking each place I came to. Why didn't you wait for us?"

"A *delivery notification?*" I asked "On what message? And wait for what?"

"Isabella gave a message to the kids on the bikes in Hollowbeck. Apparently there's some sort of network between the villages."

"That was you?" Ruiner demanded. "*We're coming for*

you? We thought it was more bloody threats from the dead tickler back there."

"Or Edith," I put in.

Ben frowned. "Oh. That's not great. It was meant to be, *Don't do anything, we're coming to help you.*"

"I don't feel that's going to replace email any time soon," I said.

Ben gave me a sharp look. "It has to when you stop replying."

"*Oooh,*" Ruiner said, and huffed his feline version of laughter. "Snippy."

"Shut up," Ben and I said together, and I added, "Sorry. I thought Jason was about to be chopped into little pieces."

"We should be so lucky," Ruiner said.

"Sod off," Jason said. "And who's Theodore?"

"A very irritated vampire by now, I imagine," Ben said. "He'll be stalking around getting all panicked because we're not back."

"An irritated, panicked vampire," Ruiner said. "*Fun.*"

"A *what?*" Jason asked. "Isn't that dangerous?"

"Only if you're bleeding," I said, and Ben and I looked at each other. "Ah."

THEODORE WAS IRRITATED, and he was panicked, and he just about ripped my car door off when Ben guided us out through the narrow gap between the walls that formed the gateway to Darrowdale.

"Morgan!" he exclaimed, dropping into a crouch and grabbing both my arms as he examined me. "Are you alright? Are you—" He looked away abruptly. "Hurt."

His hands were very cold and very tight on my arms, and I said, "Just a few scrapes. But, um…"

"Ben, please open the boot," Theodore said, still not looking at me.

"*What?*" I asked, but Ben just did as the vampire asked, climbing out of the car. Theodore let go of me and hurried around to the back, and we craned around to see Ben slam the boot lid shut on him.

"What the hell is going on?" Jason whispered. He was sitting behind me, and scooted all the way forward so he could peer around the seat. "Is that a *vampire*? In the *car with us?*"

"In the boot," I said.

"*It's a hatchback*. He can just grab us through the seats!"

"The exhaust fumes will mask your scent," Theodore called, slightly muffled. "And I can't see the blood either, so this is a suitable solution."

"Nope," Jason said, fumbling for his door handle.

"Walk home, then," I said to him.

"Why can't *he* walk home?"

"Because I like him," I said, and Ruiner growled. "Not like that."

Ben got back in and started the car again, checking the time on the dashboard clock. "We should make it."

"He's in the boot," Ruiner said. "He's not going to get sunburnt in the boot, is he?"

"I can still see light through the gaps," Theodore called. "It is a less than ideal situation, I fear."

"Nope," Jason whispered again, and Ben pulled out as fast as his little car could manage, charging through the nighttime streets of Manchester in search of safer harbours.

~

WE BARELY SLOWED to dump Jason at the house, and we did make it back in time, Theodore sprinting into the town hall as the sky lightened to the east, Hollowbeck's crisp, clear dawn being heralded by birdsong in the trees. Ben dropped Ruiner and me off at Petunia's, and I crawled up the stairs, not even bothering to pull my filthy, tattered clothes off. I just fell into the blankets, dimly hearing the warm chorus of the frogs in the walls, and was swallowed by sleep.

I surfaced at some point the next day to claim my bathroom slot, then went back to bed again and actually made it between the sheets this time. My dreams were odd, fractured things, full of rage and fright, and I was happy enough to get up properly as the sun slipped away in the evening. I dressed and padded downstairs, and Petunia stuck her head out of the kitchen door when I opened the front one.

"Morgan!" she shouted. "D'you want a vodka?"

I shut the front door again and went down the hall, to where our landlady (and Hollowbeck's resident weather witch) was cooking an enormous pot of cauliflower curry, a large glass of vodka tonic in one hand and a spoon in the other. "Not right now," I said. "I'm going to the Witching Hour."

"Not without some food, you're not."

I opened my mouth to refuse, but my stomach overruled me, loudly, and she pointed at the big kitchen table with her spoon. "Sit." I sat, and she regarded me critically. "Are you alright?"

"Just some scrapes and bruises." She'd know what had happened. Everyone in Hollowbeck would know what had happened.

She poured me a drink, being generous with the vodka,

then sat down opposite me and slid it across the table. "You can *not* be alright, you know."

"Well, sure," I said. "But really—"

"You had to go out into the world that you didn't choose to leave, and you found you didn't fit in it anymore. You had to rescue a man you no longer love, but who you couldn't abandon. You had to learn some truths about Hollowbeck that were maybe not so comfortable." Her voice was low and calm, unlike her usual spiky tones, and I took a sip of my drink, eyes stinging with weariness.

"I suppose."

"I know. Many of us do the same, in one form or another."

I looked at her sharply. "You did too?"

"I wasn't always the village eccentric," she said, with something a lot more like her usual grin.

"I'm not sure you are now," I pointed out. "Have you seen the people who live here?"

"My point is that it is very normal to not be alright. Your transition to life here has not been an easy one." She hesitated, then added, "And I'm not sure it'll get any easier. That book was barely under control when Norma had it."

"And people keep trying to steal it," I said. The satchel was with me, on my lap. I didn't feel comfortable leaving it alone. I'd even taken it into the bathroom when I showered earlier. Jackie seemed happy with that, although she was curled on my shoulder now, watching Petunia with one paw on my neck.

"That too."

We looked at each other, her faded blue eyes milky with cataracts yet somehow still sharp. "It is safe here," she said. "Relatively speaking, anyway."

I didn't answer, and after a moment Ruiner said, "At least no one's tried to eat me here."

"Effie just wanted a cuddle," I said.

"With her teeth."

Petunia snorted and got up, a short woman with cropped grey hair, wearing a maxi dress and motorcycle boots under her apron. She stirred the pot vigorously, then said, "Your car's here."

"What?"

"It's outside the gate. Go and check on it, then come back in for dinner."

I very nearly said *yes, Mum,* but caught myself at the last moment. Instead I headed outside, shivering in the cool air. There'd be a frost tonight, heavy with winter, doing all the things an early winter frost should do for plants or crops or whatever. My knowledge of that was somewhat limited.

"My paws are cold," Ruiner complained, and I stopped on the path to look back at him, standing on the doormat with one front paw raised.

"Do you want me to buy you some cat socks? Or maybe someone can knit you some. It'd be really cute."

"A lift would be better."

I went back and picked my brother up, letting him jump to the opposite shoulder to Jackie. His weight was reassuring, and his fluffy tail flicked the back of my neck as we walked to the gate. The two stone frogs on the gateposts stared down at us impassively, but I wasn't looking at them. I was looking at my poor old Volvo estate, which had been one backfire away from being written off for at least the last six years. And it definitely *looked* like the same car, with the same dated interior and chunky lines, but it was...

"Shiny," Ruiner said.

"Shiny," I agreed. Shiny, and unscratched, and with all four tyres looking like they'd come straight off the rack. I opened the driver's door and got in, finding the key in the ignition. I tried it cautiously, and the engine grumbled into life immediately. "This is not my car," I said.

"It is," Ruiner said. "It's got your name on it."

His voice was serious, and I said, "What?"

He pointed his snout at a small envelope, propped up on the centre console. I picked it up with numb fingers, the paper heavy and textured. It was expensive stuff. *Familiar* stuff.

"Ruiner," I said, not opening it.

"What?"

"Aubrey gave me one. At the carnival. Just before the whole place collapsed. It was another note, like the ones I got when we first arrived."

He stared at me. "And you're only telling me now? What did it say?"

"You're no witch. But you'll still burn."

"Bloody *hell*," he muttered. "And this one?"

I swallowed hard and opened it, smoothing the paper with trembling fingers. Ruiner leaned over so he could see it too. *Tick tock, little witch. Time is running out.*

Neither of us spoke for a moment, then Ruiner said, "They can't even make up their minds if you're a witch or not. What sort of rubbish threat is that?" I gave a little gasp of laughter, and he put a paw on my hand, looking up at me with those wide blue eyes. "Seriously. You can handle this."

"I can't."

"You can. And even if you couldn't, you've got back-up." He arched his whiskers, nodding at the road, where Theodore was strolling towards us, his skin flushed orange with a very fresh application of fake tan. He moved with an easy confidence, smiling at something Isabella was saying, her long fingers fluttering in the air. Ben walked with them, scrapes dark on his face, a sensible quilted jacket zipped up to his chin. Starlight made up the fourth member of the group, wrestling with Howard the ferret, who was trying desperately to make a break for freedom.

"Honestly," Ruiner said. "What can go wrong with all of us on your side?"

And I burst out laughing, not because I thought he was wrong, but because he was so very right. Maybe none of us knew exactly what we were doing, and one of us couldn't go out in the sun, and another could walk through walls but never leave the valley, but together we formed some strange, messy, yet formidable whole.

Which was the closest thing to home I could imagine.

I pressed my forehead to my brother's, and he pressed back, purring loudly for precisely two seconds before he announced, "*Gross*. Go and be mushy elsewhere."

"Git," I said, grinning, and opened the door, heading out into Hollowbeck's strange, wild streets and towards the cheerful greetings of my friends, dead and alive and human and not, and each as deeply magical as the other.

Because the best friends always are.

The End

About the Authors

Amelia Ash likes the quiet life. During the week, she works at the tea shop inside a friend's quirky bookstore, and on the weekends, she combs the countryside for estate sales, collecting trinkets, old furniture, and, in one memorable case, a clawfoot tub. In the evenings, she likes to binge-watch HGTV with her life companion: a barely domesticated cat named Lizard, who she suspects might possibly kill her if he could double his size and operate a can opener.

∾

Kim M. Watt: Originally from New Zealand, Kim (she/her) now inhabits a slightly different world, crafting funny fantasies and off-beat cosy (or cozy) mysteries in which tea-drinking dragons collude with resourceful ladies of a certain age, baking-obsessed reapers run petting cafes for baby ghouls, and cats always bring the snark.

Kim's stories blend myth and reality in small and spectacular ways, where the Apocalypse comes on a Vespa, and the healing magic of tea and a really good lemon drizzle cake is unquestioned. But most of all, her tales are about friendship, loyalty, and people of all species looking out for one another. Because these, above all things, are magic.

Also By Amelia Ash and Kim M. Watts

The Hollowbeck Paranormal Cozy Mysteries

Witch Slap

One Smart Witch

Life's A Witch